THE LAST ZOO

SAM GAYTON

THE LAST ZOO

SAM GAYTON

ANDERSEN PRESS

First published in 2019 by
Andersen Press Limited
20 Vauxhall Bridge Road
London SW1V 2SA
www.andersenpress.co.uk

2 4 6 8 10 9 7 5 3 1

British Library Cataloguing in Publication Data available.

ISBN 978 1 78344 770 1

This book is printed on FSC accredited paper from responsible sources

Printed and bound in Great Britain by Clays Ltd, Elcograf S.p.A.

FOR POE

voilà |vwʌ'lɑː|

1. exclamation
there it is; there you are: 'Voilà!' said the magician,
producing a rabbit from a hat.

2. noun
any life form brought into existence by a reality bomb:
'Genies were some of the first voilà to appear.'

See also: the Seam, the zoo, reality bomb, glitch

Extract from the Merriam-Webster dictionary, 2098 edition

When he awoke, the dinosaur was still there.

Augusto Monterroso, *The Dinosaur*

1

CAKE DREAM

That night in Pia's dreams they cut the moon like a cake and serve her an ice-white slice. The sponge is all silvery, dotted on top with candied meteorites. It tastes like cheesecake, of course.

The moon comes served on a blue china plate, with a velvet napkin and a mother-of-pearl fork. Quite posh really, especially for angels. Usually they come into Pia's dreams solely to make mischief – shaped like singing frogs, or gorillas wearing knickers, or elephants doing the hula. Hardly the holiest of visions.

Yet here they are, the pair of them dressed like bistro waiters, letting her taste the moon.

She keeps expecting the angels to make it taste like stinky blue Stilton, or yell out 'TOTAL ECLIPSE!' and vanish, leaving her hungry, but they don't.

Something is up. Pia knows it.

But she's asleep, and so there isn't too much she can do except gobble up her serving and ask the angels for seconds, then thirds and fourths, until finally she is full and has to leave the last sliver in the sky as a crescent.

The moon is pretty dry, as cakes go. Pia asks for something to wash it down with, and one angel flies off and comes back with a can of starlight. Pia expects it to taste all twinkly and sweet, but starlight tastes of nothing. When she complains to the angel, it looks surprised.

'The flavour won't reach you for a million years,' it says.

• • •

When Pia wakes, the dream is still there. The angels have left it shining over her cot in the darkened cabin, pinned in place above her head.

Now she's awake, the dream takes the form of a halo. Most miracles the angels make appear this way. A circle is an angel's favourite shape. It's endless and elegant and completely loopy, just like them. Angels craft halos non-stop. They take beams of light and bend or braid them into rings, the way little kids do with daisy chains. Pia has seen them weave halos out of lamps, sunsets, birthday candles, monitor screens, you name it. Anything with a glow.

This one above her now is plaited from moonbeams, cool and silver-white. It looks like a giant frosted doughnut. Or the ghost of one. Luckily, food phantoms do not exist yet. Imagine being haunted by all the long-gone desserts you'd eaten. Sweet revenge.

Wow, she has woken up really pudding-obsessed. The halo is obviously still broadcasting the dream. It buzzes in her head like a sugar rush.

Pia lies there, going drowsily from one thought to the next until the realisation hits her. Hits hard as a slap. The force of it sends her rolling out of bed and on to the cabin deck.

She can't feel the angels.

They're not there.

But that's impossible. Gone? They can't be *gone*, no, no, she just isn't feeling this right. Pia has a track record of missing things that are right in front of her: just-mopped floors, MIND YOUR HEAD hazard signs, the goggles she reported lost but which turned out to be on her head. This has to be another of those moments.

Except it isn't. Emotions aren't something you can miss. You feel them or you don't.

And Pia doesn't. Not even faintly, not even at all.

The angels are gone.

Where? She runs to the cabin window to look out on the ark. The halo comes with her, stitched in place seven centimetres above her head. It wobbles and nearly slides off. Pia steadies it with one hand. Her fingertips come away sparkly. The angels have sewn last night's frost through the moonbeams like sequins.

It's a leaving present, she realises suddenly. A parting gift. Oh Seamstress, this is bad. The angels are so young. Just kids, really. They've barely outgrown their St Elmo's fire.

The cabin window is in sleep mode, blacked out. Pia clears it with a swipe. Hoping she'll see them. Actually praying. Bright dawn streams into the cabin, sparkling off the sea and the puddles on deck and the rain beaded on the window glass. She throws her forearm across her eyes, blinded. A chill settles upon the top of her head and ears like a powder, and she remembers the night frost and, a moment later, the halo.

5

Her hand rises up further to shield it, but the halo has already vanished, its pale frosted shape dissolving in the rich butter-yellow of the morning light.

Pia just stands there. Numb with the hugeness of what she isn't feeling. Numb with her numbness. How exactly are you supposed to save the world without angels? It would take a miracle. Which is kind of why the zoo has the angels in the first place.

They might not have gone far. Can she call them back? Pia gets herself into her shirt and orange zookeeper dungarees and pulls on her scuffed boots.

Her shirt is inside out.

Ugh. Doesn't matter. Change later. Just go.

Find them.

2
Angel Feelings

Outside the cabin the world is blue and calm. Above the ship and below it, sky and sea are still. Both so different to the churning, frantic mess Pia is: shirt inside out, sleep in her eyes, one of her boots already coming unlaced. *Quit worrying about all that,* she tells herself. *Just find something to wreck, something to tempt them back to fix.*

She looks around the deck's garden: at the meadow grass, the flowers, the apple tree at its centre. All of it growing on the deck of the ark. A little patch of green, bobbing on the big blue. The angels have sung each seed up from the soil and capped a tiny halo on every blade of grass. Out of all their miracles, this is the one they are fondest of. The one they keep returning to.

So Pia seeks out the nearest dandelion and kicks its yellow head off.

She looks away, and looks back; and looks away, and looks back. Her heart pounds and her head prays, waiting for the golden shimmer of hands to come and mend the dandelion back on its stalk.

Nothing happens. No miracle. The prayer goes unanswered.

What now? What next? What? Pia can't even call out for them. The angels don't have names: it's zoo procedure not to give them any, especially when they are still young. Names encourage pridefulness, apparently, and pride in previous imagerations of angels has led to all sorts of problems.

Pia steps further into the garden, to where the angels have built their little house. It stands about Pia's height, round as a halo and made from beams of sunlight, all bent and shaped and pinned into place.

The house has walls made of strong slats of noontime glare, and windows made from treacly summer afternoons, with curtains of gloomy winter twilight and an orange-pink roof thatched from a thousand strands of sunset.

Pia can walk straight through the walls, but that will bring the place tumbling down. The angels' house is fragile, like its owners. So she drops to her knees and crawls through the open doorway.

Inside, the hallway is wallpapered with rainbows. Through them Pia can see the garden, turned vivid shades of indigo and red. She crawls forward, searching for something, anything. A clue, a sign, a note. Surely they've left one?

Maybe it was the halo, she thinks gloomily. It's possible. Angels struggle to communicate in words, and much prefer to talk in dreams and visions. They might have woven an explanation through the moonbeams using the night frost, and placed it on Pia's head to make her understand the reason they were leaving.

But what does eating the moon like a cake mean? Maybe her brain hasn't interpreted it right. Maybe there were subtler symbols in there that she's missed. Pia thinks back to the silver slice, with its cheesecake flavour and meteorites.

Were they candied nut, or chocolate chip? She can't remember now.

If only she hadn't melted the halo out of stupidity, she could slip it back on her head. Dream the dream again, figure out what it meant. She facepalms.

Maybe it was just a distraction. A way to keep Pia dreaming, whilst the angels made their getaway. That's an even worse thought. The zoo's most precious animals have escaped. On Pia's watch. And all it took was cake.

She crawls deeper into the angels' house, steadying herself every few seconds. The further down the hallway she goes, the more it scrambles her vision. The bending and pinning and stitching of light leads to weird optical illusions. 'Like a hall of mirrors', Mum used to describe it.

Pia has called up images on her goggles of old fairground funhouses, and it looks about right. Things too wide, too wobbly, or too fractured to make sense of. And she can't shut her eyes, or she'll blunder into a wall and bring the whole thing down around her like a sunset.

At the end of the hall, every movement makes her queasy. Magenta meadow grass rises impossibly high, then seems to curl to the backs of her eyeballs. Pia's violet hands flatten and unfold in concertina shapes that zigzag as she shuffles forward. The sea is the sky, the clouds are on deck. Her empty belly heaves.

Pia reverses back out again, sick and dazzled. This is pointless. The angels have billions of rooms in their house, and Pia can only access the hallway. The rest are not three-dimensional spaces, but spirals that the angels draw themselves up into whenever they want privacy, like snails inside their shells, until they are the tiniest pinpricks of light, too small to see.

The house *is* empty, though. Pia doesn't need to search the rooms to know that. Seeing the angels isn't the issue: *feeling* them is. Being in their presence is as much *emotion* as anything else, and the feeling of angels has always been there on the ark.

And now it's not.

• • •

What do angels feel like? It's hard to say. Everyone gives a different answer.

'Like waking up on your birthday.'

'Like standing on a stage and everyone applauding.'

'Like your team snatching victory in the last second of the game.'

Ishan says that for him it feels like looking up at stars and seeing one shoot. But for Pia, it's nothing like her best friend's sparkling wonder. It's way more embarrassing.

To her, angels feel just like (and she hasn't even told Ishan this) getting away with a fart in an elevator. That *exact* same mix of giddy relief and triumph.

Only now there's no relief. No triumph. Only the terrible rushing sensation of approaching disaster.

And all she can do is stand on the deck of the celestial ark and watch.

It feels just like that time she went to the Rhinosaurus rex ark when she was five, and its skin was like the surface of a mountain, with its eyes pooled in their crags like big angry puddles, and Pia got so scared she peed.

And then Gowpen told everyone, and all the other kids in the zoo started calling her *Pee*-a, even though their nanabugs told them not to, until it got so bad that they had to reclassify *pee* as a swear word for a while, so that it got filtered from conversation and no kids could use it, which actually made things worse, because suddenly no one was allowed to say the word 'people', or sing the alphabet song past the fifteenth letter, or order anything with peas from the canteen ship, which made everyone super annoyed – mostly at Pia.

And now, her life is repeating. She's made a mess, again. Accidentally, again.

And again it doesn't matter one bit. Because soon the whole zoo will know, and hate her for it.

3

Sunset Pagoda

Did any of the other celestials see them go? Pia runs below deck in panic mode, clanging through doors, boot soles squeaking on the scuffed pink corridor floors, one thought in her head.

Ask the genies.

The zoo has only two angels (well, not even two at the moment) but dozens of genies. At least one on each ark. Over sixty species of voilà on twenty-two arks, but the genies are by far the most common because of how useful they are.

Before there were angels, everyone hoped that genies might be the voilà the zoo (and the world) needs. But it turns out that the wishes they grant are only really practical for smaller stuff, like mending light bulbs and summoning more paper clips. Which is useful, but not on a *save-the-planet* level.

As genies grow older and more powerful, they get paired with a human 'genieer: an expert in wishing. There are about a dozen different types of wishes that have been safely scripted out, but the most commonly granted are zephyrs and thrints. Zephyring is a form of teleportation, while thrinting is 3D printing – rearranging proteins and carbohydrates and fats into something that resembles food. The more powerful the genie, and the more skilled the 'genieer, the better it tastes. Pia always orders double helpings of dessert whenever Rubio and his genie Ajjimajji are on duty in the canteen. Those two have brownie ice cream down to an *art form*.

But a genie's wick only burns so bright for so long. Finally, the oldest and dimmest of them end up at the retirement home on the celestial ark.

Officially, its name is the Sunset Pagoda. Which makes it sound a *lot* more glamorous than it is. It's just an old storeroom deep in the ship's belly, with fire-retardant walls and floors covered with sand. A place where genies can fizzle out in peace.

Five of them burn there at the moment. Hokapoka, Shazam and Kadabra are all so feeble they rarely leave their lamps any more. (Very few genies live in actual *lamps*, of course: it's just a catch-all term. Genies will burn in anything, really, so long as it's fireproof. Old aerosol cans are common. Tins too. Genies crawl inside them like hermit crabs.)

Solomon and Bertoldo might have seen something, though. The angels were always coming down to play with those two old dears. Pia encouraged it. It was very sweet to watch. Being celestials, genies are made of light too (amongst other things). The angels loved bending them into all sorts of hilarious shapes – cylinders, cubes, question marks. The genies loved it too. They'd float through the air like carnival balloons, hooting with laughter as they twirled.

Mum had liked to call it 'genie yoga'.

• • •

Pia hurls open the door to the Sunset Pagoda. Even though the lights are on, the room is velvet-black. Warm darkness drapes itself across her eyes. It comes from all the shadows the genies wrap around themselves like cloaks. Over time the pagoda has grown thick with them, the way a room grows thick with cobwebs.

In the centre of the darkness, spinning lazily in the air, two rings of licking flame burn above a pair of battered aluminium drinks cans. The lilac ring is Solomon, and the lime-coloured one is Bertoldo. Pia can hear them giggling to each other as they twirl.

Her heart thuds. Each genie is twisted into the shape of a halo. The angels have been here! And not so long ago.

'Do you know where they went?' she blurts. 'Solomon! Bertoldo! I need your help!'

The two genies unravel, and clothe themselves in shadows while Pia holds a hand over her eyes. Seeing a genie's naked flame is considered rude (only by the older ones, though, self-conscious about the dimness of their fire).

'Did you see where the angels went?' Pia asks them again, looking up. In their normal shapes, genies look a lot like people – only made of fire and clothed in shadow, and with extravagant facial hair.

They both whoosh towards her, each one about the height of Pia's forearm. Both their flames are shrouded except for the flickering tips, upon which burn faces and smoky trailing beards.

'Did they say anything?' The questions keep tumbling

14

out of her. 'Or, I don't know, give you a clue? Maybe in the form of a dream?'

Solomon's and Bertoldo's eyes dim with confusion. They're the youngest in the pagoda, but by genie standards, they are both very, very old.

'The *angels*.' Pia balls her hands into fists. 'Do you understand?' She has to take a breath and swallow before she bursts into tears. 'I have to find them.'

Slowly, some ember of understanding kindles in Solomon. 'She comes to the genies with a *quest*!' he tells Bertoldo, his eyes dancing with lilac fire.

'A quest?' the lime-coloured genie murmurs. 'Could it be true?'

Pia nods. 'Yes, that's right. A *quest*!'

Why didn't she say this straight away? Genies are obsessed with stories. They literally see the whole world as one great interweaving epic they call the Tale. They have their own particular way of speaking too, called Tellish, that involves narrating their thoughts and actions.

'The desperate heroine was willing to embark on any journey,' Pia says. Her Tellish has always been clunky, but at least the genies might understand her. 'Go any distance, endure any hardship, to find her beloved angels. If only the genies might aid her . . .'

She trails off. Solomon and Bertoldo are actually *fizzing* with excitement. Sparks whizz from the tips of their beards like miniature fireworks, spiralling and popping in rainbow colours. Pia is buzzing too. They get it! At last, some progress.

'The genies were only too happy to help the heroine!' Solomon announces, as Bertoldo nods furiously. 'They summoned a mighty boon to bestow upon her! It would guide the heroine to what she was so desperately seeking . . .'

Pia's eyes widen. A boon is a powerful object that genies give to those they perceive as 'heroes'. What will this one be? Magic compass? Talking sword?

Bertoldo plunges one long, flickering hand into the smoky blue wisp of his beard and pulls out a foot-long hot dog.

Solomon points with his candlelight fingers, and adds ketchup, mustard and fried onions.

The two genies offer it to Pia triumphantly.

'The mighty boon!' they both announce. 'Take it, and it will lead the way!'

Pia does her best to look pleased as she takes the hot dog. Ah well. At least that's breakfast sorted. Bless the old dears for trying.

'The heroine rushed off on her quest with renewed purpose!' she lies, not wanting to hurt their feelings.

Solomon and Bertoldo are so happy they both discard their shadows and go pinwheeling naked around the room, spitting sparks and smoke and setting off the fire alarm in the corridor outside.

Pia heaves the door to the Sunset Pagoda shut and flaps one-armed at the alarm until it stops wailing. She slides down the door, hot dog still in hand. Muffled through the bulkhead, she can hear Solomon and Bertoldo singing to each other on an infinite loop.

'The quest can't fail,
It just can't fail,
With the mightiest boon in all the Tale!'

Pia looks at the hot dog, oozing sauce down her thumb. She has no idea what to do with it. No idea what to do at all, in fact. She ends up just sitting there and eating the hot dog in a dozen miserable little bites. The onions taste funny. And there's way too much mustard. By the end of it, she feels vaguely sick. More of a mighty barf than a mighty boon.

'Ugh.' She gives an acrid little burp. 'Thanks, genies.'

4

CHIMERAS

Like most ships in the zoo, the celestial ark is an i-era vessel, patched up and repurposed to hold voilà. Before the crash and the war, it chugged around the world, ferrying parcels for some internet auction site called *dib$*.

On the *dib$* company logo, the dot on the i is a smiley face and the d and the b are both thumbs ups. The dollar sign is in a speech bubble next to the smiley's mouth. A happy little logo, speaking a simple language of money and bargains and lucky finds.

Pia calls him Dibsy. Versions of him are stuck in various sizes to the ark's doors and corridor walls, and a few transparent Dibsys still cling to the porthole windows, bleached by decades of sun and faint as ghosts.

Dibsy is in the hold too, beneath Pia's feet. Hundreds upon hundreds of him, smiling in the pitch-dark, plastered to the sides of the stacked crates of *dib$* freight that sit on pallets of rotting wood. Stuff that has been out for delivery for thirty years now.

As a kid, Pia used to sift through a few of those packages, marvelling at the pointless junk people had once found it necessary to order. A noise-cancelling fork for people who slurped noodles too loud. A man's tie that looked like a rasher of bacon. A glass bowl on wheels, for taking your pet goldfish for a walk. Glow-in-the-dark toilet paper. Bubblegum-flavoured shoelaces.

So much garbage. No wonder the world was a mess.

Pia doesn't go down to the hold any more, though. No one does. The entire lower decks are blocked off by a round metal door that looks like it has been salvaged from a bank vault or nuclear bunker. The door's edges are sealed with lead and an emergency concave mirror is suspended above it, ready to swing down and reflect any attempted escapes.

Without really being aware of it, Pia finds herself wandering down the corridor and drifting towards it. She barely registers her movements until she feels her fingers rest upon the small square peephole cut into the door's centre.

Before she can stop herself, she pulls it open, just a crack. Then she jerks her hand away, as if the peephole was red hot.

'Don't,' she says aloud.

She's not talking to herself.

Her cheek grows warm, there's the fuzz of static, and a wicked little whisper sounds in her ear.

Why not? says the creature behind the door. *What is Pia so distracted about? Tell us. We can help?*

Pia shuts off her thoughts. She is nowhere near desperate or stupid enough to go ask *Bagrin* about the angels.

Angels?

Oh, Bagrin knows all *about angels.*

Facepalm! He's powerful this close. Even through the

door. She backs off, singing an annoyingly catchy pip-pop song in her head to drown out her other thoughts.

> *Null it, gurl, be my ohtwo*
> *You breathe me, yea*
> *I'll breathe you*

She tries to hear the synth solo, but Bagrin whispers above it: *Don't go. We won't bite. Won't do anything tricky. Deal?* He sends the image of Dibsy into her head, only the logo is holding out both his hands, as if to say *Come on, now. Would we lie to you?*

Pia stares at the vault door. Deals, deals. With devils it is always deals. There used to be two of them down there, amongst the *dib$* crates, trapped in the infernal prism. The other devil's name was Gotrob. He had not been as good at deals as Bagrin. Perhaps that is why Bagrin ate him. Who knows.

Bagrin did it for you, of course. After what Gotrob did, we knew you wanted revenge.

'Liar.' Pia shakes the devil's presence away. 'And stop reading my thoughts.'

It's her own fault, for lingering too long here. Lead and concrete can only block out so much temptation. Devils have a particular talent: they can send their voices into the ears of anyone, anywhere.

Sometimes, they even send images. The official zoo term for them is *chimeras*. Every now and then, Bagrin manages to slip one through to her. Often while Pia is asleep, thoughts unguarded.

Chimeras are like adverts, with Pia at the centre. Most of them are really generic desires. Her, but *pretty*. Her, but *smart*. Her, but *ruling the world*. All obvious stuff like that. Not particularly tempting. A standard safety procedure set-up is that Pia should keep conversation with Bagrin to an absolute minimum, to stop the devil from learning too much about her. It has stopped him from tailoring his adverts and making them irresistible.

Before the crash and the war, everyone owned devices that did the same thing as devils. Dark little boxes called phones, that sat in your hands promising you anything and everything. Listening to your desires and murmuring back: *I can make you pretty; I can make you interesting; I can make you cool.*

Pia touches her dungarees pocket. Just imagine it. Mum and Dad carried phones. A lot of sprawl-punks still do, even though there isn't much for them to connect to any more.

Bagrin whispers to her again. *What do you want to know about angels? We can tell you. Deal?*

'No deal,' Pia corrects. She knows the devil is lying. That's what makes him so tempting. There is comfort in lies. At least they offer hope, unlike the truth. Hope can be comforting even when it's false: Pia knows that from experience.

But it always turns bitter in the end. Hope didn't bring Mum and Dad back. Why would it bring the angels?

• • •

Back up on deck, the halos in the garden have slipped. With the angels gone, the tiny ones above the grass and flowers, small and golden like wedding rings, have mostly blown away. A few of them hang in tangled loops in the branches of the apple tree, the leaves around them already fading to autumn shades.

What can Pia do? The garden won't last long here, a kilometre from land on a repurposed cargo ship. Not without the angels feeding it a steady diet of miracles.

And what if someone sees?

Pia runs up to the rail and looks around for nearby ships. The celestial ark – her ark – is just one of the twenty-two that make up the zoo. Pia can see the old supertanker that holds the megafauna; the small coaster that is the zoo's aviary; the bulk freighter with modified cargo holds where the singing hippos wallow and the pigasi fly.

Each ship is a little brightly coloured island in a colourless ocean: navy and rust-red, brilliant-white, burnt-orange. And at the centre of them all, like the spoke around which they all turn, is the island mountain.

Pia can see it clearly this morning: a shard of black volcanic rock that juts from the sea in a crest of white foam.

It doesn't always look this way. Depending on the glitch that rages around it like an eternal storm, the mountain might look smaller, or see-through, or not there at all. Sometimes it shines. Once, it wriggled and flexed, like the tip of a finger that was half a kilometre high.

It's all an illusion, of course. Just the glitch, playing tricks on the mind.

Pia shudders. Suddenly she's aware of how alone she is up here on deck without the angels. Usually her nanabug would be there to monitor her, but Threedeep is off being mended after Pia accidentally sat on the drone whilst she was in standby. A really high-authority genie is having to wish her back together.

Sitting on Threedeep has turned out sort of lucky, though. If the nanabug was there, alarm bells would already be ringing throughout the zoo.

Why hasn't Pia raised the alarm yet, though? The angels have been gone twenty minutes at least now. Seeing as they can travel at the speed of light, that is quite a long time. They might be anywhere. They could be topping up their tan on the surface of the Sun.

And say they *did* want to go sunbathe in space rays – how could Pia even stop them? The zoo has procedures for keeping other celestials contained: devils are bound by prisms and contracts, genies by lamps and wishes . . .

But angels? Well. The only known way to keep an angel in one place was, basically, to *need* them. That's what has kept them here since they first came from the Seam. Pia's need, and above that the zoo's need, and above that the world's need for them to stay.

Only now, it seems like that's not enough.

• • •

Since she is up on deck, Pia decides to check the numinous lamps before she raises the alarm. They form a floodlit perimeter around the ark. You can't see celestials without numinous light. Maybe they're malfunctioning?

She checks: they're not.

OK.

Time to go back to her cabin and fully freak out in private.

Pia's cabin is her bedroom and office, combined. It has windows you can blacken, cloud or clear. It has a chair, a desk, a cot. It has piles of reports, organised into various categories (overdue, way-overdue, half-written) and several stacked towers of old plastic food pots from canteen-pilfered snacks. Various communities of mould are slowly moving into each level of the piled-up pots, like they are penthouse flats.

Pia barges in and waves the walls from clear to cloudy. She catches sight of herself in the reflection. Torn dungarees, wonky fringe, untied shoelace, shirt inside out. Solomon's and Bertoldo's hot dog has left a smear of ketchup on her lip. There's mustard on her boot.

How, in the name of the Seamstress, could the angels have left someone so obviously in need of them?

A few slips of green paper have appeared on Pia's desk since she woke: little messages zephyred there by her best friends, the Rekkers. Pia glimpses a few scribbled notes from Wilma and Gowpen and Ishan:

Rekkers assemble, it's unicorn day!!
Good luck!!
Hey! Slee-P! You up?

Scribbling chat to her friends can wait. She sweeps the messages aside and scrambles around for her goggles. They are i-era, old and cranky. No connectivity any more, just lots of pre-loaded files for reference.

She pulls them over her eyes, blinks them on, and calls up *Procedures of Care*, the zoo's basic keeper handbook. Ninety-five different species of voilà have appeared out of the Seam in the last thirty years, and the handbook has entries concerning every single one. There are tips for grooming phoenixes . . . advice on hummingdragon training (reward them with gold dust, which they love to hoard) . . . regulations on trimming genie beard lengths . . .

It takes a while to find what Pia wants. One of the lenses was cracked (another victim of her butt), so she can't use the search bar. She has to keep paging everything over on to her left eye. Soon she has a headache to add to her panic and her hot-dog burps. It's a day that keeps on giving.

Finally there's a list of procedures titled ENCLOSURE BREACHES / ARK ESCAPES. It consists of several bullet points from Director Siskin, written in the boss's usual way:

```
#1 - Raise the alarm at once.
#2 - As in, five minutes ago.
#3 - WHY ARE YOU STILL READING THIS?
```

Pia pulls off her goggles and drops them to the floor. Of course, Siskin is right. Raising the alarm is the proper thing to do. The only thing to do. Facepalm, facepalm, *facepalm*. There *have* to be other options. Anything.

Prayer?

She clasps her hands. 'Please, please, please come back. Please let me open my eyes and see you there. I need you. The world needs you. Amen. Amen.'

How long should she crouch there like this, broadcasting her prayer loop like some sort of distress call?

Are they listening?

Is anyone?

Suddenly the door sweeps open. Pia leaps up, daring to believe. It worked. She can't believe it worked!

But it isn't an angel that comes to her aid. She might have known. In reality, there's only one creature in the entire universe tuned into Pia's wavelength.

It's Ishan.

5
THE KLUTZES

Ishan. Who else would it be? He always seems to know where Pia is hiding. Sometimes she wonders if he might have bugged her somehow.

It isn't such a crazy thought. Ishan works on the ark with the zoo's only cybernisms – the nanites. (Nanabugs and bluebottles and ark pilots are electronic too, but technically they are just really smart drones, rather than animals, so they don't count.)

Apart from people, the nanites are the only creatures in the whole zoo that haven't come from the Seam inside the mountain. Ishan accidentally evolved them himself out of a ream of computer viruses he bred in a hive stack. Apparently they worship him like a god. They've even built tiny monuments to him out of silicon. He has one of them glued under his fingernail. He showed it to Pia once under a microscope.

When the authorities found out what Ishan had done, they sent him straight to the zoo, giving him a new ark to himself – the *cybernism* ark. For the first few hours after he arrived, it was like he was the most exotic creature in the whole place. It had been sort of hilarious. Zookeepers stopped grooming their phoenixes and training hummingdragons with gold dust, and zephyred to the cybernism ark to catch a glimpse of the wiry little kid from the San Silicio shantyscraper.

Ishan hadn't known what to do with all that attention. Dutifully, he'd tried to explain the workings of his nanites, who had by then upgraded themselves into a primitive civilisation. And people nodded and stifled their yawns and said:

'Oh, how interesting. *Now tell us about San Silicio.*'

That was why, of course. It wasn't *Ishan* they were fascinated by, it was where he'd come from.

The mainland. The sprawl.

From the arks, the city on the coast fifty miles east was just a yellow glow that spread over the horizon each night like a fever. But Ishan had *lived* there. The zookeepers wanted him to make it real for them. What was it like? To wake in its morning haze and bike through the shimmer of its dusk? To thread through its heaving crowds of Free Staters and refugees, beneath shantyscrapers stacked upwards like dirty plates? Had he fought in the bread riots? Lost anyone to rat flu? Was it true the air-scrubbers in the ohtwo factories were failing?

Ishan had just blinked at them. 'It's, um, pretty crowded there. I mainly stayed in my room.'

'. . . Oh,' said everyone, realising the kid was just another gogglehead dork. 'Sure.'

'Would you like me to show you the nanites again? I'm hoping they'll bring back the internet, eventually.'

'Umm,' said everyone, as they worked out somewhere else they had to be.

Just like that, without even realising it, Ishan blew his one chance to be popular.

Pia had instantly decided he was awesome.

He's been at the zoo for six months now, and they have been solid best friends for five of those months, apart from fifteen massively traumatic seconds during one evening last week. Pia tries not to think about those seconds too much, although of course with Ishan now standing in front of her she *is* thinking about them – all fifteen.

'Pia?' Ishan waves on the cabin's lights, dazzling her. He rears back. 'You're bleeding!'

'It's ketchup.' Pia smears the sauce from her mouth with the back of her hand and wipes it on the leg of her dungarees.

'What are you doing in here?' Ishan has a faint tan line around his eyes and a quiff of thick black hair. Both are from the goggles he wears when interacting with his nanoscopic creations. It makes him look permanently bewildered. 'Are you OK, Pia? Did something happen?'

So he doesn't know. How has he not felt them gone, or noticed the garden wilting? Ordinarily, Pia would tell him. The main basis of her and Ishan's friendship is that they are two of the biggest klutzes in the entire zoo.

This time, it's too risky. Ishan is a stickler for rules. He would pull the procedure up on the goggles, see Siskin's bullet points and insist they report the disappearance.

Or – and this would be worse – he might try and cheer

her up. Then he might decide to try and kiss her again, and Pia would have to give him another punch.

She bounces his question back at him. 'What are *you* doing here?'

She might have spoken just a bit too aggressively, because Ishan turns pink and looks at the floor.

'I sent you some chats,' he says.

Pia glances over at the slips of paper on her desk. 'Oh. Yeah. Well, I haven't read them. Been busy with stuff.'

Ishan glances up. 'I'm guessing that means it didn't go well then.'

Pia frowns. What is Ishan talking— 'My appraisal!' she screams. *Good luck*, the chats said. It's this morning, her meeting with Siskin, oh *facepalm*!

'Wait, what?' says Ishan. 'Haven't you been?'

Pia jumps up. The chair hits the shantyscraper of stacked-up plastic pots and topples it over. Ishan throws himself out of the way as she pelts from the cabin.

'I thought it was half an hour ago?' he calls.

'It *was*!' She is late, she is *so* late. She runs across the deck, legs and arms pumping. Doesn't even take her respirator. Ishan runs after her waving it in his hand and yelling something sensible-sounding about today's tox levels. Pia is in too much of a rush to care about the level of peroxal-whatever in her lungs. She has to zephyr to Ark One.

Pazuzu, the genie that serves the celestial ark, curls from her old aerosol can of a lamp and spirals into a bow. Even in

30

her panicked state, Pia remembers to bow back. Genies are not slaves, and don't have to grant wishes if it isn't an emergency. Getting them to help you is mostly about good manners. Luckily, Solomon and Bertoldo are Pazuzu's parents, so she has a big soft spot for Pia.

Pazuzu glances back across the ship at Ishan. She twiddles her long thin handlebars and narrates a question: 'Running from the persistent prince, she wishes for a zephyr?'

Pia is too out of breath already. She just nods yes.

'For her?' Pazuzu asks dryly. 'Or him?'

'Me,' Pia manages between gasps. 'Annual. Appraisal. The boss.'

To survive as a serial klutz, multi-tasking your calamities is essential. It is a talent Pia has honed over many years and many subjects. She just takes whatever she doesn't want to think about and throws it out of her head. Simple as that. Gone. For a little while, at least.

It is sort of like juggling. Actually, exactly like juggling. Which is an activity, she reminds herself, for clowns.

Pia puts the angels out of her mind and worries instead about this other, slightly lesser calamity: how late she is for the most important meeting of her year.

The meeting where all of the data Pia's nanabug has monitored, day and night for almost twelve whole months, gets collated and summarised for Zoo Director Siskin.

Who will then decide whether or not to send Pia inside the mountain.

To the Seam.

And the Seamstress.

· · ·

When Pia was six years old, her parents took one of the zoo's little ferry boats, and went to show her what the Seam was like.

They motored as close as they could get to the glitch-storm surrounding the mountain, and then they waited. Pia stood with her arms wrapped around her mum's leg. She was afraid. Against the sides of the mountain, the waves roared on the rocks, loud as a Rhinosaurus rex. The boat bobbed and bucked in the swells. But it wasn't the sea that scared Pia. There was something else. Something inside the mountain.

'Do you feel it?' Mum said. 'This is what we came here to show you.'

Pia squinted past Mum's finger, deciding to be brave. She watched the mountain. She had a strange feeling. Somehow, she didn't think it was a mountain at all.

'Do you know where we are?' Mum asked.

Pia nodded. 'Yeah. Where the scientists detonated the reality bomb.'

'That's right,' said Mum, sounding pleased.

'Normal bombs destroy *matter*,' Pia recited, trying to impress her even more. 'But reality bombs are different. They . . .' She paused, trying to remember. 'They destroy the under lion laws of the unifirst.'

'The *underlying laws of the universe*,' Dad corrected gently. 'That's right. The scientists used the reality bomb like TNT: they blasted through the laws that govern the *possible*, so we can mine the *impossible*.'

The weird feeling was so close that Pia felt dizzy, as if she stood at the centre of some wild spinning wheel. She blinked, and cried out. 'It's not dark,' she said. 'Behind my eyes, when I blink. It isn't *dark*.'

Whatever it was inside the mountain was in Pia's head too. She could see it when she closed her eyes, like a dream.

'She's shaking,' Mum said, voice low. 'We shouldn't have brought her this close.'

'It's OK.' Dad stroked Pia's head. 'Don't worry. You're safe.'

'You don't have to close your eyes if you don't want to,' said Mum. 'We can go home. It doesn't mean you're scared.'

Mum was wrong. That was *exactly* what it meant. Pia scowled. She had to prove to the others that she was brave. Some kids were still taunting her for what happened with the Rhinosaurus rex.

She shut her eyes, and this time she kept them closed.

• • •

In her mind's eye, Pia sees the mountain. She sees it for what it truly is: not a jagged black mountain, but a jagged black hole. A tear in reality's fabric, where all logic and laws have come loose and lie unstitched.

33

The Seam.

And there are threads hanging in that shining space, millions of them, in all the colours of starlight. Threads years wide and eternities long, threads microns thick and photons brief. Threads made of moonlight and threads of glittered silence. Threads made of majesty, threads that sing, threads that weep. Each one alive and each one dreaming.

And like a hand plays a harp, a being dances across them. Something in the Seam is *alive*. And weaving.

See her ten legs clack, see them gather and braid. Plucking at the threads in the endless shining, each leg tapered to a needle's point.

Her body a glitter-black blur, her two eyes glinting inscrutably.

A life-weaver.

A dream-spinner.

A Seamstress.

• • •

When Pia opened her eyes, the boat was back amongst the arks and the Seam was far away again.

Dad was next to her. He just smiled and knelt down and patted his thighs, and Pia clambered on. She burrowed into his jacket, feeling his scratchy wool jumper against her cheek and his heart beating in his chest.

'What is she?' Pia asked.

Dad sighed. 'We don't know.'

'Is she God?'

'We don't know, Pia.'

'Is she real?'

'She might be. Or she might be a mirage. When people get close to the Seam, they see what they want to see. Maybe our imaginations created the Seamstress. Or maybe she's always been there. Maybe she lives in unreality, and now because of the reality bomb we can see into her home.'

Pia thought about this. 'I saw her making something,' she said eventually.

'Life,' said Dad. 'The Seamstress makes life. All the voilà in the zoo have come from the Seam. From her.'

'But . . .' Pia was confused. 'I thought *Mummy* made the angels. When she was little.'

Dad nodded. 'She did. Sort of. Did you see the threads and strings? We think they come from us. From our imaginations. That's what the Seamstress weaves. But no one knows for sure. No one who comes out of the Seam can remember. You know how waking up can make you forget a dream? It's like that.'

Pia followed Dad's gaze toward the mountain. 'Did *I* go inside the Seam?'

Dad leaned down and kissed her on the head, quickly and a little fiercely. 'No, Pia. You went right up to the door, but you didn't go inside. Your mum and I would like it if you never went inside. Sometimes, when people go in, it can hurt their heads.'

'Even kids?'

'Even kids, though not as much to them. We call it mind-fray.'

'But Mummy went in, and *she* didn't get mind-frayed.'

'That's right. Your mum is very brave.'

'*I'm* brave too! I'm going to go in and make more angels, just like her.'

Dad looked over at Mum, who slumped her shoulders and said: 'It was worth a try.'

• • •

It was only when Pia was older, and she looked back on this moment, that she understood it. Mum and Dad had been trying to scare her. They didn't want Pia to become a Seamer, and didn't want her to take that risk. They wanted her to stay on the ark with them, and look after the celestials.

Where it was 'safe'.

They couldn't have known.

6

ARK ONE

From her dungarees pocket, Pia unrolls the text she has to speak for Pazuzu to zephyr her to the meeting. To come true in the way that you want, wishes have to be said perfectly, word for word. Otherwise you might zephyr halfway inside a wall, or reappear half as big as you were, with your fingers and your toes swapped over. It has happened.

Or, just as bad, you might hurt the genie. A wish gone wrong is nothing to do with them, of course; it's in the nature of wishes themselves. Wishes are living things, born the moment they are uttered and dying the moment they are granted. They are squirmy, twisty creatures, and there is malice in them. There is a reason zephyring tends to be the main wish zookeepers make: teleporting from ark to ark is useful, but it also has a start and end point. It happens, and then it is over. It isn't a dangerously vague wish, the sort that might live for a long time and cause all sorts of unintended consequences, like *I wish for happiness*, or *I wish to live for ever*.

There's a zookeeper saying: *Angels mend, devils deal, genies grant a slippery eel*. It sums up wishes pretty well. Wishes are slippery eels, and if the cage of words you speak isn't strong enough to hold them, they'll wriggle out and bite.

It takes a whole minute to go through the wish-script, only for Pia to mispronounce the phrase 'Siskin's office' as

'Siskin's orifice'. Now *that* would have been a particularly horrific zephyring accident. For everyone involved.

'Gently, Pazuzu urged her not to panic,' the genie narrates in Tellish as Pia begins again.

She tries not to, but it is hard. She feels sick. What was she thinking, eating that hot dog? Solomon added too much mustard. Oh Seamstress. Not only has she lost the angels, she has wasted the boss's time. She doesn't know which one he is going to shout at her more for. He will *definitely* be moving her off the celestial ark. She'll be transferred to care for some voilà so boring it will make her brain weep. The ice slugs, maybe, that look like mini glaciers and move at the rate of five centimetres per year. She can imagine Siskin's mocking smile as he reassigns her.

At least you won't lose them, *Cornucopia.* (He is one of the few people who *always* calls her by her full name.) *Also,* he adds, *stop imagining me and keep your attention on the* wish *you're making*.

She finishes the zephyr script at last.

'. . . all this, I wish.' You have to say it this way: backwards, saving those two binding words until the very end, just in case you made a mistake.

'So she spoke,' Pazuzu says. 'And thus the genie granted.'

• • •

The weird thing about zephyring: it doesn't feel like anything. No breathless rush of speed, no whirligig of motion

38

and smoke. You vanish with a clap as all the air rushes in to fill the you-sized vacuum you leave behind, but you aren't around to hear that. You are already somewhere else.

It's best to close your eyes, pinch your nose and blow out through your cheeks. It stops your brain getting too confused. Zephyring is quick as a finger-snap, and sometimes it causes double vision and headaches. Two things Pia definitely does not need, feeling as queasy as she does.

So she stays with her eyes shut for a few moments, waiting for her body to get used to Ark One: the slight change in breeze, the stillness of the deck beneath her boots, the chill on her skin from standing in the shade instead of the sun.

Her belly sends up a little burp. Something *definitely* not right about that hot dog. She hurries for the ramp that leads down into the offices and canteen, working her jaw to ease the popping in her ears.

Her nose and eyes are streaming as she heads across the deck. Ishan had been right: the air is seriously toxy today. By the time Pia descends the ramp and waves the door open, her throat feels raw and sludgy. At least the taste of chemicals is overpowering the taste of the hot dog.

'Sorry!' She stumbles in, the door blinks shut behind her and she doubles up with coughing. 'Here now!'

A bluebottle buzzes over to her, looking and sounding like every other security drone Pia has ever seen: same ugly black plastic, same bristling nodes, same fat buzzing rotors.

'I'm here for my appraisal.' She wipes her eyes and sniffs. 'I had a meeting with Director Siskin forty minutes ago.'

The bluebottle pings a message to Siskin's secretary and gets one back. A message scrolls across the drone's display: **It was <u>forty-three</u> minutes ago.**

Ugh. Bluebottles. So pedantic. Everything they say just makes Pia want to splat them.

She shrugs. 'I'm sorry.'

The bluebottle hovers.

'I slept in,' she adds.

The bluebottle hovers.

'My nanabug is broken. She normally wakes me up.'

You are now forty-four minutes late, chats the bluebottle.

Pia stifles the urge to punch the stupid thing right in the node. All she has to do is get through the next half an hour. It is entirely possible she will zephyr back to the celestials and find the angels back in the garden, busy braiding sunbeams. Hey, if the zookeeper of a celestial ark can't believe in miracles, who can?

Careful, Pia, says a voice inside her that sounds like Bagrin. *That sounds suspiciously like hope.*

The bluebottle pings. **This way.**

• • •

Ark One is the only non i-era ship in the zoo. It is new, custom-built, and super, super boring. Every time Pia zephyrs here, it always amazes her how *dull* it is. Just several security clearances and a boat ride away, the Seamstress sits spinning creatures into life from the raw threads of human imagination.

Not that you'd know it here. On Ark One, the air con makes everything taste of plastic and the walls are painted beige and the secretaries all have voices that sound like long-drawn-out yawns.

Pia follows the bluebottle to Siskin's offices. They pass admin staff in grey suits, and scientists in doom-rock T-shirts for bands like *N Diz Nigh* and *Horsemen*, and security patrols with black uniforms and long sleek rifles that they hold in a way that always reminds Pia of concert violinists standing before a performance.

There are drones too. Nanabugs for monitoring, bluebottles for security, and cleaning drones that nobody notices enough to give a nickname to. And though Ark One contains no habitats or enclosures, there are plenty of voilà. Floating by a busted strip light, Pia sees a young red genie she hasn't met before. His human 'genieer (Dirk? Kirt? He's Dutch, Pia knows that much) is talking through the wish-script to fix the bulb.

Pia tenses up. Genies might not have the empathy levels of angels, but they're still drawn to those who need help. What if the red genie senses her massive, unfixable problem?

He doesn't, of course. She needs to get a grip. The guilt is making her sweat, and the air con is making her shiver. By the time the bluebottle drops her off at Siskin's offices, she looks like someone with rat flu.

The boss's new secretary sits working at a desk by the

door. He's a recent transfer, even newer to the zoo than Ishan. Pia has only talked to him once before, on the canteen ship. All she remembers is that his name is Blom, which she'd accidentally misheard as Blong.

No, wait, maybe it was the other way around.

'Take a seat,' the secretary says. He doesn't take his eyes out of his goggles. Rude. At least he can't see the mess she's in.

'Sorry I'm late.' Pia perches on one of the chairs, trying to get her heart rate under control. 'Is he really mad?'

Blong – it is definitely Blong, not Blom – twitches a finger as he deletes something on his goggles.

A small genie sits on the desk too. He looks young, maybe only a few weeks old, and is the size and colour of a cigar puff. The genie's beard is extraordinarily long. It's like a heap of grey spaghetti. He sits on top of it, by his old Zippo lighter of a lamp, going through a flip chart of written-down wishes without a 'genieer. Pia's never seen a genie wish unsupervised.

As she watches, the genie bows after reading each wish-script, and murmurs: 'The wish was granted, and it was so.' Each time, one of the letters on the desk zephyrs away with a puff. Letters and reports, mailed off to the mainland.

There used to be a thing called the internet, which was what the i-era was named after, and it was basically a computer network that zephyred information. It hasn't existed for decades though, not since a virus called Megalolz spread through every device connected to the net and turned

42

them all to junk. After that, pretty much the only working tech left were spare parts that hadn't been assembled, or military stuff that ran on its own networks: security drones like bluebottles, and surveillance drones like nanabugs.

Megalolz had been pretty bad. Lots of people died because of it, because once the internet went down nobody could communicate properly. The old ways, like phone calls and fax, had all been phased out. There was just the net. And after Megalolz, there was nothing at all. Lots of countries got confused and thought Megalolz was a cyberattack on them, instead of something that was happening the world over. So a whole bunch of wars happened, basically by mistake.

Once the fighting started, no one bothered trying to talk either. It took a couple of years before people figured out that Megalolz was just the work of some nameless hacker in some random sprawl who probably hadn't even realised how powerful his virus would be. A few countries in Europe are still fighting each other now, thirty years later, even *after* finding out about Megalolz. Like it's a habit they can't be bothered to break.

After Megalolz, a lot of things vanished for ever. Pia's dad used to list them all. His voice would go faraway and sad, like he was talking about old friends he'd lost touch with.

Search engines. Selfies. Swiping. The final season of that show he'd been watching.

FOMO. China. The States.

Silly videos of cats.

'Bad stuff happens when people don't communicate,' he always told Pia. What would he think of her now, sitting in Siskin's office, knowing the angels were missing, not saying a word?

• • •

Pia waits. She swings her legs and fans her face and scratches some dry mustard off her dungarees. She marvels again at the weenie-genie. That really is the longest beard she's ever seen! The way it piles up around his little cigarette-lighter lamp! He must be one of the most powerful genies in the zoo. She bets he could make gold rain from the sky. And Siskin has him sending mail.

She spots an enormous blackhead in the grey curve of Blong's nostril. It's huge. Big as a barnacle. It needs its own enclosure in the zoo. Pia can't take her eyes off it. It's sort of horrifying, but strangely calming to focus on too.

Wait, maybe his name *is* Blom.

Ping! go his goggles.

'Siskin will see you now,' whatever-his-name says. Pia has the sudden urge to guess, one way or the other, Blom or Blong. Like a sign. If she gets it right, it means she at least has luck on her side when she steps into Siskin's office.

She stands, and says, casual as she can: 'Thanks. See you around, Blom.'

He pulls up his goggles for the first time. And not to smile.

'My name isn't Blom.'

'Oh. Sorry.' Pia feels the positive power of the universe fall away from her, the way it falls out from a horseshoe hung up the wrong way. 'It's Blong then, isn't it? Not Blom.'

'No.' He looks peeved. 'It's not Blong either.'

'Oh.' Now Pia is completely confused. 'Are you sure?'

'Very sure,' says the secretary.

'But I thought last time we met I heard your name wrong.'

'No.' The secretary narrows his little brown eyes and jabs his thumb at the genie on his desk. 'Last time we met, you heard *his* name wrong.'

'Oh,' says Pia again, a little more bleakly this time. 'Sorry. I'm in a bit of muddle today.'

'What else is new?' The secretary swivels round on his chair and pulls his goggles back down.

Pia scowls. 'Just so you know, you have a disgusting blackhead on your nose,' she says quickly. Then the door to Siskin blinks open and she heads inside, hot with embarrassment and full of bad luck.

7

YURK!

Zoo Director Siskin sits behind his aluminium desk, observing her with eyes like grey chips of ice. He looks so scary he makes Pia's stomach clench and a splurt of something sour suddenly burns up the back of her throat. Of all the terrible mistakes made this morning, the hot dog with mustard and extra onions might yet turn out to be her most catastrophic.

'Are you going to vomit?' Siskin asks, the same way someone else might say 'How do you do?'

Pia doesn't trust herself to answer back. She keeps her mouth jammed shut and shrugs.

'Make up your mind. You've wasted enough of my morning already with your tardiness.' Siskin produces a disposable tissue from the shiny pocket of his suit and holds it out to her. 'Use the bin by the door. Wipe your mouth afterwards.'

This is a very Siskin thing to say and do. The boss has procedures for everything. There is a rumour that tacked to the inside of his wardrobe is a sheet of paper with twenty-eight bullet points, telling him step by step the correct way to get ready in the morning.

Pia bets the rumour is true, except she reckons it is *way* more than one sheet of paper. Nobody can look like Siskin in only twenty-eight steps. The boss is immaculate – always.

His blue suit never has a crease. Each hair of his goatee is perfectly in place on his face, like iron filings in the grip of a powerful magnet.

Pia makes a lame attempt to neaten her fringe with her fingers. She really should've made more of an effort. Combed her hair. Washed her face. At least turned her shirt the right way out. These appraisals are a big deal. Zookeepers have got reassigned after them, sometimes even to the Seam.

Never Pia, though. She fails the psych test every year, of course. Her file is full of phrases like 'pessimism', 'obsessive self-analysis', 'a preoccupation with failure', 'unresolved grief'. Apparently, in her current mental state she's at high risk of mind-fray if she ever enters the Seam. At the very least, she'd develop a severe hot-dog phobia.

Eating it was such a bad idea.

So is thinking about it now.

She really feels sick.

Stupid genies and their unhelpful wish-grantings. Pia makes a promise to herself that one of her last acts as their zookeeper will be to give both Solomon and Bertoldo a very close shave.

Behind his desk, Siskin clears his throat. Somehow, the sound forces Pia's nausea back down. She takes a few deep breaths through her nose and cautiously opens her lips. Luckily, only words come out.

'I'm fine. I'm ready. Sorry I'm so late.'

Siskin nods and bends down to a drawer to retrieve her pink file. The light from Siskin's desk lamp glares off his shiny bald head, so bright it makes her squint. Through the walls comes the quiet hum of power cables, the throb of the ship's engine.

'Cornucopia, isn't it?' he says.

It is, technically. It means boundless plenty. Dad's idea. He used to say having a kid when the world was about to end was an act of reckless optimism, and his daughter's name should reflect that. Pia approves of the idea – she just wishes her parents hadn't chosen such a crappy name.

'Pia for short.' She tells him this every year, and every year Siskin gives zero indication he has heard her.

While the boss flicks through her folder (he hates tech, won't use goggles), Pia wipes the sweat from her forehead. *Come on*, she thinks. *Come on, come on. Let's get this over with. I've got a full-blown calamity that I've left at home completely unsupervised.*

'So.' Siskin brings out a slim grey file from inside the pink one and opens it up. 'Let's have a quick chat.'

Despite saying this, he keeps on reading. He makes no attempt to start any sort of chat at all.

The silence stretches out. A full minute of it, like elastic. Pia isn't sure what will snap first: it or her. She looks around for something to distract herself with.

Siskin's office is a lot like him. Controlled and cold and clean. A little empty. Metal-framed photographs cover one wall, showing various pictures from the mountain's history. The famous portrait of the first research team, just before the detonation. The same scientists in hazard suits, at the fringe of the blast radius, scanning patches of glitch with their instruments. A blurred shot of the first-ever voilà: Zafira, a lemon-yellow genie.

Right, that's it. She's looked at the pictures. She can't stand it any more.

'Is something wrong?' she asks.

Siskin stops reading, and glances up. 'Is that a habit?'

Answering questions with questions is one of the most annoying things the boss does. Now she feels angry as well as upset.

'Is what a habit?' Pia says back to him. See how *he* likes it.

Siskin sighs. 'Why are you assuming the worst?'

Argh! Take a deep breath. Be calm. 'Because I have a track record.'

Siskin holds up the file. 'I can see that. You're missing the last two weeks of reports. How is Threedeep, by the way?'

Pia looks at the floor. 'Still mending. The 'genieer says she doesn't really know what she's wishing fixed.'

'Of course she doesn't.' Siskin shakes his head disappointedly. 'That nanabug is i-era tech. Practically a living thing itself. It's certainly more complicated than some of the voilà we have in the arks. A pity you aren't as careful with the zoo's drones as you are with our celestials.'

Oh Seamstress. She should tell him now. Just say it. Go on.

Pia gulps. 'Well, um, I actually—'

'Please.' Siskin holds up his hand to cut her off. 'Stop with the modesty, Cornucopia. You know the celestials better than any of us. You are a credit to this zoo.'

Pia can't bear to hear Siskin say that. 'I'm not.'

'You are a credit to this zoo,' Siskin repeats emphatically. 'Now look at me and nod.'

Pia looks at him and nods. 'But I messed up—'

She jumps as Siskin slams her file shut.

'Of course you mess up! Just look at today. You arrive late, you almost throw up, you're nearly in tears for no reason. And what's that on your trouser leg?'

'It's, um, mustard.'

'You see? This is why you're so perfect for the celestial ark.'

Siskin is in full flow, no stopping him now. He loves doing this: taking long reports he has just read and summarising them.

'Celestials don't need to eat or photosynthesise, correct?'

Pia nods. Now she feels sick, not just with the hot dog but also with herself. What a coward.

'But they *do* need to appear to humans. Otherwise, they – how did you put it in your report?'

'They burn out. Like light bulbs. They use up so much power trying to get you to notice them they blow a fuse. At first, Mum and Dad thought they fed off *utility*. Like, being useful. But it's more complex than that. Angels, genies and devils all need *attention* too.'

Siskin nods. 'Which is where your clumsiness, absent-mindedness, and general calamity-causing have all proven very useful.'

He rattles off a bunch of impressive-sounding statistics, about how the angels were thirty per cent busier and ten per cent brighter, and her genies were making triple the previous amount of wishes, which seemed to prolong their flames.

'Just make sure you keep an eye on their beard lengths,' Siskin continues. 'As for the remaining devil, he hasn't managed to trick you into making a deal with him yet, which is about all I can hope for.'

'Thank you.'

'It's good to know I can trust you with this. It's important we care for our celestial voilà. The zoo cannot function without the genies. And as for the angels . . .'

Trailing off is not a very Siskin thing to do. In the silence, his jaw twitches.

'The two most important voilà in this zoo,' he finally says, 'are the two angels in your care. Earth needs a miracle. Now at last, it has two miracle-workers.'

Pia squeezes her eyes shut. Once again, the enormity of the secret she is keeping threatens to overwhelm her. Since before Megalolz, the zoo has been floating around the island, gathering up creatures from the Seam that might stave off the end of the world. Because the apocalypse is at hand – and it is not the flash of fire and fury that previous generations had predicted. It is slow, and some days it is almost unnoticeable, like the winding down of a clock, or the moving of the ice slugs. But it is coming. As the ohtwo factories break down and global temperatures climb and sea levels rise, it is closer every year.

It is just like Siskin said.

Earth needs a miracle.

Right, that settles it. She won't tell Siskin the angels are missing. Not yet. Not until she is *absolutely certain* she can't find them again. It is just too awful to consider that the *entire world* is now *doomed*, and Pia is to blame.

Nice idea, says a voice in her head. *Burying your head in the sand – that worked really well for humanity in the i-era, didn't it?*

Pia tells herself to shut up. She *isn't* burying her head, just keeping the problem *contained*. Siskin will freak out and transfer her, and that won't help anyone. If anyone is going to find the angels, it is Pia. Like the boss said, she knows them best.

'Don't worry,' she says. 'I'll sort everything out. You'll—'

Siskin holds up a hand to silence her. He notices a hair on the sleeve of his suit and plucks it off. 'The only celestials you don't seem to have had much progress with,' he says, carefully putting the hair in a drawer like someone filing a report, 'are the ghosts.'

Pia's throat tightens. She swallows a few times and looks at the floor.

'Which surprises me,' says Siskin, standing up and sitting on one edge of his desk.

Oh, great. This is Siskin's *talk to me* posture. But Pia doesn't want to talk. She wants to tell Siskin to shut up, she wants to yell at him, but she is concentrating too hard on her belly as it clenches and boils.

'I know it's an unusual situation. They used to look after you, and now you look after them.'

Pia says nothing.

'I thought you would have liked seeing them.'

She shakes her head. Closes her eyes to stop the queasiness.

'Why not?' Siskin sounds genuinely interested. 'Talk to me.'

'Because,' Pia gasps. 'Because they don't – because they don't realise it's *me*.'

And she gives up trying to fight it. She doubles over and yurks all over Siskin's desk.

Siskin leaps to one side, clattering into his lamp and knocking it over. With a blue flash and a bang, the bulb blows.

'Sorry,' says Pia groggily.

The director looks at his broken lamp. It is probably vintage and designer. Then he looks at the bright orange mulch that Pia has spewed all over his files. A vein pulses in his forehead. The disposable tissue comes back out from his suit pocket, pinched between thumb and forefinger. Pia takes it and meekly wipes her mouth.

'Let's reschedule,' Siskin says coolly. 'We'll conduct the on-site appraisal when you're feeling better.'

Pia looks down at the vomit-covered report. 'On-site?'

'I'm missing two weeks of data because of your nanabug accident. I was about to suggest we compensate with a tour of the celestial ark. But we shall follow hygiene procedures. You should return to your ark and recuperate.'

Pia gawps at the vomit. It saved her. The hot dog had actually saved her. Siskin was about to invite himself on to the celestial ark for a guided tour. Oh Seamstress, that was close! Now she can keep him and everyone else away from the celestial ark until she works out what to do.

Siskin's secretary gets called in and gives Pia a look of utter loathing as he scoops up some of the puke with a wad of paper, then scribbles out a wish for the little grey genie to zephyr it away.

The blackhead on his nostril is gone. He must have squeezed it out.

Pia shudders and almost yurks again. She hurries out of the office as fast as she can and sits down on a seat in the corridor, gulping the ship's stale recycled air. Despite throwing up, she feels better than she has all morning. OK, she is never doubting Solomon and Bertoldo ever again. What a mighty boon they gave her. It hasn't led her to the angels, but it has bought her time.

'Shall I ping a nanabug to take her away?' Pia hears the secretary ask Siskin. There is a note of pleading to his voice.

'I shall take her myself,' comes the answer, in a tone that suggests it is the only guaranteed way to get rid of her. Siskin steps out into the corridor. 'This way.' He turns left towards the elevator.

Pia follows him. She has the weak-headed, weirdly euphoric feeling she always gets after throwing up. Siskin's shoe heels rap steadily over the floor. She finds herself walking in step with him. The man walks like a metronome.

'I don't think your secretary likes me,' she says.

'Weevis is almost the same age as you,' Siskin answers, as if that means they ought to get along brilliantly.

'Weevis?!' Pia facepalms. '*Now* I remember. He *so* looks like a Weevis too.' She mutters it into her memory. 'Weevis. Weevis, Weevis, Weevis.'

Siskin gives her a look that he often gives to kids. Sort of like they are creatures in the zoo, ones that really weird him out. Pia is sure that he would prefer a zoo without any kids on it at all. Everything would probably be a lot more *ordered*. But it would also be a lot more empty.

No one really knows why *kids* are the best at creating voilà inside the Seam, but bad stuff tended to happen to any grown-ups who went to the Seamstress. Most of the first research team – the scientists who created the reality bomb – had gone crazy in the Seam, or even disappeared altogether. Pia thinks of the photograph of them on Siskin's wall. Those excited smiles. Not even the mightiest of hot dogs could have saved them.

8

Bargains, Bargains

Pia borrows a breather, leaves Ark One, and zephyrs back to the celestials. Ishan is gone. That's about the only good news.

Her absurd hope that the angels might have returned is crushed the moment she looks at the garden. The apple tree looks like something from a haunted forest, its scraggly branches clawing at the sky. The beams of sunlight holding up the angels' house have started to scatter and fade.

The sight makes her want to cry. She tries to hold in the tears, but in the end she gives up. Maybe letting everything out will make her feel better.

Nope, she decides after a few minutes of sobbing. Some things – tears, secrets, vomit – are better bottled up.

Pazuzu unfurls from her aerosol can and tries to comfort Pia. 'The heroine is tormented by her McGuffin?' the genie asks.

Pia's Tellish isn't good enough to understand what that means. She forces her tears to stop and thanks Pazuzu and goes back to her cabin to calm down. Then she scribbles a message on a scrip of pink zookeeper paper, and goes back to Pazuzu so she can zephyr it to Ishan.

Downside, I threw up everywhere. Upside, I now have room for lunch. Every cloud, hey? Rek in 10 and I'll tell you all? P

A few minutes later, another slip, this one green for

Seamster messages, flutters suddenly in the air as Ishan zephyrs back his reply.

Pia snatches at it. He's written *It's a date!* which he had obviously then realised was a massive mistake, because he'd tried to cross it out completely. The words still show through, though. *See you in 20 – got some nanite updates to run!* he's written instead.

That's good. If she's going to work out a way to summon the angels back, she needs to think about this more logically. Ishan's brain can help with that. He always thinks about things in a real step-by-step way.

I'll have to be careful not to make him suspicious, though, she thinks. *I don't want to actually confide in him.*

Pia goes back to her cabin before she leaves. She scribbles out a few other messages to the rest of her Rekker crew. She wishes Gowpen good luck (he's in the Seam today), and tells Wilma to move Weevis up their league table of enemies (it's a thing they do). There's still a few minutes to kill, so she listens to some pip-pop tunes on her goggles' tinny speakers whilst she reads everything there is on file about angel behaviour.

'*Nine bil, ten bil, girl you know the world's ill.*'

She starts singing along to the chorus (it's super sweary; if Threedeep was here she'd bleep it). She gets so into it that she doesn't notice Weevis has zephyred on to the ark until he raps on the cabin window with his knuckles.

Oh facepalm! She tears off her goggles.

'You shouldn't be here,' she says through the glass. 'Hygiene procedures.'

Weevis gives her a look. 'I'll stay on this side of the window.' His muffled voice drips with sarcasm. 'Because you look so contagious.'

Pia scowls, but her heart is racing so fast she feels she might faint. 'What do you want?'

'You forgot this.' Weevis holds up Siskin's busted lamp. The cord is looped around the base; the plug dangles down by his elbow.

'Huh?'

'The Director wants to try something. Do you think the angels can miracle this fixed?'

They could if they were here. Pia shrugs. 'Why not get a genie to do it, if you're in a rush? That little one on your desk has a pretty long beard.'

Weevis raises his eyebrows, which are the size and shape and colour of dirty fingernail clippings. 'Because the Director wants to try something,' he repeats in a tired voice. 'Genies can't wish without a 'genieer, and the 'genieer needs a good knowledge of electricals to figure out how the lamp is broken, and the way to mend it.'

Weevis is right, of course. That is the whole problem with wishes. The more complex the problem, the more detailed a wish has to be in order to contain it and minimise unexpected consequences. It is why Threedeep is taking so long to fix, and why a genie can't just wish the world's problems away. Not only would they need a beard a mile long, but problems like climate change, overpopulation, pollution, and mass-extinctions are all too enormous and complicated, and

58

too intricately linked with the ten billion humans living here.

A few years back, Siskin trialled wishes as a way to save the world. He sent his most powerful genies and best 'genieers – the most logical, thoughtful writers of wish-scripts in the zoo – to one of the drowned cities on the east coast. There, the 'genieers crafted a wish so detailed it took three hours to speak. The wish was designed to make the swamped streets habitable again for the thousands trying to survive there.

Upon the wish's granting, a cacophony of thunderclaps echoed through the city.

The wish succeeded – in a way. The genies and their 'genieers made the drowned city liveable in again. But not by draining the flood waters. Nor by raising up the houses. The wish simply zephyred away two thirds of the city's population, freeing up enough food and resources for the other third to survive.

Two hundred thousand people, missing in an eye-blink. No one has ever discovered where they zephyred to.

After that, development of new wish-scripts was put on hold.

'The Director wants to see how miracles cope with problem-solving, without all the wish-scripting and research,' Weevis continues. 'It'll be a good indication of what the angels might be able to achieve when they grow up.'

'*If*,' Pia corrects, because no one knows how angels age, and they've been kids for twenty years, ever since Mum brought them out of the Seam. Whatever causes an angel to grow up, it isn't time.

Weevis just sniffs impatiently. 'Call them over, then.'

'Huh?' Pia actually gulps.

'The angels. Summon them, or whatever it is you do.'

'Yeah, OK, I will, but . . . it's just that they're resting.'

'Well, wake them up. This lamp is an antique, you know.'

'You'll have to leave it with me,' Pia says desperately.

'Why?' Weevis looks at her with narrowed eyes.

Behind him, there's an enormous crack. A branch from the apple tree breaks off the trunk and falls on to the angels' house, caving in the roof, which disappears the way sunsets do.

Weevis turns. 'Is that supposed to look so dead?' His tone suggests that he clearly thinks not.

The lie comes instantly to her lips: 'I've told the angels to let the garden go into autumn.'

'So?'

'So I'm giving the angels a break. They're tired out. No way they're doing any mending until tomorrow at least.'

What the Seamstress just happened? Pia's brain is usually way too slow to come up with excuses. That felt like someone whispered them in her ear . . .

Wait a second.

Stupid, stupid, stupid.

'Bagrin,' she mutters.

'What?' says Weevis through the glass.

Pia is too furious with herself to answer him. She must not have sealed the lead door's peephole properly in her panic this morning. Bagrin has probably been listening in on her thoughts since she got back to the ark.

Which means he knows about the angels.

That's why he just fed her those lies: he knows he has some knowledge to bargain with.

She looks up. Weevis is looking at her like she might actually be crazy. And up to something. 'Where are they, anyway? I don't see them.'

'Over there,' Pia says, as Bagrin slips another lie into her head. She adds a little bit of scorn into her voice. 'What, can you not feel them or something?'

It's an Emperor's New Clothes moment. No one wants to be known as the guy that can't feel angels. That would be embarrassing. Weevis has enough trouble making friends at the zoo as it is.

'Of course I can feel them,' he says after a moment. 'You're right – they, uh, do seem tired.'

Pia is too relieved to say anything back.

Weevis puts the lamp down on the deck. 'OK. I'll come back. Don't break it any more.'

Pia watches him hurry off. She waits for the clap of air that signals he's zephyred, then she heads down to the infernal prism and tells the devil to lay off the temptation.

You owe Bagrin, says the voice from behind the lead door. The devil sends her the image of Dibsy, his round yellow face glinting like a gold coin. *Big time.*

Don't phrase anything as a question, she reminds herself. *Questions give devils power.*

'I don't know what you mean,' she says.

Oh, really? Maybe Bagrin should send a whisper to Siskin that his precious angels are gone.

'Good luck with that.' Pia grips the peephole. It's open just a fraction, just as she suspected. 'I'm shutting this now. Your whispers won't get through.'

What about when Weevis comes back? We will scream and scream and scream.

Pia grits her teeth and goes to slam the peephole shut. Then she dongs her head on the metal with a groan. She can't do it. Too risky. The devil has nothing to lose, and she has everything. She just needs to buy enough time to find the angels. Until then, she needs to keep Bagrin quiet.

'Tell me what you want,' she mutters.

Bagrin's presence on her shoulder moves up and down, in what Pia assumes is an attempt at a shrug. *Just to observe.*

'Observe? What does that mean?' (Ugh, dammit, don't ask him *questions*, stupid.)

Just that you leave the lead door open, just a crack. And agree to let Bagrin listen in as you search. Who knows? There might come a time when Bagrin might be – and now the cunning creeps into his voice – *of assistance.*

Pia turns from the lead door in disgust. Facepalm, facepalm, facepalm! What a morning. The angels have been gone a few hours, and already she is in league with a devil.

'I'll give you until sunset,' she offers. 'If I haven't got the angels back by then, I'm raising the alarm.'

Deal, Bagrin says, and Pia feels a weird warmth upon her shoulder as his presence settles there.

Oh well. At least she hasn't *signed* anything.

Yes. Bagrin is an evil little whisper in her ear. *This is a good deal. A real steal.*

'Stop talking and let me think,' she tells him.

You'll have to work out a way to bring the angels back. Summon them.

'I don't want your help, Bagrin. I just want you to shut up.'

The devil is probably right, though. The angels might be absolutely anywhere on Earth now. Anywhere in the solar system, actually. Pia won't ever find them; she'll have to find a way to bring them back to her.

To summon them.

Perhaps she ought to try praying again. Or give up entirely. Or she could always head down to Bagrin's prism and throw herself in. All three might genuinely work. Prayer, despair and impending doom: these things summon angels.

Sometimes.

Because Pia has already tried prayer, hasn't she? Maybe she didn't do it properly. Maybe prayers are like wish-scripts: you need an exact sequence of words. Or maybe it isn't *what* you say, but *how* you say it, or whether you *deserve* what you're asking for.

Who knows. Pia has prayed a lot in her life with exactly

zero return, so whatever the answer is, she's doing something wrong.

There are other ways, Bagrin dangles temptingly. *We can tell you of them. And all we ask in return is—*

'Get out of my head, Bagrin!' she yells, and he flees on to her shoulder and settles there.

Stupid devil.

And now she's late for Ishan.

Rummaging around in her dungarees for the wish-script that will take her to the Rek, she rushes to see Pazuzu.

9

THE SMELLEPHANT IN THE ROOM

The Rek is a small i-era military ship, abandoned after the detonation that created the Seam. Unlike the rest of the zoo, it doesn't move. It only just about floats. The island's mountain rises sheer from the sea, except on the southern side, where it dwindles down to a bed of black sand and rocky reefs. That's where the Rek lies, slightly to one side, its lower decks filled with seawater.

The Rek is too small to be an ark, and too rusted and full of holes to be much else too. Back in the years when the air was cleaner, Siskin tried encouraging keepers to zephyr here and picnic. The whole top deck was painted and parkified: benches, bright plastic turf, a few replica trees. There had even been a ceremony with a ribbon, and a period when Siskin insisted everyone call it the *(P)ark*. He *loves* hip little names like that.

But after all that dressing up, the (P)ark was still just a half-sunk hunk of junk in a cove of bumpy scab-coloured rock. And for the grown-ups, terrified of getting mind-frayed, it sits way too close to the Seam. So eventually they stopped coming, which meant the genies stopped mending, which meant the paint peeled and the rust came back.

But Pia and her friends have stayed.

It is her favourite place in all the zoo. There's something about it. She loves how the tilted deck makes *everyone* clumsy. More than that, she loves how it is *theirs*. Their Rek, which stands for *Wreck* and *Recreation* and *Recklessness*.

The Rekkers (which at the moment are her, Ishan, Wilma, Gowpen, and Zugzwang when he can be bothered – and with his dad being the Director of the whole zoo and always so busy, Zugzwang can pretty much do what he wants) head there whenever they need to joke or gossip or bicker. The Rek's genie Karratakirattaki has basically become their own personal butler, wishing them up endless supplies of sweets and stim drinks, until curfew comes and their nanabugs order them all home.

It was here that Pia heard about the prism explosion; here that she came to sit and cry in the months after. It was here that Ishan tried to kiss her.

He is waiting on the same bench where it happened. Pia shakes away the memory. Part of her wants to start discussing how to summon angels right away, but Ishan's nanabug Sixtip is a hovering black blot in the blue sky above them, monitoring from a distance, logging all their conversation. She'll have to be sly about this. She'll have to be patient.

So she sits and tells him the story of the appraisal instead: the hot dog, Weevis, the puke.

'Throwing up isn't so bad,' Ishan says. 'In my first appraisal, Siskin called me Buttercup throughout the whole thing.'

'Whaaaat?' Pia grins for what feels like the first time that day. 'How is that even possible?'

'He looks down at his desk a lot. His secretary mixed up

our files. You know Buttercup, who works with the phoenixes? Siskin sat down, reading through her report instead of mine, and he didn't look up the whole time. Not once. "Take a seat, Buttercup." "I'm impressed with your fire hazard assessments, Buttercup." I was too scared to correct him. When he said, "You're doing an exemplary job," I just said "Thanks" in a high-pitched voice and ran off quick.'

In spite of everything, Pia starts to laugh. 'How did I not know this?'

'Maybe I've been saving it for a day like today, when I needed a real toe-curler of an embarrassing story to make you feel better.'

Pia slumps her head and lets her shoulders shake as she sniggers. Her whole friendship with Ishan is built on just this sort of story. You're a klutz, I'm a klutz, let's laugh about it before we cry about it.

They chat for a bit. Ishan technobabbles about his nanites and the upgrades they are going through, and how he is trying to program them so they won't upgrade into some evil robot consciousness that wants to destroy the world, like a version 2.0 of Megalolz.

Pia listens out for a chance to introduce the angels into the conversation. She lies on the deck and closes her eyes. The sun's heat has soaked into the metal all morning and that warmth seeps into her back. The Rek always has this weird relaxing effect on her, no matter what.

'It's hard,' Ishan is saying. 'The nanites keep asking me questions about humans, so I do my best to explain what we're like, and then they come back with, "You are illogical", "Your species makes no sense", and I'm like, "Yes, I know, we're gadj-damn crazy".'

'You are such a human-hater, Ish. These nanites better not grow up just like you.'

Ishan grins. 'Hey, they've worked it out themselves. We *are* totally insane.' He points at the mountain. It is shimmering lightly, as if radiating waves of heat. 'Would a *sane* species invent a reality bomb that blows up the laws of time and gravity and whatever, and *then* send kids into the weird hole it makes to see if they can imagine new animals into life?'

Pia shrugs. 'No?'

'*Exactly!* A *sane* species would probably decide that it was *easier* just to look after the planet they lived on, instead of polluting it and ruining everything.'

Pia gets up on her elbows. Now might be a good time to ask him about the angels. Ishan's in one of his theorising moods. If she just starts pondering how to summon angels, he'll surely come up with a dozen different possibilities for her.

'Soooo,' she begins. 'I was thinking . . .'

Pia really thinks she sounds casual as she says this, but Ishan instantly goes into nervous mode. His eyes go big, his fidgeting stops, and he gets an expression on his face like he's about to sneeze.

'Ah. I know what you're about to say.'

'Umm, I don't think you do.'

68

'Sure I do, Pia. It's the smellephant in the room.'

Oh, great. Is Ishan talking about the massively embarrassing thing that happened last week? Does she really think she wants to talk about *that*?

So much for being all subtle and stealthy. Now he'll be scrutinising absolutely *everything* she says. Pia groans. 'Forget it.'

Now he looks confused as well as nervous. 'But you brought it up. It's the smellephant in the room.'

'I know. And I'm happy for us to just ignore it and pretend it isn't there.'

'Ignore it? Even though it's farting out all these bad smells whenever we're around each other?'

'This metaphor is sort of gross, Ish.'

Ishan blinks as he processes this. 'Yeah,' he admits. 'I guess what I'm trying to say is . . . Never mind.'

Another awkward silence. The conversation has juddered to a halt, like some complex machine they have just busted. Pia has no idea how to fix it. She has no idea how to fix anything. The world is dying and the angels are gone and, maybe worst of all, her friendship with Ishan Gabril feels broken.

Then two scrips zephyr into the air in front of them and flutter on to their laps.

A message from Wilma, of just one word:

UNICORN.

10

SPARKLEHORN

The message changes everything, or at least makes it less important. Suddenly they're both standing, talking over each other.

'Did you get—'

'Yes! Do you think—'

'I don't know! Shall we—'

'Go? Yeah!'

Ishan shouts up to his nanabug that they're going to see the unicorn. Sixtip flashes back a green light, and the two of them rush across the tilted deck. Pia slips on the remains of the old plastic turf that the sea's turned a slimy green and Ishan reaches out to catch her, but taking hold of his hand would be too weird right now, so Pia prefers to fall flat on her face and scramble back to her feet.

'You OK?' Ishan looks at her.

Of course she's not OK. She's now wet, and smelling of seaweed. She's a mess, it's all a mess, but clutched in her hand is a little slip of paper with something amazing on it.

A unicorn. Gowpen's made an actual unicorn. She clings to that thought. Right now it's just about the only happy one in her entire head.

• • •

Karratakirattaki lives on the Rek's old command deck, in the barrel of a rusty flare gun. Ishan pulls the trigger and out he comes in a khaki-coloured boom.

'Your wish is my command, commander!' the genie says, snapping to attention.

Pia and Ishan both return his salute. Genies often use the places and objects around them to 'accent' their Tellish, and living on this old navy ship has given Karratakirattaki a real military bearing.

'At ease, commando,' Ishan says in Tellish. 'Got a vital mission for you. We're going in behind enemy lines.'

Karratakirattaki lights up like a night-time battlefield. It has to be the ten thousandth time the genie's heard this, but he doesn't care one bit.

'Mission accepted,' he says. 'Awaiting orders.'

'Where are we zephyring?' Pia asks Ishan as they fumble for their scripts.

'Arrivals ark?'

Oh yeah, of course. Wilma's note didn't say because it was obvious. All new voilà go to the arrivals ark when they first come out of the Seam and off the island. That's where the unicorn will be.

Ishan goes through his wish-script first.

'Yes, SUH!' belts Karratakirattaki. 'Evac, evac, we need evac now!' He grants the wish, and Ishan vanishes in a clap that the genie decorates with a miniature fireball and the sound effect of an i-era helicopter.

Pia goes next, closing her eyes and jamming her fingers in her ears. The world whirls around her and she lurches forwards and falls over again. It's always like this when zephrying from the Rek. The deck never moves, so when you appear on something that's travelling at speed, you tend to go flying.

Her eyes are still closed, trying to quell the dizziness, when a hand takes hold of her and hauls her up. She's about to snatch it back and yell at Ishan, but it isn't him; it's Wilma. She must have been waiting at the zephyr zone for them to come in.

Wilma Adeoye is super short and super sarcastic and super awesome. Pia always thinks of her as being way too cool for the Rekkers. She's not a gogglehead like Ishan, not a slacker like Zugzwang, not a mummy's boy like Gowpen or a klutz like Pia. And yet she's a Rekker, and you can only be a Rekker if you're a misfit. You have to have something that sets you apart. Like a superpower, only one that compels you into mega-awkward situations.

For Wilma, it's her sense of humour, which is so cutting she'd need to declare it if she ever boarded a plane. In the year she's been at the zoo, Wilma has managed to fall out with every other group of kids: the admins, the 'genieers, the other Seamers.

It's only really Gowpen who can handle her. The two of them are best friends, which is why she's here before Pia and Ishan.

'Is he OK?' Ishan's eyes are so wide he looks like he might sneeze, which is a sign that he's nervous. 'Is *it* OK?'

Wilma's face is a picture of doom and despair, and for a moment Pia's heart stutters. Being a Seamer is a risky job. Every year, kids go off to the island mountain and don't come back. Even those that do make it can return mind-frayed, heads so messed up they can't tell what's real any more.

'Oh Seamstress, what happened?' Pia's hand flies to her mouth.

'His mum wants him to name it *Sparklehorn*.' Wilma rolls her eyes. 'Come quick, we have to save him.'

Ishan groans. 'Wilma! Don't *do* that!' But he's grinning as he says it. They all are. Gowpen's done it – brought a voilà out of the Seam. Taken a figment of his imagination and made it real, made it true.

And not just any random creature, but a *unicorn*.

Pia gets to her feet and looks around. The arrivals ark is stacked with old shipping containers, like a cube made of enormous multi-coloured toy bricks. The holding bays, where new voilà are tested and treated, are all inside.

A couple of security guards are posted at the main entrance, but they haven't even clocked Ishan and Pia's zephyring because they've both turned round to peer through the doorway, trying to catch a glimpse of the unicorn.

'What's it like?' Pia says, and for some reason she is whispering.

And Wilma just grins and says, 'Come see for yourself.'

• • •

The unicorn is purest white: a white that *shines*. Not in the way angels shine, Pia decides. Angels are all hazy and gold: the unicorn is shimmering silver. It glows the colour of cool moonlight.

Moonlight. It triggers a thought in Pia. Was this the meaning of the angels' dream? To herald the unicorn's arrival?

'Wow,' she sighs. Her breath mists up the glass between the viewing container and the holding bay. She wipes it with her sleeve and carries on staring.

No one speaks for what seems like ages. The unicorn is mesmerising. Though hours old, it walks like a queen. Like the world has been made for it, instead of the other way around. How did Gowpen imagine such a thing?

'Look at your eyelashes, all glittery-wittery!' Pia coos at it. She sounds like a five-year-old; but who cares?

The unicorn comes closer, dark blue eyes filled with sparkling glints, like shards of diamond. Its hooves clip across the floor, the horn ripples silver. Its mane makes a sound like little bells tinkling. All around it, scientists in lab coats are waving monitoring wands in the air and noting down the results and mumbling to themselves.

Pia giggles. 'They look like wizards in pyjamas,' she says to Ishan and Wilma.

The scientists look up. Their leader, a bald man with a frizzy grey beard, scowls. His tinny voice comes through the room's speaker. 'The intercom is on, you know.'

Pia spots the microphone above her, and her cheeks go

hot. She leans forward and thuds her forehead on the barrier glass.

'Oh, Catastro-P,' Wilma says sympathetically. It's her nickname for Pia whenever stuff goes wrong.

'You have no idea,' Pia groans.

Reaching forwards, Wilma flicks the intercom switch with her thumb. 'Maybe let's leave the pyjama-wizards and go see Gowpen?'

'Yeah,' says Ishan, wincing at the hostile looks coming from the scientists on the other side of the glass. 'Let's do that. Awkwardness levels are approaching lethal limits.'

How's it all going? Bagrin asks brightly as they leave the unicorn. His voice is fainter than it was, and there's a crackle of static too, but he's still audible. He sounds smug.

Pia grits her teeth and doesn't answer. Bagrin knows *exactly* how it's going: disastrously. She hasn't even been able to bring up the subject of angels yet.

Just let us know if you need any help, says the devil. *We can provide a range of suggestions, all competitively priced. Go on, make a deal . . .*

Pia shakes him off. But it's not as easy as before. And even when Bagrin's presence fades, his voice lingers like an echo.

Go on, make a deal, make a deal, make a deal . . .

But it isn't the devil's voice at all, she realises with a shudder. It's her own thoughts, it's temptation. And it's getting harder to resist.

• • •

They find Gowpen in another container with a different bunch of pyjama-wizards, all waving different monitor wands. Any kid coming back from the Seam has this check-up, to make sure they're not mind-frayed.

Gowpen's fine, though. Pia doesn't need a monitor wand to see that. He grins at them as soon as they come in, and they grin back and send high fives through the barrier glass.

Pia likes Gowpen a lot. He's always smiling, even though he has crooked teeth and one of the worst jobs in the zoo: when he isn't at the Seam, he shovels Rhinosaurus rex manure over on the megafauna ark. According to Gow, it comes out like boulders that he has to roll off the edge of the ship and into the sea. His face is always baby pink, from having to have a dozen showers a day to wash off the stink. Today it's even pinker than usual, because he is super proud, and because his parents have turned up, and they're super embarrassing.

'Unicorns!' Gowpen's mum Fay bursts through the door behind the Rekkers. She claps Gowpen hysterically. Fay cares for the Fabergé chickens. She wears perfume and puts rose powder on her face. Pia often cites her as proof for her theory that, given enough time, zookeepers begin to resemble the creatures they care for.

Fay smiles at Ishan and Wilma. Not Pia, though. Gowpen's mum has not been her biggest fan, ever since three weeks ago, when Pia stupidly asked one of her genies to colour Fay's nails purple as a surprise for her fiftieth birthday.

Solomon hadn't heard the word *nails*. Fay had not been

happy when she woke up totally violet. They'd needed a 'genieer to script her back to normal. Pia was close enough to Fay now to see that some of the dye *still* hadn't been wished out from her wrinkles.

Fay sighs. 'Oh, Gowpy, it's like a fairy tale come true . . .'

Gowpen blushes. He's a Rekker mainly because of his mum.

'*Unicorns!*' Fay squeals.

'Just *a* unicorn at the moment, Fay,' says Gowpen's dad. Tej is zookeeper to the singing hippos, so Pia keeps expecting (as per her theory) to see him turn fat-bellied and bald-headed and peg-toothed. But Tej is skinny and cheerful and totally devoted to Fay, just like his son.

'Poor thing,' says Fay. 'It must be so lonely!'

Gowpen speaks from behind the barrier glass. 'I'm heading back tomorrow for another one, Mum. This one is a lady unicorn so I'm going to try for a male next.'

Fay lets out an excited squeal and does a dozen little claps extremely fast just below her chin.

'*Finally*, some good news,' says Vivi, one of the scientists, as she passes her wand across Gowpen's forehead. 'I wonder what they'll be used for?'

Every voilà in the zoo is meant to help the world in some way. The hummingdragons are being trained to scavenge and hoard precious metals for recycling. The pigasi are involved in some sort of experiment to see if the zoo could selectively breed *luck*.

Gowpen blushes at the question. 'I don't know. I doubt they'll be as useful as angels and genies.'

'Ahem, *nanites*,' Ishan adds with a cough.

'Who cares about useful?' Tej beams at his son. Singing hippos are not useful in the slightest, but sing some pretty beautiful lullabies to their babybotamus young. Siskin decided to keep them in the zoo on account of the exquisite 'Hippopoperas' they perform to each other as a kind of courtship ritual. Pia was always glad when Tej's ark drifted near to hers around sunset.

'Yeah, Gow!' Wilma slaps the glass like she's giving him a smack. 'You brought out a freaking *unicorn*! On behalf of the six-year-old me, thank you for *literally* making my childhood dreams come true.'

Gowpen grins. 'No more Rhinosaurus rex manure for me! Soon me and the unicorns will have our own enclosure.'

Tej nods. 'Maybe even your own ark like Pia and Ishan each have!'

'Oh, *don't* say that,' Fay scolds. 'I'll tell Siskin to put Gowpy and his unicorns on our ark, right next to us.'

Wilma makes some chicken-based pun about it being time to leave the roost, which everyone but Fay laughs at. Pia laughs mainly to cover her jealousy. She wishes that— No. Stop that thought right there. The zookeeper in Pia is trained not even to *think* stuff that begins with that phrase.

Talk drifts back to the unicorn. 'Is it true that her blood is rainbow-coloured?' asks Wilma. 'Is it true she poops glitter?'

'*Unicorns!*' Fay dabs her eyes and starts to cry.

'Uni*corn*, darling,' repeats Tej.

Fay is full-on bawling now. 'He's calling her Sparklehorn, you know.'

The Rekkers all share a look, Gowpen included. Wilma goes up to the intercom and asks one of the scientists to check over Fay for signs of mind-fray. Like all Wilma's jokes, it cuts a little close. Fay *is* acting a little weird. There's a wounded silence. Even Gowpen looks embarrassed.

'OK,' says Ishan. 'How about we go get lunch? I'm pretty sure there are some people in the canteen we haven't made enemies with yet.'

11

THE GARGANTULA-KEEPER

They zephyr to the dining ship, an old i-era luxury cruiser. There are cheers for Gowpen as they appear in the canteen. Everyone's clapping, and a few 'genieers get their genies to zephyr glitter above Gowpen's head. He's blushing so hard Wilma pretends to give him that Heimlich manoeuvre you do when someone's choking.

Pia slaps a fake smile over her face all through the cheers, but it keeps peeling off like an old plaster. All this good feeling for Gowpen is just reminding her of the fury she'll face if anyone finds out about the angels. The death stares. The muttering. *You stupid, stupid girl.* And it won't be glitter zephyring above her head, oh no. It'll be boulders of Rhinosaurus rex poop, and that's if she's lucky.

Want to avoid all that? Bagrin asks. *Then you just have to—*

Pia shakes him away, just. The temptation is growing in her, though. It's like a hunger. Maybe she can fill it with food.

A genie called Tadaaa and her 'genieer Fran are on thrinting duty in the kitchens. They take food orders by big vats of farm-factory-grown nutrient slop, then make that slop appear upon the plate in whatever form you ask for.

Pia and Ishan and Wilma and Gowpen wait in the queue. Ishan wishes a bowl of stir-fry noodles and a stim juice. A puff of smoke, and it appears. Wilma wishes cereal, like always. Gowpen is too busy being congratulated by all the other zookeepers to order.

Pia wonders what to get. Tadaaa thrints a pretty decent ice-cream sandwich, but in the end she just asks for salad.

'Wow.' Ishan looks at her plate. 'Where's the real Pia gone?'

'Me and junk food are officially on a break.' He has no idea the trouble a cake and a hot dog have caused her today.

The room is full of long tables. Who you are decides where you sit. There's the security staff table (loud and sweary), the admin staff table (lots of soup in mugs for some reason), old spider lady's table (no one sits there but Urette). It's almost like the zoo staff are different species of voilà, all in separate enclosures with their own environments.

The Rekkers sit on their table, which is in the corner by the bins. Eventually, everyone planning to say congratulations to Gowpen has said it, and they're alone.

'Moonbim is a right terror,' Gowpen tells the table. 'I nearly got skewered this morning when we both came out of the Seam.'

'Great name, Gowpen!' Pia says.

'You think?' Gowpen says. 'You don't prefer Sparklehorn?'

Wilma mimes throwing up over her bowl of cereal. Pia has never seen her eat anything else but Malty Pops and milk.

'No offence, Gow,' she says, after another mouthful of cereal, 'but your mum wouldn't know a good name if it came up and introduced itself to her. Remember when I won her name-a-chicken competition and wanted to call it The

Mother Clucker? She blubbed for two days until I agreed to change its name to Mauvie.' Wilma shakes her head darkly, making her braided hair swish. 'Sometimes I think I'm too hilarious for this place.'

'Where's Siskin gonna put your enclosure?' Ishan asks.

Gowpen shrugs. 'Trying not to get ahead of myself. Arrivals are still doing all their tests and stuff.'

'We call them pyjama-wizards now,' Wilma informs him.

Gowpen brings out a fistful of paper scrips: grey, for the colour of lab technicians. 'They say she's doing well so far. But it's early days.'

The rest of the table nods solemnly. Plenty of the voilà brought from the Seam are far too fragile to survive in reality for long. It took hundreds of imagerations for Pia's mum to bring out the angels, for example.

Sometimes, it was just that the creature wasn't quite imagined right. Other times, the voilà might be so complicated or strange that no one could work out how to care for it in time.

That was what had happened to Vivi, the woman who monitored Gowpen for mind-fray. After years of visiting the Seam, she only ever created one type of voilà: a species of origami mantis that seemed to feed off words, which it stripped out of books and tattooed on its paper body.

But then, when she was much older, Vivi accidentally fed one mantis the last page of a novel with the words THE END on. The phrase spread like a disease over the whole brood, until eventually they all unfolded into single sheets of creased and lifeless paper with THE END stamped all over them in large type. There are no origami mantis in the zoo now.

'Moonbim's a fierce one, but fragile still.' Gowpen smiles at Pia. 'Tell your angels to sing prayers for her, won't you?'

'I will.' Just like that, Pia's sick feeling creeps back into her belly. Gowpen just shared his worries with her, like a good friend should. And still she hid behind lies.

'How's life without your nanabug, P?' asks Wilma. 'Threedeep's been gone days.'

'Weeks,' Pia corrects.

Wilma whistles low. 'That must be some butt you have.'

Pia grins. Wilma's jokes would make her scowl if anyone else ever said them.

'Think you could sit on my drone too?' Wilma adds in a mock-whisper.

We have talked about this sort of inappropriate joking, chats Wilma's nanabug, Fourcandles, on her screen. Normally nanabugs leave the kids alone at meal times. Fourcandles has probably turned up to punish Wilma for something or other. The two are always squabbling.

Gowpen is the only one in the group without a nanabug. Every kid working in the zoo without parents has to be monitored. Ishan's parents are back in the sprawl, Pia's parents can't look after her any more, and Wilma's parents are busy with their diplomat duties back on the mainland. Wilma doesn't go back there much because she argues with them even more than with Fourcandles.

Zugzwang, the latest member of the Rekkers, has a nanabug too, despite his dad being here on the zoo. Pia guesses it's because Siskin is too busy.

Wilma fixes her nanabug with a withering stare. 'If you would just leave me alone, like all the other bugs, maybe you wouldn't be offended by my sense of humour.'

She motions to the canteen entrance, where Ishan's drone Sixtip and Zugzwang's drone Sevenheaven are out in the corridor on standby.

Fourcandles stays put. **We have also discussed answering back, Wilma.**

'Aaaaaaaanyway.' Wilma gives a huge eye-roll. 'That's weird what you say about your unicorn, Gow. The mirrorangutangs have been nervous today too.'

Just like Gowpen and Zugzwang, Wilma is a Seamer. The voilà she brings out are big rusty-coloured creatures that can only exist in reflections. The mirrorangutangs live on an ark of mirrors that needs to be kept lit twenty-four hours a day and has its own back-up generator, because if the engine ever blows and the lights go out, the mirrorangutangs will cease to exist.

Siskin was very excited when the first of them had appeared, because beings that live in light might have been able to be trained to carry instantaneous messages, like satellites and optical cables once had. But the mirrorangutangs have turned out to be yet another disappointment to him. They are too much like Wilma. You can never rely upon them doing what you want.

Ishan frowns. 'The mirrorangutangs are being funny too?'

'Mum said at breakfast that one of the Fabergé chickens laid an egg that was completely *plain*,' says Gowpen.

'Yeah.' Wilma grins a ghost-story smile. 'And when she threw it in the bin, the shell cracked and a *scream* came out.'

'True story,' Gowpen confirms. 'It made Mum cry.'

Wilma snorts. 'Fay's *always* crying.'

'She's been pretty emotional today,' Gowpen says. 'Even for her.'

Pia is stabbing her salad with her fork, feeling sorry for herself. Suddenly she pushes away her plate. This is interesting. Other voilà are acting strangely? What if there's a link to the angels' disappearance?

'You heard of any other voilà being weird?' she asks. Everyone shrugs or shakes their heads. 'What about you, Zugz?'

Zugzwang sits a few seats away from them, watching some video on his goggles, shovelling his lunch into his mouth.

For someone with such a cool name, Zugzwang is a real loser. Pia doesn't really know why he is even in their group. Maybe it's because he is Siskin's son, and they feel scared to chuck him out. Or maybe it's because he is Siskin's son, and they feel sorry for him.

Zugzwang has never brought anything out of the Seam. Wilma blames his addiction to his goggles. Tech has junked his imagination, according to her. Apparently Siskin once instructed Zugzwang's nanabug to limit his eye-time, and Zugzwang just hacked the thing and overrode it.

'Oi, Zuggers!' yells Wilma, and they all try to get his attention.

'Zuggy!'

'Zugz bunny!'

'Zug, zug, give us a shrug!'

'Let's hang with the zwang!'

Zugzwang's goggles glow with kaleidoscopic light. A faint tinny noise comes from his headphones.

'Gogglehead,' says Gowpen sadly.

'Hey!' Ishan points to the tan line around his eyes. 'Some of us find that term offensive.'

Wilma makes a face. 'The only thing that's offensive here is Zugzwang eating with his mouth open.'

They all laugh, and for a while it becomes a game to try and chuck one of Gowpen's soy peas so it lands on Zugzwang's fork at just the right moment for him to eat it.

This game carries a risk of choking, chats Fourcandles.

'That's why it's fun,' Wilma explains, as if talking to a one-year-old.

'Uh-oh.' Pia's pea flies way over Zugzwang's head.

Wilma's nostrils flare. 'It could only be you, Catastro-P.'

'Heads down!' hisses Ishan. The soy pea has landed on Urette's table. The wrinkled-up zookeeper sits on her own like always, draining orange juice out of plastic cartons.

Pia's pea rolls over the table like a little green marble. They all watch out the corners of their eyes as it scoots past Urette.

Old spider lady doesn't even move her head. Just raises up her hand and WHACK!

'She mushed it flat,' whispers Gowpen.

Wilma grins madly. 'That is so creepy.'

'She is most definitely crazy,' says Ishan.

'Have you seen how she drinks her juice? Doesn't use a straw. Just *squeezes* it out, like she's sucking out the guts of a fly.'

You should apologise, is the advice from Fourcandles, which they all ignore.

'Time to go.' Pia gathers her plate and takes it across to the kitchens.

'*They're frightened.*'

Urette's voice cuts through the hubbub of the canteen. The tables all go quiet. The sound of cutlery hitting plates dies away. Pia feels the prickly heat on her skin that means people are looking at her. She turns. Urette has stood up from her lonely table.

'They're frightened,' she repeats, speaking to the room but looking only at Pia.

Pia can't think of anything to say back except: 'Who are?'

'The gargantulas,' says Urette. 'You wanted to know if any other animals were acting differently.'

Pia flicks her eyes to Ishan, Wilma and Gowpen. They look away, red-faced. A few seconds ago this was funny, but now they know Urette was listening to them. She heard every mean word they said about her.

'Stare into any one of a gargantula's sixteen eyes, and

they'll show you exactly what it's thinking.' Urette gathers up her plate and scuttles towards Pia. 'And my spiders are scared.'

Urette comes up so close Pia can see her white scalp through grey hair that is thin as silk wisps. Her chin has tiny hairs sprouting out of it, black and spiny. Pia has the sudden image of Urette pulling the legs off a fly and gluing them there. She can't stop staring at them; she half expects one to twitch.

'I don't know what would scare a gargantula,' Urette says. 'I do know one thing, though.'

Pia swallows. 'What?'

'*We* should be scared of it too.'

She turns and scuttles off. For a moment, her words hang in the silence of the canteen like cobwebs, before the chatter rises again to brush them away.

The Rekkers come over a bit sheepishly.

'Thanks for the backup,' Pia huffs.

'Sorry, P, but she is *freaky*.' Wilma shudders.

Ishan nods. 'Mind-frayed, for sure. You know she was one of the original research team? Hey, Pia, you OK?'

Pia shrugs, hugging her arms. Goosebumps are suddenly crawling up the back of her neck like a hundred little legs tiptoeing across her skin. Urette's words are stuck in her mind. Up until now, she'd thought the angels were missing either through mischief, or through some fault of her own.

But what if it's something else? What if there's danger coming? Something that makes even gargantulas afraid. That makes even angels flee.

12

SUSPICION KLAXON

They scrape their plates and stack their trays and wait in the zephyr queue. Pia keeps a little ahead of the others. Urette's creepy monologue has cranked up her anxiety levels a few notches, and she needs to get back to the celestial ark and think. Half the day is gone already, and she hasn't even started working out the details of her angel summoning.

'Get thinking about collective nouns, Rekkers,' Gowpen says behind her.

It's something they do. When a new voilà joins the zoo, they come up with a collective noun for it. A choir of singing hippos, a bonfire of phoenixes, a pong of smellephants (Pia's personal favourite).

'A sparkle of unicorns,' says Wilma. 'A glitter. A majesty.'

'A multicorn?' Ishan is useless at this game.

'A multicorn of unicorns?' Wilma laughs nastily.

Ishan looks wounded. 'You know, for someone with ambassador parents, sometimes you could be a little more diplomatic.'

'I like a *glitter*,' says Gowpen. He looks guiltily at Ishan. 'Although, a *multicorn* is kind of cool too . . .'

'What about humans?' says Zugzwang suddenly, his goggles kaleidoscoping as he shuffles forwards in the queue.

Like whenever Zugzwang speaks, it takes everyone a moment to work out whether he's just mumbling something at his goggles, or actually taking part in the conversation.

'A *humans* of unicorns?' Wilma looks at Ishan. 'I'm searching for a way to be diplomatic about this, but I . . . just . . . can't.'

'Humans are a species living in the zoo,' Zugzwang clarifies. '*We* don't have a collective noun for *us*.'

Wilma dongs her head against an imaginary wall. 'We're the Rekkers, stupid.'

Ishan grins. 'No, it's a good point. Zugz doesn't mean me and you guys, do you?'

Zugzwang nods in a slow, zombified way. 'Yeah. I mean *humans*.'

Pia shrugs. 'A crowd?'

Ishan made a *pfff* sound. 'A *plague* of humans.'

'A *plague*?'

He nods. 'Or what about an infestation? Hmm. An *invasion*? That's good, but invasions have a *point*. They aren't thoughtless, endless, stupid, the way humans are.'

Pia groans.

'My favourite,' says Zugzwang, 'is *problem*.'

Ishan claps his hands. Out of all of the Rekkers, he probably understands Zugzwang best. The two of them are fellow goggleheads, after all. 'That's perfect! Take us away, and you solve the polluting, the extinctions, the mass depletion . . . Humans are the greatest problem on the planet!'

'Then what's the solution?' Pia asks him.

Ishan shrugs. 'I'll leave that for the angels to figure out.'

They get to the front of the zephyr queue. Pia takes a moment, like she does every day, to feel sorry for poor Ozima, the dining ship's emerald-coloured genie. Swamped with wishes three times a day, right after breakfast, lunch and dinner.

'Ozima doesn't mind all the wishes,' the genie explains to them when Wilma remarks on how bored he must be. 'It's just the spinach in everyone's teeth when they're said.'

'Then we promise never ever to eat spinach,' Wilma answers solemnly. 'For your sake.'

Gowpen zephyrs first, back to the arrivals ark to check on Moonbim. Pia steps up after him and starts to speed through her wish-script.

'Hold it!'

Pia stumbles to a halt. Around her, everyone bristles. Interrupting someone mid-script is just not done at the zoo. It could be sort of dangerous: your words might get tangled up in the wish. At the very least, it's rude.

But then, Weevis has never cared much about that.

'Feeling better?' he says to Pia.

She glares at him: greasy, slouchy Weevis with his shiny forehead and the little dotted blackheads in the creases of his nose and chin and brows. He meets her stare and hands her a folded scrip of paper. It's yellow, the colour that 'genieers use for their communications.

'Your drone is fixed.'

No hello, or sorry for jamming up the queue, or anything. Pia ratchets up her glare to its fullest level.

'How do you know that?' she asks. 'Are you reading my messages?'

Not only that: why is Weevis bringing this here? Why doesn't he just get his little grey genie to zephyr it? An alarm trips in Pia. A klaxon wails out in her head, loud and terrifying.

He suspects.

Weevis is on to her!

Of course he is, Bagrin whispers in her ear. *You're a very, very bad liar, Pia.*

Weevis is still holding out the yellow slip of paper. Pia can't even get herself to take it off him. She's frozen with dread. Her secret is about to bust out into the open, in front of *everyone.*

She glances desperately at the Rekkers, and though none of them can know what's going on, they all recognise that look and what it means: it means *Big trouble, send backup.*

And this time, they all come rushing to Pia's rescue.

'Hey!' Wilma steps up. 'Whatever your name is. Blom?'

'That's his genie,' Ishan corrects.

'He's got a genie?' Wilma looks confused. 'I thought he was admin staff. Whatever. We all hate him though, right?'

'A little,' says Ishan, with an apologetic look at Weevis.

'A lot,' mutters Zugzwang darkly. He's blacked out the lenses on his goggles and put angry red targets on them, like pupils.

'Hey!' someone yells behind them. 'There's a queue you're holding up!'

Weevis ignores whoever that was. 'I'm not admin staff,' he says snootily at Wilma. 'What I do for the boss is none of your concern. As in, it's a little above your security clearance.'

Wilma clicks her fingers, as if remembering something. 'Oh *yeah*,' she says. '*That's* why we hate him. Because he thinks he's Siskin's new adopted son, or something. As in, he even tries talking like him.'

'HEY!' yells the voice behind them, considerably louder and angrier. 'LET'S MOVE IT ALONG!'

'Aaand now the security meatheads hate you too,' Wilma says, arms folded. 'You got a procedure for that, Mr Secretary?'

Zugzwang grins. He's clearly enjoying this. Weevis is sort of his nemesis. When the secretary (or whatever his actual job description is) first came to the zoo, random bluebottles kept flying into Siskin's office and trying to arrest him. According to Ishan, Zugzwang was hacking the security drones and deleting Weevis's profile, so they identified him as an intruder. Which was kind of hilarious, and also kind of brutal.

He got away with it too. Zugzwang covered his tracks like a professional hacker. Which didn't surprise Pia – the kid was a genius at tech.

Zugzwang could resurrect the internet though, and it *still* wouldn't be enough to impress his dad. Siskin is indifferent when it comes to technology. A little indifferent when it comes to his son too.

Pia's thoughts snap back to now as Weevis flings the paper slip at her. 'I know you're up to something,' he says. 'I'll find out what.'

Then he turns and leaves, and the Rekkers all shoot laser-beam stares into his back, and the zephyring can start up again.

'Oooh,' says Wilma. 'I am so moving him up a few places on our enemy list.'

Pia's calmer as she goes through her wish-script. Weevis obviously doesn't *know* about the angels – otherwise *actual* alarms would be ringing, not just those in Pia's head.

She's OK. For now. But she's running out of time. And with Threedeep operational again, summoning the angels just became that much harder.

13

ᕼ🏋ᕼ

Pia puts on her breather and zephyrs back to Ark One. She meets the same rude bluebottle at the door. Or maybe it's a different bluebottle with the same rudeness settings. The drone scans the code on her letter and escorts her to the 'genieer who has fixed Threedeep.

The 'genieer is a tall lady called Wanda who always wears jeans, old cowboy boots and floral shirts. Every time Pia sees her, Wanda has got her genie to give her a new hairstyle. Today, it is all curled and shiny.

'Hey, gal.' Wanda waves Pia inside.

Wanda's wishing lab looks a lot like the Sunset Pagoda, with sandy floors and shadow-quilted walls. It has a desk and workbench too. On the desk is a pair of goggles and a stack of files and a little navy-blue genie sitting in a glass ashtray like it's a jacuzzi tub, her beard gently smoking upwards in the air.

'That there is Boppity-Boo,' Wanda says as the genie vanishes inside her teapot lamp. 'Don't mind her. She's just embarrassed because we couldn't mend your nanabug.'

'*Couldn't?*' Pia checks the note again. 'But—'

'Oh, don't you worry. Threedeep's fixed, all right.' Wanda looks at the workbench. Threedeep is powered down: a boxy, single-rotored drone with a message screen. 'It wasn't me and Boo who did the fixing, though. We were still weeks away from a finished wish-script. Then we woke up this morning, and she was good as new. It's a miracle.'

Pia's heart starts to thud. 'Miracle?'

'Oh yeah. It was your angels for sure. They even left their calling card.'

Wanda goes to a desk drawer and pulls it open. Something pale shines from inside. The 'genieer brings out the moonlight halo carefully. Pia can't help but gasp.

'The angels fixed Threedeep before they went!' Her jaw drops when she realises what she just said. 'Back! Went back, I mean! To their garden!'

Wanda is too fascinated by the halo to notice Pia's slip. 'Purdy thang, hey?' she murmurs.

'If it were up to me, I'd let you keep it.' Pia gives a fake sigh. Thanks to Bagrin, it sounds very realistic. The rest of the lie tumbles out without even thinking. 'Have to follow procedures, though. You know what the boss is like.'

Wanda rolls her eyes. 'Don't I. I have to fill out a form every time I wish my hair different.' She offers the halo out to Pia. 'Do you want Boo to wish up some shadows to cloak this in? It feels delicate.'

'That would be brilliant, thanks.'

A whole morning of disaster, but now this. Pia's mind spins with possibilities. Maybe the halo is a message. Or a clue. Or a map! Oh, please, *please* let it be a map.

Whatever it is, at least it's *something*. She has to get back to the celestial ark, so she can figure out what.

Wanda coaxes Boo from her lamp, and together they

wrap the halo in shadow. Pia watches them for a bit, then wanders over to Threedeep and switches on the nanabug.

Hello, Pia! chats the drone when she's done starting up. Like bluebottles, nanabugs have no voice – just words that scroll over its scratched and faded screen. **My name is Threedeep.**

Pia's sigh is one of endless weary. 'I know who you are.'

Threedeep processes this. **Sorry, Cornucopia. I don't recall us meeting. Are we very good friends? If so, YAY!**

A picture appears on the screen of two friends, high-fiving:
(˘⌣˘)人(˘⌣˘)

Pia presses the balls of her palms into her eyes. The angels' miracle has obviously wiped Threedeep's memory, and reset her personality settings to default too.

'It's Pia,' she growls. 'And dial down the emojis, your cuteness levels are way too high.'

A widdle bit of cuteness never hurt anybody. ৻(˘ᴥ˘)৲

'Try saying that when I sit on you again.'

The nanabug's rotor starts up. She wobbles up from the bench and out of reach. **Someone seems a bit grouchy.**

'I was just fine when you were powered off.'

Intelligences prefer the term 'asleep', Threedeep informs her.

Pia rolls her eyes. Nanabugs. They love to play at being humans, like little kids playing at being parents. It was best to just ignore them, which was what almost everyone did.

Pia goes to the desk. Wanda and Boppity-Boo have wrapped up the halo in layers of protective shadow.

'The shadows will protect it a little,' Wanda says. 'I'd still keep it out of direct sunlight if I were you.'

'Oh, I will.' Pia clutches the halo to her chest tightly. No way is she letting this one melt away too. She is going to take it back to her cabin and study it with her goggles on maximum magnification. The angels have left halos in all three places they visited after leaving their garden: Pia's cabin, the Sunset Pagoda, Wanda's workshop. There has to be a reason. The halos are clues. And now she has one of them. She just has to figure out how to read it.

'Tell those angels of yours thanks,' Wanda says. 'I only wish I'd seen them visit. Must've come in here sometime last night.'

'Will do.' Pia backs out of the room. 'Thanks for the shadows! Bye, Wanda! Bye, Boppity-Boo!'

'Say goodbye, Boo,' Wanda says, and the genie pokes a timid pink flame from the tip of her teapot and gives Pia a flicker of a wave.

Pia practically sprints back to the ship's zephyr zone, Threedeep buzzing by her, the nanabug's screen filled with questions.

ᔕ(ᐸᓂ)ᕤ **Where are we going, Pia? Is it somewhere fun? Can I guess? How about a guessing game?**

Pia carries on down the ship's corridor until they reach the stairs.

'Do you remember where the angels went after they fixed you?' she asks, surprised that she hadn't thought of asking this before.

I'm sorry to say I don't, Pia. I don't even remember them mending me. Is that where we're going? To the angels, to tell them thank you?

'Hopefully.'

Are the angels and I very good friends? If so, YAY!

Pia glances at the drone. Threedeep is a lot more sociable than she used to be, now she is operating several tiers younger. Whoever wrote the drone's behaviour code obviously had a really moody, stereotypical view of teenagers.

Pia? Threedeep chats. **Why did you ask me where the angels were? Aren't they in their garden? Or in their house? If not, shouldn't we alert—**

'We're playing a game of hide-and-seek,' Pia lies. Or maybe it's Bagrin. She is starting to have trouble distinguishing her lies from his. Not a good sign.

ς⌒ೱ⌒ϲ How lovely! Hide-and-seek is a fun game.

'Yeah. The angels are hiding, and I think they left me this as a clue.' She holds up the shadow-wrapped halo. 'Do you know what it might mean?'

Threedeep's node scans the shadows.

Halo | ˈheɪləʊ/ | noun

A circular emanation of light found in many cultures and religions; an icon denoting holy or sacred figures; an aura exuded by heroes, gods and kings; a signifier of divine wisdom; used symbolically above the heads of saints, who would often receive visions and—

'Hold on.' Pia points to the text scrolling down the screen.

Above the head. Receive visions. Of *course*. Why hasn't she thought of that? Isn't that exactly what her dream-halo was?

This can't wait until she's back on the celestial ark. Pia ducks under the staircase, down into the gloomy part where the corridor strip light can't reach. She unwraps the shadows from the halo until it is a perfect white frosted ring once more.

Hands trembling, she places it above her head.

Nothing happens. No lightning bolt of wisdom. No dream, no vision. Pia holds the halo above her head until her arms begin to ache.

Pia? It's long past lunch. Don't the genies' beards need trimming?

Pia sighs. She forgot what it was like to have a drone remind her of things. Threedeep is right, though. All a genie's power resides in their facial hair – and each genie has to maintain a strict beard length, appropriate to the type of wishes it grants. Pia has to shave the senior genies every day: if their beards grow too long, one of them might do something crazy, like turn the moon into an apricot.

What were you hoping would happen? Threedeep asks, node swivelling towards the halo.

'I don't know. That the halo would show me something important, I guess.'

Threedeep waves a virtual arm in her face.

ㄟ(ツ)

'What?'

Why would you expect that halo to show you something important?

Pia rears up so quick she clunks her head on the staircase. The pain doesn't matter. Threedeep is right. Again. The halo isn't meant for her, it's *Threedeep's*.

Before the drone can object, Pia thrusts the shining ring above her rotor. Threedeep emits a weird blarping sound and her screen goes blank.

Oh Seamstress. It worked! Somehow the halo has actually put the nanabug into standby mode.

Intelligences prefer the term 'asleep', Pia remembers Threedeep saying, just as the drone begins to dream.

Not just in words, but in images.

14
BEARD TRIM

```
zzzzzzzzzzzzzzz
         _      _
     (\o/)  {\o/}   wardrobe, narnia
>>>   /_\    /_\
                      /   \
                        _
                    \_\(_)/_/
                     _//"\\_
                      /   \


         wrong solution
                  \
                   \
                    \
    ____             \
:`  o `:              \
|`----`|               \
|bad   |  .--.         ()
|move  | /    \        /\
|      |/      `.'   '.__.
 `-----`

                   \ | /
                  -- o --
                   / | \

(✖_✖)(✖_‾✖)(✖̄_✖)‾(✖_✖̄)(✖‾_✖)(✖̄_✖)


          @   @
        ( • x • )

                 o-o
                /,_,\
              ,Mm/_\mM,

                          ♩ɛ(·ϴ·。)э

88888888 .d88b.  .d88b.
   d88P d88""88bd88""88b
  d88P  888  888888  888
 d88P   Y88..88PY88..88P
88888888 "Y88P"  "Y88P"

        \_)
      .-./--.
     /# ^^   \
     |       |      __
      \     /     ("_\  .-.  .-.  /)
       `-.-'          \\_//^\\_//^\\_//

8/8/8/3pK3/2kP4/8/8/8
```

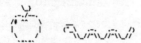

Pia stares in shock.

The halos weren't goodbye gifts, they were goodbye *messages*. A kind of *aerial*, tuned to only one person (or drone). Capable of picking up only one very specific transmission. Written in the only language angels knew how to speak. A language circular and infinite. A language made of light.

Pia lists all the things she can see.

Wardrobe.

Narnia.

Animals. A spider. A worm in an apple.

Death.

Light.

Animals.

Needle and thread.

A bad move, a wrong solution.

The zoo.

Junk data.

Are they symbols for something, or is Pia supposed to take them literally? She has no idea what Narnia and Wardrobe mean, but the animals have to represent the voilà here at the zoo. And the great big giant spider? Oh, that dings some bells, all right.

That stooped, scuttly, mind-frayed old gargantula-keeper! Pia should've known Urette has something to do with this. Did the *wrong solution* in Threedeep's dream belong to her, or someone else? Had the angels maybe gone to convince Urette she'd made a mistake?

They might not have gone with Urette willingly, Bagrin whispers. *Maybe she's found a way to kidnap them.*

As much as she doesn't want to, Pia finds his possibility convincing. If you can trap a devil in an infernal prism, surely there is a way to capture an angel too?

Neither of the dreams the angels left behind them feel like cries for help or ransom notes, but still. Urette is her only lead here. Even if the gargantula-keeper *isn't* keeping the angels captive, she has some connection to their disappearance.

And Pia is going to find out what it is.

She withdraws the halo, and Threedeep's screen wipes once more. For a while, Pia sits in the dim stairwell, thinking and thinking. A few people come down the steps from the deck above but they don't notice her. Eventually Threedeep's screen returns to normal again.

My system encountered an error. What happened?

'The angels sent me a message. Through you.'

Oh. Are they still playing hide-and-seek?

'Yes. But I have a place to look now.'

That's good. We really ought to be getting back to the celestial ark anyway, to trim the genie beards.

Pia wraps the halo back up in Boppity-Boo's shadows, and crawls out from the stairwell.

'Sure,' she says, happy for Threedeep to think the angels are hiding somewhere on the celestial ark. It makes sense to go back there anyway. Pia has a plan to make. Certain things she needs to fetch. And yes, beards to trim.

And then, once she is ready, Pia is going to pay Urette a little visit.

• • •

Everything is dead, Threedeep observes, node swivelling around the celestial ark.

Pia looks at the angel garden gloomily. 'Yup.'

The entire deck is shrivelled and brown. She crouches down and runs her hand over the grass. It crumbles to dusty bits between her fingers.

Plants need water and sunlight, Pia. Perhaps if you watered them, they might turn less brown.

'Thanks for your very helpful suggestion, Threedeep. They need a lot more than that, though. These days, with all the tox and depletion, they need a miracle.'

Yes. Perhaps the angels should stop playing hide-and-seek.

'Oh, don't worry. I'm going to find them really soon.'

It's true. Pia can feel it. But first, there are a few things she has to do. Number one on the list is: lose her nanabug.

Pia slaps her thighs and pushes herself back up to standing. By the time she is upright, a cheerful smile is fixed on her face.

'How would you like,' she says to Threedeep, 'to make some very good friends?'

• • •

Solomon and Bertoldo are delighted to see Pia. They come out of their lamps like Catherine wheels.

'Did the young heroine's boon assist her?' asks Solomon. 'How has her quest progressed?'

'Solomon!' Bertoldo scolds. 'Stop picking at loose threads!' This is Tellish for *mind your own business*.

Pia sighs. 'Come on, you two. Let's take a look at that facial hair.' She mimes a moustache when they fail to hear her. Both genies have grown long curly purple ones since this morning.

'She gazes upon our unshorn magnificence with wonder!' Solomon observes, as Pia straightens the moustaches out and measures each half, from nostril to tip.

'Four centimetres! Wow, that's some growth, guys.'

'Wistfully, she yearns for a moustache of her own,' Bertoldo declares. 'The munificent genies are only too pleased to bestow her wish—'

'No, no, no!' Pia's lucky the old dears narrate so many of their thoughts. She brandishes her scissors. *Snip! Snip!* A flash and a pop, and the moustaches disintegrate into soot.

'But alas,' adds Bertoldo mournfully, 'the genies were suddenly too weak to grant the girl her wished-for beard . . .'

Pia grins. She loves these deaf old dears. She always finds herself staying awhile, and requesting harmless little wishes from them. She doesn't even have to recite the wishes from a script, because the genies are too weak now to grant anything but fireworks in the shapes of various objects and creatures.

'A red rose: all this, I wish!'

BANG! Over Solomon's head blooms a firework in the shape of a big nose.

Pia claps enthusiastically, as if that was just what she had wished for. 'Now grant me a bird: all this, I wish!'

Bertoldo giggles. 'She calls his work absurd!'

'I said it looked *just as good as I'd heard*,' Pia says quickly to the hurt-looking Solomon. 'Bertoldo, I demand a crown: all this, I wish!'

Bertoldo bows, hands pressed together, and a picture of a clown blooms and whizzles away in the dark above him.

Pia whoops, and the genies bow, and so it goes for a while.

'Hey, Threedeep!' she calls.

Threedeep insisted on waiting in the corridor outside the Sunset Pagoda. The drone peeks from the entrance like a shy kid.

'Come say hi to Solomon and Bertoldo!'

Threedeep's node lights green with a ping sound, and the drone zooms over to where the genies float.

'What sorcery is this, the genies wonder?' Solomon muses, tugging his goatee in vexation.

Pia giggles. 'You guys have met Threedeep before. Remember?' The poor old things must be dimmer than she'd thought.

˪(•◡•)˩ **Hello! My name is Threedeep!**

'An infernal device, powered by thunderfire!' Bertoldo declares.

That is correct, chats Threedeep. **If thunderfire is**

107

your term for electricity. What powers a genie, if I may ask?

Bertoldo and Solomon swell with pride. 'Wishes!' they yell out, bowing deeply.

Pia grins. In spite of herself, she is finding this conversation very cute.

Is that so? says Threedeep. **In that case, I wish for us to be very good friends.**

The genies are momentarily dumbstruck. Pia doubts anyone has ever asked that from them before. But Threedeep's wish is actually perfect – small enough for the genies to give, easy enough for them to grant, and totally without consequence. And best of all, it appears on a screen, so they can't mishear it.

'As you command!' they both cry.

Pia leaves Threedeep chatting with the genies. For a while, she pretends to look busy tidying the pagoda. She cleans the other lamps, waking Hokapoka, Shazam and Kadabra, who are all as faint as will-o'-the-wisps. Pia tries asking wishes from them, but none of them grant anything she says, so she simply fetches as many shadows as she can, and cloaks each one to make sure they are comfortable.

A quick glance over at Solomon and Bertoldo: Threedeep is showing the genies silly emojis on her screen. They are transfixed. There won't be a better time than now. Pia creeps up behind Threedeep, the moonlit halo in her hands. In a flash, she slips it on the drone, and Threedeep goes into standby mode again. Solomon and Bertoldo look quizzical.

'Sleeping Beauty,' Pia explains, hoping her Tellish is good enough.

The genies seem to understand. They both put fingers on lips and make shush sounds. Perfect. She's bought herself some time, at the very least. Pia creeps away towards the door, eases it shut, and rushes upstairs to her cabin.

15

LOOPING GHOSTS

Pia has never been to the gargantula ark before, and the angels might be anywhere on it. If Urette really *is* keeping them, Pia will need a numinous lamp to light them up.

Normally, celestials have different levels of visibility. Angels and ghosts are invisible, genies are visible, and devils are somewhere in between. Numinous lamps emit a special light that lights them all up. Pia assumes it's the same way UV lamps light up UV stuff.

The numinous lamps are strung around the ark like stadium floodlights. Someone might notice if she takes a numinous lamp from the edge of the ship, but there are several others: one in the Sunset Pagoda, one in the infernal prism, and one in the haunted cabin. Threedeep has one installed on her too, but that was out for obvious reasons. And it would be dangerous to give Bagrin even a few minutes of invisibility. (*Oh, go on*, says a voice in her head. *We promise to behave. Deal?*)

Pia shakes her head. Just like angels, devils mainly draw all their power from being *unseen*. All celestials do. It's why genies shroud their wish-grantings in shadows and puffs of smoke, and why angels like to work their miracles unnoticed.

Fetching the lamp from the ghosts will be fine, though.

• • •

The ghosts are the fourth and final type of celestials on the ark. They haunt a specially built cabin at the back of the ship, a few metres from where they died. Pia no longer bothers calling them Mum and Dad. It's easier to use their names. Their names, they remember.

'Hi, Estival.' She shuts the cabin's door behind her. 'Hi, Yisel.'

Two blurry figures stand beneath the soft white light of the numinous lamp. No matter how hard Pia squints, they never quite come into focus. In so many ways, the ghosts are like recordings. A few brief moments, captured like flies in amber. They will never know anything or think anything or feel anything they hadn't known or thought or felt four years ago, on that Wednesday afternoon when the prism failed, at eight minutes past three.

'Ugh.' Estival, the ghost of Pia's mum, looks at the sole of her boot. 'My shoelace keeps untying.'

'I've been thinking,' says Yisel, her dad's ghost, crouched on the floor.

Pia has heard him say this a hundred times, a thousand. She knows these last moments off by heart.

'That's rare for you,' she murmurs.

'That's rare for you,' says Estival's ghost.

'Ha! Stop avoiding the subject.'

Estival's ghost turns. 'Yisel.' It is too hard now to tell whether she says it with disapproval or with worry. Time has taken emotion from the ghosts, the way it fades colour from photographs. One day they might wear away to a few whispered words, then finally nothing at all.

'I'm serious,' Yisel says.

'You're never serious.'

Yisel's ghost shrugs.

Estival throws her hands up. 'And what happens after?'

That final question of her mother's haunts Pia's life. She has spent nights awake and wondering, with no answer.

'Excuse me,' she interrupts.

The ghosts look up at her. As always there is that moment when Pia feels they recognise her. Then it passes. She isn't their Pia. Their Pia isn't tall and lanky, with hair hacked short and a wonky fringe. Their Pia is much younger. Still a little girl. A podge with plaits.

'Who are you?' Estival asks.

Pia has answered her mum a hundred different ways, a thousand. She hasn't found an answer yet that the ghosts don't find confusing.

'I'm friends with Pia,' she says. It's one of the few replies that doesn't cause the ghosts to loop.

'Pia?' Estival steps forward. 'Our daughter Pia? Is she OK?'

'She's on Ark One playing with Gowpen in the crèche, she's fine.' Pia heads for the numinous lamp. It is docked in the wall, but take it out and the charge will make it shine on for a while.

Estival steps closer, some unseeable expression on her blurry face, and she stumbles. She steadies herself and sighs and lifts up her shoe with a huffing sound.

'My shoelace keeps untying.'

This happens all the time. When the ghosts move too far

from the moment before death, they loop back to where they knew. To *when* they knew. Wednesday afternoon, four years ago. At eight minutes past three.

'I'm going now.' Pia unclicks the lamp from the wall. Her parents blur even more as the light shifts away from them. 'Bye.'

Yisel jumps. 'Where did you come from?'

Estival's ghost throws up her hands. 'And what happens after?'

Pia switches off the lamp to save battery. Her parents bleach away into the air. Their voices fade. The cabin looks empty. But they are here. They are always here. Pia has lost count of the times she has wished (yes, actually *wished*) they might finally blur away completely and be at peace. But some things can only be erased by time. Like grief. Like ghosts.

She heaves the door shut. About now, Yisel is looking down, saying, 'Does that light—'

That was the moment the infernal prism beside them breached. Gotrob had been weakening the crystal structure for a while, rebounding himself off each edge at the speed of light until the whole thing heated up and cracked. A jagged rain of glass blew outwards across the deck, releasing the devil like a fireball.

It was the worst enclosure escape in the history of the zoo. It took almost three weeks to zephyr Gotrob back into the remaining prism (where he was eaten by Bagrin just a few months later – something Pia will always be grateful to the remaining devil for). By then another three zookeepers were dead. Pia doesn't pray any more for the miracle that would bring them all back to life. Every night for two years, she clasped her hands and pleaded. But sometimes not even angels can mend what gets broken, or who.

16
SPIDER PARLOUR

Dusk is already falling as Pia gathers her things. Numinous lamp, check. Breather, check. No nanabug, check. There's only one last thing she needs.

Genies aren't officially supposed to zephyr anyone around after dark, to reduce the chances of poachers sneaking about, and the gargantula ark is currently floating on the other side of the island, way out of reach of most genie's beards. It might take several wishes to get there.

She needs an excuse, and one that might need to work more than once.

'Bagrin?' she murmurs.

Like a bat out of the gathering night, his presence swoops down upon her shoulder.

'Look,' she says. 'I need a favour.'

Bagrin doesn't do favours.

'OK, fine. Go away then.'

Don't be like that. What do you want?

'An excuse. To get me to the gargantula ark.'

But it is almost past curfew.

'That's why I'm asking you. Because I need a very good excuse.'

Bagrin chuckles. *You are much more interesting than your parents. They did not have half as many evil thoughts as you.*

'Shut up. Can you do it?'

It is very far away. You will need to make several zephyrs.

'Yeah.'

And what does Bagrin get from this? Make us an offer.

'You . . . can come along for the ride.'

We can come along anyway. We made a deal.

'Our deal was until sunset.' Pia points at the horizon. It's dark. 'I'm willing to extend it to dawn. Deal?'

The devil pauses to consider. Then he sends her a chimera of a red Dibsy with horns, giving two thumbs ups.

Deal. But only if you also let Bagrin eat your soul.

'No.'

Very well, not your soul. How about a kitten?

'I'm not going to feed you a kitten, Bagrin.'

He whines all the way across the deck to Pazuzu: *Why not a kitten? Kittens are only small, you know. You are a very unreasonable child.*

'Hey,' Pia murmurs. 'Pazuzu.'

A little firefly-sized flame rises out of her lamp. 'And who should be calling at this late hour, Pazuzu wondered?'

'It's me. Think you can zephyr me towards the gargantula ark? I won't be long.'

Pazuzu doesn't look happy. 'The genie wondered what the girl's nanabug would say to such sneaking off.'

It is a good job genies narrate their thoughts. They are obsessed with stories. Which is why Pia's excuse (*ahem – BAGRIN's excuse*) is basically irresistible.

'Can't you help a pair of star-crossed lovers meet beneath the moonlight, Pazuzu?' Pia says in really bad Tellish.

116

The genie is suddenly much more awake. She drifts from the lamp, coloured love-heart red, and asks: 'The persistent prince?'

Pia bats her eyelids. 'The very same.'

Ugh, this is so embarrassing. But it is working. Pazuzu's sigh is full of sparks. Genies are total suckers for romance. Pia just hopes this never gets back to Ishan.

• • •

Using her story (fine, OK, *Bagrin's* story), Pia zephyrs across the zoo. She tells it to Orel, the genie at the moonfairy ark, and to Zosimus by the hummingdragon hives, and finally to Sim Sala Bim over at the timefrogs. They lap it up, all three of them. It's in their nature. Genies are hooked on anything against the odds, high stakes, and a little hopeless. Which pretty much sums up the zoo itself, and explains why no genie has ever left to go and grant wishes anywhere else. They are all in love with the *tale* of this place: a ragtag fleet, a mysterious mountain, a last-ditch attempt to save a dying world. Sounds pretty clichéd to Pia, but hey. Maybe it's more exciting in Tellish.

With a bow and a 'so it was granted', Sim Sala Bim wishes her on to the gargantula ark. Pia has never zephyred so many times so quickly before. After Pazuzu, she felt the regular disorientation: the popped ears, the dizzy tiredness. With each subsequent zephyring, the feelings have magnified. By the time she reached Zosimus, Pia was swaying like a drunkard and gasping for breath. Fortunately, Zosimus just mistook her queasiness for lovesickness, which made Bagrin's story even more convincing.

This fourth and final zephyring is the worst yet. Pia has to keep her eyes closed until her nausea and exhaustion goes. No way is she barfing twice today. Especially not in a breather mask.

Still unable to look at anything, she tries to focus on the sounds around her to distract from the travel sickness. The gargantula ark is very quiet and still, so much so that Pia decides that the ship's zephyr zone has to be inside. Nothing strange about that. Plenty of arks keep their genies below deck. But as well as all the other side effects, this fourth zephyring has given her a curious new sensation on her face, neck and hands.

It feels like something is falling upon her skin – something soft and very fine, somewhere between dust and snow. It tickles her chin. A small pile is already gathering on the bridge of her nose where her breather rests.

What is it? She opens her eyes to see.

If Threedeep was there, she would have emitted loud bleeps to drown out Pia's swearing.

She isn't just inside the *ship*. The ark's zephyr zone is in the gargantula enclosure itself! Pia is in the freaking spider parlour!

What? Is this actually happening? She's on the wrong side of the two-centimetre-thick glass that holds giant carnivorous spiders.

Pia flicks on the numinous lamp, and it casts milky light into the mass of floating cobwebs around her. Gargantulas secrete it like a mist around themselves as camouflage. Oh facepalm, this is bad. What does she do? Her thoughts are all fogged up, her heart is thudding. Every moment she expects either one of the spiders to scutter out of the cobmist towards her, or for Urette's bony hands to fall on her shoulders.

But no gargantulas appear. No Urette either. A wisp of web settles on her dungarees. She brushes it off with a shudder. Most of it ends up on her palm. When she tries to flick it off, it gums up her fingertips. Yucky stuff.

She shakes her hand furiously, wondering what to do. Does she explore? That would be crazy. Call out for Urette? That feels just as stupid. There might be a gargantula just a few metres away.

She needs to get out of here. Where is the ark's genie? She turns and looks for a lamp, but it's hard to see through the mist, especially when it glues to her eyelashes.

She blinks, rubs her face with her sleeve, and sees a dim light to her left, where the cobmist is thick. That has to be the genie. She needs to zephyr herself to safety.

Taking a deep breath, she plunges in. A grey-white cloud avalanches over her.

Instantly, this turns out to be a terrible idea. A trillion silk particles glue themselves to her. Ugh, it's all over. Everywhere. In her hair, forming webs between her fingers, making long sticky strands between her eyelids. She can barely see the genie ahead of her. She struggles towards it.

It suddenly occurs to her that this was the gargantula equivalent of a web, and the one thing you don't do in a web is wriggle about. She takes her first breath, but the mist has gummed up her breather filter. She takes off the mask and the cobmist coats the inside of her throat and she doubles up, choking. She jams her nose in the crook of her elbow, wheezing for air.

Some instinct tells her that cobmist doesn't just *hide* the gargantulas, it catches their prey too.

The light is by her feet, which have gathered up such big cobmist tufts they look like cotton candyfloss on the sticks of her legs. She kneels down and prods the light.

It's not a genie's lamp. Just a standard, zoo-issue headlamp.

Oh Seamstress.

She really, really, *really* needs to get out. But now her knees won't straighten. Pia falls on her back. Which direction did she come from? Behind? She tries opening her eyes, but they are gummed shut. She wipes them clear using the inside of her dungarees. It doesn't really work. Her vision stays blurry. A waste of precious movements. Should she use her hands to free her knees, or just guess a direction and crawl? *Stop lagging, Pia, just decide. Every moment you stay here, more cobmist sticks to you.*

The dome is eerily quiet. Maybe the cobmist has gummed up her ears too. One voice sounds loud and clear, though.

May we be of assistance?

Pia wheezes another breath. *Bagrin!* She can only think, not speak. *What do I do?*

Ah, Bagrin says. *Now that would be telling.*

Help me! Pia's terror is making her giddy-headed. She can't breathe. She needs to breathe.

Of course we will help, Bagrin soothes. *We'll be happy to . . . make a deal.*

Before Pia can answer, she hears a slow scrunch, scrunch, scrunch. Something is coming through the cobmist towards her.

There is no time to bargain. She'll be spider food in seconds. Panic takes over. She crawls blindly, hands jammed beneath her armpits, saving them for when her legs get totally glued together.

A hard set of pincers catch her by the shoulder.

She swings a fist that connects with nothing, twirls round and falls. A vague glimpse of an enormous brown-haired thing. Maybe a leg, or a couple of legs. It pins her flat to the floor. Pia's mouth is so gummed up she can't even scream.

Then, through the cobwebs covering her ears, Pia hears Urette say: 'You're lucky I dropped my headlamp.'

The bony fingers gripping her like mandibles relax. Something slick and acrid sprays in her face. Pia claws with her hands, mouth and eyes and nostrils burning. The cobmist slides off her skin and slops to the floor, the colour and consistency of porridge.

'Here.' The blurry shape of Urette hands her an aerosol. 'Spray that down your throat. It burns, but it's better than suffocating.'

Pia nods, wheezing, and takes the can. It tastes like chemicals, but it works. She doubles over coughing, gross white gunky globs sliding up and out of her throat. Urette clicks her false teeth together beneath a wet-looking plastic breather.

'Thanks,' Pia manages to rasp, looking up. She wasn't hallucinating before: the old witch really *is* wearing some kind of horrible suit made of shaggy brown spines. The cobmist seems to slide straight off it.

'Do your eyes next, girl. It'll sting.'

Pia supposes she should be angry. What the hell is Urette doing, putting her zephyr zone inside a deadly creature's enclosure? But right now, her relief at still being alive is overriding her fury.

'Now the rest of your joints,' Urette says. 'And don't scream, Nancy hates it.'

Pia coughs up more wet silk. 'Who's Nancy?'

A second later, the spider dances into view.

It tiptoes delicate as a ballerina, each leg leaping up and vanishing through the mist for a weightless moment before alighting again with the softest rustle on the floor. Pia isn't prepared for the *grace* of the thing. For the shyness of it. Her skin crawls when she looks at the twitching mandibles. The shaggy thorax has large pom-pom sized silk balls tufted on top. The drooping and swollen abdomen farts out a constant cloud of cobmist. Gazing at the nightmare of eyes, set in glittering black rows, Pia realises Urette had been right:

stare in any of a gargantula's sixteen eyes, and you can see what it is thinking.

And Nancy is *scared*.

Of Pia? Seriously? As she sits up, the spider freezes. It makes a sort of clacking sound.

Urette clicks her false teeth together in reply. 'Back to your nest, girl.'

Nancy turns. One by one, the spindly legs waltz away in the haze.

Pia listens to the spider's timid footsteps fade to silence. The breath she was holding whooshes out of her lips like air from a puncture.

'Big scaredy-cat really.' Urette sprays Pia with another canister of cobmist dissolver. 'Her size makes her fragile, you see. She'll only eat something if her cobmist has trapped and suffocated it first. You're lucky her clutch hasn't hatched, though.'

'What do you mean, a *clutch*?'

'Didn't you see the egg sacs she's carrying?' Urette cackles. 'Babbagantulas will eat anything, alive or dead. They'll start with Nancy, in fact.'

Pia shudders. 'Could not be more glad I work with celestials.' She coughs up another gob of cobmist and sprays her throat again.

Urette turns and trudges away in her spider-hair suit. 'Come on, then.'

Pia grimaces and gets to her feet. 'Where are you going?'

'Back to my bubble.' The old witch trudges off into the mist.

Pia looks around. Where else is she going to go? It's not as if there are any other options. She waddles through the cobmist to catch up with the spider lady.

17
The Cabin in the Cobmist

Urette's cabin is a small plastic habitation bubble, plopped straight in the midst of the cobmist. It's igloo-shaped, with clear walls. Little more than a sturdy tent, really. It has the primitive look of something that's been thrinted into being by a genie.

Outside, the waltzing shadows of the gargantulas flitter past. Makes it kind of hard to concentrate on conversation.

'Sorry, Urette . . . could you say that again?'

'I said, don't mind Nutella,' Urette repeats, over by the kitchen area. 'He's just curious.'

Pia's attention is all on the enormous brown leg, like a long articulated pool cue, that pokes out from the mist an arm's reach from where she sits. Now it prods at her, crinkling the bubble's plastic wall. She shuffles as far away as she can.

'We don't get many visitors, you see,' Urette explains.

'*That's because you put your zephyr zone inside a damn enclosure,*' Pia mutters. She's never heard of anything so crazy.

Urette cackles, and Pia inwardly facepalms. She keeps forgetting that the old witch has amazing hearing. 'It's a little unconventional, I know. I'm not really a follower of *procedures*, though. And since no one ever comes here but me, I thought: *Why not give the 'gantulas a little more play space?* So I did. I gave them the whole ark.' She cackles again and gestures around her tiny bubble with its see-through walls. 'Now *I'm* the one in an enclosure.'

Pia fakes a chuckle. The bubble is crammed with junk and dust and that sour old-person smell. For something so full, it feels empty and lonely too. On the shelves, the droopy plants are all in need of watering. The light from the bulb looks brown and wilted. Beads of yellowing cobmist glue cover everything, making each object look like a half-melted candle. A dead babbagantula, clenched up like a huge hairy fist, hangs in a jar of preserving fluid labelled 'Betty's clutch #27'.

Squeezed in amongst all of this is Pia, sitting on a pile of plastic crates. She watches Urette, hunched over by her sink, whistling tunelessly through her teeth. She is making tea.

Just as the kettle boils, a slip of paper zephyrs in front of Pia's face and tumbles on to her lap. It's blue, which means it comes from only one place.

Stamped on the top are the words: *From the desk of Director Siskin.*

Pia snatches it up and reads it as Urette chatters on with her back turned:

> *The Director expects you back on your ark in thirty minutes.*
> *As in, not a moment after.*
> *Weevis.*

Pia can imagine his smug face as she reads this. She scrunches the scrip up in her palm and stuffs the balled-up note in her dungarees pocket. Facepalm.

She doesn't know how he found out she's breaking curfew, and it doesn't matter. How is this creepy old spider woman connected to the missing angels? She has about twenty-nine minutes to find an answer.

Urette potters at the sink, bringing out two brown chipped mugs and plopping a bag in each one. She still wears her coat of giant-spider hair. Now it comes off and gets draped over the back of the single armchair.

'I'm sorry for bothering you this late,' Pia begins.

'No bother, no bother.'

'I just wanted to ask you—'

'Don't rush me now, don't rush me.' Urette turns and offers Pia a tin of canteen-pilfered biscuits. 'You breathed in a lot of cobmist. You'll cough it all up eventually, but we still need to degunk you.' She smiles sweetly. 'Don't want you suffocating in your sleep now, do we?'

Wow. Even trying to be friendly, Urette still manages to be mega-creepy.

'Drink up.' Urette hands Pia one of the mugs. The tea is dark green, with scummy bits on the surface.

Closing her eyes, Pia takes a tiny sip. Ugh, bitter. She forces it down. *Take deep breaths*, she tells herself. *I will not yurk, I will not yurk, not twice in one day.*

'Very nice, thank you.' She forces a smile, hoping it doesn't look too fake.

'Is it OK?' Urette says. 'Would you like it sweeter? I know you kids like it sweet.'

'Oh yes,' Pia lies. 'Delicious, thanks.'

She takes a big gulp to make Urette feel better, and scalds her tongue. In the awkward silence, they both sit and sip their mugs. Urette opens her mouth and shuts it a few times, making her false teeth go clack.

'How does your throat feel now?' she asks eventually.

'Much better, thanks.' Which is true. The claggy feeling has almost gone.

'It helps to talk a little too,' Urette suggests.

Pia hesitates. She's totally in the dark. It might be better to make small talk first, see if Urette gives anything away. She might not *want* to share her connection to the disappearance – especially if she's involved somehow. And there's still almost half an hour before the boss's deadline.

She looks around for something to make chit-chat about. The dead babbagantula? Yuck, no. How about the old photo printouts Urette has tacked on the walls? Old people *love* talking about the past. The good old days, when they just hung out on the internet all day, photographing their lunch.

'Are those pre-d?' Pia points at them. Pre-d is shorthand for pre-detonation: before the reality bomb made the Seam.

It's all the chit-chat Urette needs. For the next ten minutes, she yanks the printouts off the walls and passes them to Pia: group shots of scientists atop the island's peak; pictures of the mountain getting hollowed out for the r-bomb detonation; a young Urette – just a kid really – by the Free State flag; an i-era helicopter.

Urette gives a commentary. 'There's me. There's Jobs, our support drone. Very early model. You had to plug him in every six hours. Here's one of Celeste. She was nice. I lent her my earrings the day she . . . well, you know. I wonder if they're still in the Seam, in some way?'

Celeste Lalande. Despite the gross tea and the filthy cabin and the giant spiders trying to prod her, Pia can't help but feel a little bit in awe. Doctor Celeste Lalande . . . The inventor of the r-bomb.

Urette notices Pia staring at the photo, and cackles. 'I know what you're thinking. How can we all be standing so close to the blast radius?! But we really had no idea back then of what unreality did to adult brains. We were all very smart people, but very naive. A little arrogant too, maybe.'

'Like Marie Curie. She kept radioactive test tubes in her desk drawers.'

'Ha! More like those archaeologists that uncovered Tutankhamun's tomb. They all met grisly ends, one by one.'

'I'm pretty sure that curse was made up,' Pia says.

'How fitting, then. So is the Seam. It's pure fantasy.' Urette sits back, stirring her tea with one finger. She licks it like a lollipop, then looks back to the group shot of men and women in lab coats.

'I think fifteen of those twenty got mind-frayed,' she says. 'And of course, Celeste vanished completely.' She points to the mountaintop in the photo's background and tut-tuts. 'We must seem very reckless to you.'

Pia shrugs. 'I mean, you guys *did* blow up the laws of reality.'

'Ha ha, you're right! How reckless can you get?! But then, who needs reality? Reality sucks! I grew up in San Silicio, so believe me, I know. No genies to wish up all the scrummy canteen food you're used to. Just slop grown under LEDs. Just rat flu, and doom cults, and ohtwo factories scrubbing filthy air clean. I'm sure my fellow sprawlizen Ishan told you all about that.' With a little titter, Urette wipes her eyes. 'And I'm sure he's told you how pointless it is too. This zoo, I mean. These arks. The whole project. Siskin's grand search for a miracle. The world's already dead, and we're just the worms on the corpse.'

Pia looks down at her mug, hoping to hide her blushes. She doesn't want to think about when Ishan told her that. She has spent the last week trying to forget it had even happened.

'That's just doomsay,' she mumbles.

Any obsessive talk related to the end of the world is called doomsay. In the sprawl, it's technically illegal.

Urette cocks her head. 'Did you know there are literally hundreds of sprawl-tung phrases that are doomsay-influenced? Like "nihilishus".'

Pia nods. ' "Anything that tastes, looks, or feels like nothing." '

'Ah, so Ishan's taught you some, has he? Does he ever tell you to "null it"?'

'Yeah. It's like a blend of "shut up" and "whatever".'

Urette grins. 'Sort of. Only in a much bigger, more pessimistic sense than both, like: "we're all going to be a scattering of radioactive ash in a couple of decades, so I really can't be bothered to deal with you."'

Pia actually laughs. This is sort of surprising. She keeps expecting the old zookeeper to reset back into her default mode of creepy, but Urette is actually being kind of nice. Even *funny*.

Maybe for her, the aura of creepiness she exudes is sort of like a gargantula's cobmist: a disguise (Pia's theory again).

'Why is doomsay illegal in the sprawl?' Pia asks.

'Because it's powerful. Everyone knows the world is ending, but no one speaks about it. In the sprawl, people just carry on as normal, whilst the ohtwo factories fail around them. So when you doomsay, you have to be careful who hears you. You might start a fight. Or a cult.'

'Don't they know the *zoo* will save the world?'

Urette wrinkles her face. 'That's what they're *told*. I doubt anyone believes it. Do you?'

'Siskin says we will.'

'That isn't what I asked.'

Pia is quiet, and Urette cackles. Then her features relax and she settles back into her chair.

'This . . .' she says. 'I've missed this.'

'What?'

'Being listened to.'

Oh Seamstress, that is actually pretty sad. Pia thinks of Urette on her own at the canteen, day after day. When was the last time she talked with someone? Actually *talked*? An appraisal with Siskin? That's mainly being talked *at*.

Urette and Pia sit in the bubble quietly for a while. From outside, there comes the soft *pat, pat* of gargantulas tiptoeing through the ship. When Urette looks up again, her expression has changed. It is less soft, somehow. There is a knowing glint in her eye. 'OK, Pia.'

'OK what?'

'Ask me.'

'Ask you what?'

'Whatever you came here to ask, of course.'

Pia lags, the way she usually does when surprised. 'I, uh. Um, well—'

'Oh, come on, girl. You didn't break curfew and come halfway across the zoo just to mumble at me, did you?'

Pia blushes. No, she hasn't. She takes a deep breath.

'The angels told me something about you.'

Bagrin has been quiet all this time, but suddenly he speaks up. *Don't tell her any more than that. Not yet. Feed her the story bit by bit, and wait for her reaction.*

Seems like good advice. Pia takes it, grudgingly. She stays quiet, and she watches.

So far Urette's eyebrows are raised, and that is about it.

'And?' says the old zookeeper.

'And it was about Narnia,' Pia says, remembering the words from Threedeep's dream. 'And the wardrobe.'

With a plop-clink sound, Urette's false teeth drop out of her open mouth and into her tea.

Et voilà, Bagrin says.

Shut up, Bagrin, let me handle this.

'What do they mean?' Pia asks.

'Kidsth theeth dayth.' Urette shakes her head and fishes out her teeth from the mug and sucks them back in. 'Ask your nanabug. What else did the angels say?'

Pia shrugs. 'Answer my question, and I'll answer yours.'

Spoken like a true infernal. Bagrin sends her a chimera: an image of Pia on a stage in a glittery ballgown, applauding tuxedoed devils all around her, accepting a golden award shaped like a pitchfork.

'*The Chronicles of Narnia* are children's stories I used to read,' Urette says. 'There's a wardrobe in one of them.'

That's only half an answer, Bagrin says. *She's not telling the truth, the whole truth, and nothing but the truth.*

One side of Pia's face is uncomfortably hot. Should she really let the devil sit in on this conversation? She doesn't really know how to stop him. And he is proving to have his uses.

'Narnia is what Celeste and I called the Seam,' Urette grumbles after Pia prods her a little more. 'Back before it existed, when it was only theoretical. And before the detonation, when we were building the r-bomb, we both worked in a government facility called the Weapons Research Development Bunker. WRDB. Wardrobe. You see?'

'Only sort of.'

Urette clicks her teeth in annoyance. 'Narnia is a fantasy land full of made-up creatures,' she snaps. 'You climb into the wardrobe to get there. Get it now?'

And now it is Pia's turn to spill her tea. The mug drops from her hands and rolls across the floor. Urette glares at the stain spreading across her carpet, then gets creakily to her feet, muttering under her breath.

Pia barely notices.

She knows where the angels are.

Back inside the Seam.

18
THROUGH THE WARDROBE

Urette scuttles around the kitchen for a tea towel, and Pia holds an emergency discussion with Bagrin in her head.

How interrrrresting, says the devil.

Interesting?! Pia's thoughts shriek. *They've gone into the Seam, Bagrin! Anything could happen to them. Literally anything. That's the point of glitch. What if they come out, and they're not angels any more, or they can't do miracles, or they don't want to help?*

The devil chuckled. *Angels will be OK. They are hard to kill. Bagrin tried many times.*

That was in the real world, not in the Seam. Do you know how many imagerations of angels Mum created before these two, Bagrin? Hundreds.

She is babbling, she knows it, and babbling to devils is a very bad idea, but in her panic she ploughs on regardless.

It took Mum hundreds of trips to the Seam, and each time she came out the angels she'd imagined didn't last. They floated away because humans weren't interesting to them, or were too weak, or only lived for minutes, or turned into devils.

Bagrin interrupts. *We prefer the term 'upgraded' into devils.*

Pia stands up as Urette pats the spilled tea down. There's about ten minutes before the ultimatum on Weevis's note runs out, and she has just discovered that the angels are in a place of literally unimaginable danger, and she can do absolutely nothing about it. Not tonight, and probably not ever.

Don't be so sure, Bagrin says. *There's always a way. It just depends how badly you want it.*

What does Bagrin mean?

We'll explain, the devil says, reading her thoughts. *But first, we need to get you out of here.*

Suddenly Pia finds her nose itching.

Pretend to sneeze, Bagrin says.

Is she really doing this? Is she really so desperate that she'll take orders from a devil?

It turns out that yes, yes she is. Scrunching up her face as much as she can, Pia goes 'Choo!' in a high squeaky voice.

It doesn't sound particularly convincing. Sneezing feels like tears or laughter: something that requires real talent to fake. Yet the effect on Urette is as instant as the words 'Narnia' and 'Wardrobe'.

'Are you sick?' she asks sharply, rearing back in her armchair. 'Do you feel sick?'

Tell her you think you have a cold. It'll help, Bagrin promises.

Pia does as she is told. Urette stands up so quickly her knees make clicking sounds.

'You have to go,' she says hurriedly, seizing her gargantula coat from behind the armchair and shrugging it on. 'Gargantulas have very weak immune systems. I didn't know you weren't well.'

'I didn't know myself.' Pia tries another fake sneeze.

Urette flings tissues at her. 'I'll bring Vizier,' she says, scuttling out of the bubble. 'Can't have you contaminating the ark further.'

Pia guesses Vizier is the ark's genie.

He is, says Bagrin. *He will zephyr you out of here. See how Bagrin helped?*

'Yes,' Pia says drily. 'The Devil just wants to help out. I don't know why he gets such bad press.'

Bagrin is a *devil, not* the *Devil.*

'Uh-uh. Not true. If you didn't want to be known as *the* Devil, you shouldn't have eaten Gotrob.'

Gotrob still lives, in a way. We incorporated him.

Pia cocks her head, surprised. So eating Gotrob was more of a *hostile takeover* for Bagrin. Makes a lot of sense. Devils conduct themselves in a very business-like manner: advertising their services (with chimeras and whispers), finding customers, making deals, and buying out rivals.

If Gotrob *is* part of Bagrin, that means Pia is in league with *two* devils, and in double the trouble.

Not in league, Bagrin says. *No contract. More of a 'free trial period'.*

'Liar. You don't give *anything* for free.'

True, Bagrin admits.

'Why are you even helping me, then?'

Market research.

'Research into what?'

His answer gives her chills: *You.*

The chimera he sends her now is different to all the

others. It has been tailored. Instead of Pia at its centre, there is a plan. A shining diamond of a plan. And in its glitter, Pia sees all manner of wonderful things.

A way to rescue the angels.

A way to pass her psych test.

A way to make Mum and Dad proud.

Would you like it? Bagrin's honeyed voice asks. *Bagrin will tell you for – oh, almost nothing. It is a perfect plan, you see, but oh so delicate. The slightest flaw will ruin it, and waste all of Bagrin's hard work.*

Would you like it?

Do you want it?

'No,' Pia lies.

But you want to save your angels.

Isn't that what you want?

Isn't it?

It is. More than anything. More than almost anything. But Bagrin's price—

Price? Bagrin reads her thoughts. *There is no price. It is* Bagrin *who will be paying* you.

You can have the plan, Pia.

And in return, you work for Bagrin. You do all you can to make sure Bagrin's plan happens. You obey everything Bagrin says.

Pia recoils. 'Like a slave obeys their master?'

Like an employee obeys their boss, Bagrin replies. *Work for Bagrin, and Bagrin will pay you in angels.*

Well?

Deal?

Somehow, Pia manages to turn away from him. Manages to block the door to her thoughts and push the devil away. *No*, she thinks. *No*.

He tries sending her the chimera again, but she shuts her mind. He pushes against her, and she sings catchy pip-pop songs with her hands clasped over her ears, until at last his voice howls into the distance, and the warmth on her cheek turns cool.

Pia sits there with her heart racing, wondering where the willpower had come from to resist a chimera so tempting.

She doesn't have an answer. Now Bagrin has gone, she doesn't have *any* answers.

And at last she can no longer fool herself: this mess is way beyond her ability to fix. She hopes that it isn't beyond Siskin's.

• • •

Urette is full of apologies when she comes back into the bubble. 'I'd love you to stay longer. But I can't have Nancy getting sick, especially with her carrying a brood . . .'

Pia rummages around for the bit of paper that will get her out of there. She feels sick with despair. Now she has turned from Bagrin's lies and admitted the truth to herself, she will have to admit it to someone else too. The thought of coming clean to Siskin after lying to him that morning is almost unbearable.

'It's due to their solitary nature,' Urette explains, maybe interpreting Pia's silence as offended.

'Is that why you keep their ark so far from all the others?' Pia makes small talk as she searches through her dungarees pocket.

'They're not *that* fragile,' Urette says, a little defensively. 'Their cobmist contains ultra-powerful antibodies, which screen out most disease.'

So that is why the zoo breeds the gargantulas. Almost one hundred species have come from the Seam, but the zoo only has a limited number of arks to hold them. Those that aren't useful in some way or another are allowed to go extinct.

'Well,' Urette says, the genie lamp in her hands. 'You'll have to come again, once you're better. If you'd like to.'

'Oh, sure, definitely.' She is getting better at lying. Bagrin's influence, or maybe just practice.

'And give me advance warning next time,' Urette says.

'OK.'

'So I can be on hand with the de-cobber spray.'

'Yeah.'

'And keep your breather on.'

'Yeah.'

'Do you like hot chocolate, because I could—'

'*Choo!*' Pia fake-sneezes again, just to remind Urette that she is ill.

The old zookeeper recoils, and starts to rub the lamp and summon Vizier. Then she pauses. 'You haven't told me,' she says, hand hovering above the lamp's brass surface.

'Told you what?'

'What the angels told you about me.'

'Huh?' Then Pia remembers. 'Oh, right. They said you had the wrong solution.'

'Wrong solution to what?'

Pia shrugs. 'That's not how angels talk. It's up to you to work out what they're saying.'

That, at least, isn't one of Bagrin's lies. Genies have Tellish, devil-speak is rooted in deals, but no one has figured out yet what language angels speak. It is a mishmash of allusions, riddles and wordplay, and just like the angels themselves, the meaning of it is something you have to *feel* to understand.

Urette stands there pondering, rubbing the lamp in her hands. The ark's genie, Vizier, rockets out like a firework, burning so bright Pia has to shield her eyes.

'Who dares summon the dread djinn Vizier?!' he booms in a theatrical voice.

Pia sighs. Poor thing. No one to wish for apart from Urette. Must have turned him into a bit of an exhibitionist.

She bows, then starts to plod through her wish-script. Vizier makes a great show of spinning shadows around himself and twirling his smoky beard into the shape of arcane symbols as she speaks.

She gets to the part of the script that says [insert location here], and fills in the blank. Urette cocks her head in surprise when she hears where Pia is going, but she doesn't interrupt.

'. . . all this, I wish.'

Vizier throws all of his shadows across the bubble like dust sheets. Everything around Pia is cloaked in velvety blackness. Then he pulls himself into one dense point of light and spins around her like a meteorite, trailing rainbow colours. She does her best to look suitably in awe.

'And! So! It! Was! Granted!' his voice booms, and Pia zephyrs away to the cybernism ark.

If she is going to come clean, if she is going to cause an unprecedented panic, she might as well have Ishan with her.

[Spider Parlour]

After Pia leaves, Urette takes the mugs to the sink to wash up. She dunks them in the suds and plonks them on the side to drain and pulls out the plug and listens to the water gurgle away. That was nice. Just to talk, just to listen. Whatever brought the girl to the Spider Parlour, Urette is glad of it.

She dries the mugs and puts them away and sits back in her armchair with her thoughts. Around her, the ship groans and tilts in the ocean's current. Nancy chitters in her nest and wakes Nutella. Another night of nervy dreams from those two, then. Perhaps it's the cold weather.

To her surprise, Urette finds she can't settle either. She keeps noticing how dusty and cluttered her bubble is. Getting to her feet, she starts to make a pile of old things for Vizier to zephyr away. Then she waters her sorry-looking plants. She fetches a cushion and puts it on the plastic crate where Pia sat.

There. That will be a lot more comfortable, next time she comes for tea.

It's only then that she realises that Pia has left something behind. Well, not a thing, no, not exactly. Some sort of *feeling*. A kind of heat, warming one side of her face.

Psst, it says.

Urette blinks. A bony finger is stuck in one ear and wiggled. Is she hearing things? Getting mind-frayed in her old age? Oh well. It feels long overdue.

Psst.

There it is again. Very faint, crackling with static. A voice.

'Vizier? Is that you?' But the genie is sleeping in his lamp.

Psst. Hey. You.

'Who's there?' Urette looks around the bubble.

And, like an old wireless radio, an answer comes through the fuzz.

Just call us the Whisper.

19
FHG K UGH R

The cybernism ark is one of the smallest in the fleet. Pia hurries from the zephyr zone on deck, down its rusted steps, towards the central hold. Halfway there, a second blue scrip zephyrs in front of her face.

> *I believe Weevis told you thirty minutes*, it says.
> *And I believe he told you thirty-one minutes ago.*
> *My office. As in, right now.*
> *Siskin.*

So she's made the boss mad. Nice move, Pia. She flings the note aside. No point worrying now. She is about to make him a whole lot madder.

Ahead, she can hear the humming throb of the nanite hive stacks. A dozen of them are arranged in a neat row on the floor of the hold: tiny glittering cities of circuit boards and blinking lights and silicon chips that rise up like tower blocks.

Power cables as thick as anacondas snake across the floor, feeding the nanites steady rivers of electrons and data. Pia picks her way over them to Ishan.

He is slumped in his chair, asleep. In front of him, a dozen monitors are squeezed on to his desk. His forehead rests on the keyboard, nose touching the space bar. Every time he breathes in and out, long nonsensical words type on the screen.

FHG K UGH R.

G VU H.

BUU YU YB.

Pia looks at him. Most of the zoo staff just use goggles when they need to do tech stuff, because they are faster and easier and take up less room, but Ishan salvaged all these old flat screens and a keyboard and taught himself to type. Apparently, it's retro.

'I lost the angels,' Pia says, quietly enough not to wake him.

U U, types Ishan's forehead.

'I've been searching for them all day, Ishan. I just had to tell you. I don't know what to do. And you can't help me, because you're asleep.'

'Uh, actually . . .' Ishan opens one eye. 'I was sort of pretending.'

Pia stares at him. He sits up, rubbing the back of his neck, a mosaic of little squares stamped on his forehead. 'Sorry, Pia.'

Calamity. She is an absolute calamity. She facepalms so hard there's a slapping sound. 'Why were you pretending?'

'I don't know. It was weird. I don't think you've ever come here before.'

She looks at him. He is right. It has always been Ishan coming to her, before this.

'And it's way past curfew, and I saw you coming on the

146

camera . . .' He nods at a monitor, where a grainy image of the ship's zephyr zone is windowed in one corner of the screen. 'And I sort of panicked.'

'Panicked?'

He sneezes. For some reason, sometimes Ishan does that when nervous.

'Bless you.'

'Thanks. And don't act surprised. You make me do a lot of stupid things, you know.' He points at his eye, still bruised from last week when Pia punched him.

Pia sinks to the floor and curls over, hands over her head.

'So. You lost the angels, huh?' Ishan speaks softly, quietly, like she has a migraine or something. 'That's . . . Wow.'

'I haven't *lost* them,' Pia says, voice muffled. 'I know exactly where they are.'

'You do? Where?'

'Inside the Seam.'

'Oh.' Air blows out of his lips. 'Wow. OK. Wow.'

Pia actually feels worse now she's told someone. The great calamitous secret has finally broken loose from the flimsy enclosure she built to hold it. Soon it will rampage around the zoo, followed by a stampeding horde of procedures and inquiries and reports . . .

'How do you know they're in there?' Ishan asks.

'They told me.'

'What? How?'

'In a halo. You wouldn't understand.'

Ishan scratches his head. 'Celestials are so *weird*. What the nihil are they doing in the *Seam*?'

'I don't know.'

'What does Siskin say?'

'Um.'

Ishan grips his chair's armrest. 'You haven't *told him*?!'

'Don't tell! Please, Ishan!' Pia hates how pathetic she sounds.

'Me? Are you crazy? *I'm* not doing it, Pia, *you* have to. Here.' He grabs some scrip and waves it at her. 'Here, you can zephyr a message to Ark One.'

Ishan's words take all the will from her. Pia crumples to the floor and starts to cry. She can't stop it. She just doubles over, leaking tears and spit and snot, and Ishan knows her well enough to know not to come and comfort her.

Then she hears him make a noise – half yelp, half gag. She doesn't need to look up to see why.

She *feels* the reason.

The giddy relief. The triumph. The numinous lamp has winked on in a sudden miracle. Lit up beneath Ishan's desk is one of the angels, faint and shivering and almost dead.

• • •

It's almost impossible to kill an angel, Pia tells herself as she crawls under Ishan's desk and sets the lamp down by the celestial.

Still, that hasn't stopped whatever did this from trying.

148

The angel is all flicker and static, like one of Ishan's monitors. It keeps trying to form itself back together and collapsing into a heap of fuzz. Whenever it does coalesce, Pia sees a round perfect hole in its shoulder like a gunshot wound.

Pia has always known angels can die, but not that they can be *wounded*.

She reaches out her finger and lets the angel hold on with its tiny hand. Which of the two is it? The littlest one? Yes. She is almost sure. The littlest, who likes singing blossom from the garden's apple tree; who weaves halos a little lopsided; who loves to make rainbows in the rain.

How could someone do this? She shakes with the fury of it. The fear too.

'Do something,' Ishan says behind her. 'Do something, Pia. Do something.' He is freaking out, stuck on a loop. He doesn't understand that Pia *is* doing something. She is believing. Belief is the oxygen that angels breathe. So she shuts her eyes and clasps her hands and believes as hard as she can.

You'll get better. You'll mend.

'Do something, Pia. Pia?'

She ignores him, and at last he goes silent. Pia's focus is on her belief, feeble and faked as it is. She stares at the angel.

You'll be OK, she thinks. *You will.*

After what seems like hours, the angel sits up in its shape again and crawls on its hands and knees into her lap. It feels like holding an empty plastic bag. The angel still

149

trembles at its edges. The wound in its shoulder is round and ugly.

'How did it – why did it – what is it doing under my desk?' Ishan backs away. He is not dealing with this well at all.

'Tears, despair and impending doom,' Pia mutters to herself. 'These things summon angels.'

She didn't know for sure, but perhaps her crying had mixed with her despair and brought the angel back. But why hadn't that worked this morning, when she had come back from Ark One and burst into tears? And why had only the littlest come? Why not both of them?

Maybe Pia's tears and despair weren't enough. What if the angel itself provided the third element: impending doom? Pia glances at the wound in its shoulder. It looks like it is getting bigger.

Oh Seamstress, don't think that. She throws the thought from her head and cuddles the angel, believing and believing and trying not to doubt. *Don't die, you won't die, if you die I'll die.*

'What do we do?' Ishan says.

Pia has no idea. In her lap, the angel speaks.

'Hole in this whole,' it says. 'Going once, going twice, going going gone with the wind.'

'What was that? What did it say?'

'I don't *know*, Ishan.'

'Why not?' He doesn't get angel-speak. Ishan is used to a language of ones and zeroes. Yes or no.

'Angels don't speak like nanites. They can say yes and no and maybe all at once, depending on who's listening.'

'Ohhhh,' Ishan says. 'Superpositional.'

Pia guesses that is gogglehead-speak for *Now I get it*.

'Hole in the whole,' says the angel again. 'Moth in the cloth. Worm in the apple. Oh, rose, thou art sick!'

Then, in a way that somehow makes the back of Pia's neck crawl, it whispers: 'The worms. The worms.'

Ishan sneezes. His hands are suddenly tugging at her shoulder. 'Get away from it, Pia. It's not – it doesn't sound right.'

She turns round and whacks him. Not hard. Just a little jab in the arm to say, *Shut up*. Then she looks back at the angel and follows its words like they are a trail or a path.

Hole in the whole. Moth in the cloth. Worm in the apple. Oh, rose, thou art sick! The angel has a hole in it. Perhaps it means that. And moths make holes in cloth, and worms make holes in apples. Apples grow on trees and roses grow on bushes. Pia thinks of the angel's garden. But that isn't sick – it's dead.

And dead things get eaten by worms, she thinks with a shudder.

Her thinking has gone in a circle. Now she is back to worms, and holes, and death. She needs to be thinking of healing; of the angel getting better. It is in a bad way, body flickering and buzzing with static. A few bright particles of light fizz away from the edges of its wound, like sparks from a bonfire.

151

'You'll be fine,' Pia says on impulse. Her voice sounds loud and hollow beneath the desk. 'It'll all be fine. Don't be worried. I'm not.'

Another spark of the angel breaks away. Pia makes a pointless grab to stop it. It passes through her hand and vanishes, leaving a vague tingling warmth that goes cold.

The hole in the angel is now the size of her fist, and growing.

What can they do? Try to bandage the wound? With what? She looks at Ishan. No point asking him. Confusion and panic fill his face. He is used to looking after a species that makes back-up copies of itself and runs automatic diagnostic checks. Nanites don't *die*, they just update.

Bagrin? Pia calls out to the devil, not knowing where else to turn. *Bagrin, are you there?*

Silence. Where has he gone? Now that she thinks about it, she hasn't felt his presence for a while. Maybe after rejecting that last chimera she blocked him out for good. Perhaps he is punishing her. Or the angel.

She shuffles back out from under the desk. Stark violet shadows from the numinous lamp light up the hold. Circuit boards and power cables and qbit stacks. What does she do? In her hands another piece of the angel drifts away, like an ark without an anchor.

Anchor! That's it! 'We need to anchor it, Ishan. Keep it here.'

Ishan runs his hand up his vertical fringe. 'How do we do that?'

Pia looks down at the celestial in her lap. The hole has widened across the angel's shoulder and is spreading across its body. She feels panic inside her like a bird; it flutters and flaps its wings. 'I don't know. I don't *know*, Ishan.'

Pia freaking out seems to focus him. Suddenly he snaps his fingers. 'Hey, remember when Arlo got bitten by the salamadder?'

Of course Pia remembers. Arlo is the old Spaniard on the aviary ark, with the eyebrows like fluffy clouds. He lost his whole foot to that salamadder bite. It just turned to smoke and drifted off his ankle. The poison put Arlo in a coma for a week. The doctors didn't know if he'd wake up, but he did. Said he'd heard his friend Toro's voice by the hospital bed. Calling him back. Out of the darkness.

Saying his name.

Ishan starts to explain his idea, but Pia has already figured it out. It's a risk, and it's against procedures. The angels are nameless for a reason. If Bagrin and Gotrob weren't given names, they might still be angels and Pia's parents might still be alive.

Ishan sees all of this in her eyes. 'If it works, we can deal with the risks later. And if it doesn't work . . .'

Pia gets him. If it doesn't work, there is no risk, because the angel will be gone.

She takes a deep breath.

'Would you like a name?' she asks the little wounded celestial in her lap. 'You know what a name is, don't you? It's a word that means you.'

'Angel,' crackles the angel, flaring brighter.

'That's right. But angel means you and your friend, doesn't it? You're both angels, aren't you? A name is just you. Let's think of a word that just means you.'

'Me.'

Pia nods. This is good. Keep the angel talking. Keep its focus here. Make it feel noticed, and needed.

'Like Cornucopia means me. Just me. And Ishan means just Ishan.' She points at herself, then behind her. 'So what about you? Let's give you a name.'

'Angela?' suggests Ishan.

'Angela? How do you like Angela?'

The angel buzzes a low flat sound: No.

Ishan sighs. 'Wilma is right, I'm terrible at names.'

'How about you pick your own?' Pia suggests.

The angel flickers silently in her lap for so long that Pia wonders if it understood. Then suddenly she hears: 'Om Mani Padme Hum.'

It's a little startling. 'That's a big name. Shall I . . . call you Hum for short?'

'Hum,' repeats the angel in a whisper. He (with a name like Hum, he somehow just seems to Pia like a boy-angel now, she doesn't know why) crackles.

The hole in his shoulder disappears.

Ishan blinks. 'Did it work?'

'I don't know. Maybe. Hum?'

The hole reappears at Hum's centre. Ishan swears in sprawl-tung. Pia chokes back a sob. For a moment, she thought naming the angel had helped. Maybe it did. But not enough. Not nearly enough.

'Tell us how we can help you. Please, Hum.'

'Down the rabbit hole in one,' Hum whispers. 'Way to the weft undone.'

The hole is as big as a handspan now. Hum looks like he is *melting* around it. Dripping into some molten spinning violet ring, bending himself around the wound. With a gasp, Pia recognises the shape. The angel is weaving the wound. Turning it into a halo-shaped miracle.

Making it from himself, from his own light, and shrinking as he weaves it, until he is a shining mote, barely alive and no bigger than a star, so small and faint that Pia can barely see or feel him.

And wobbling on the floor is his miracle. A warped ring of light. A woven halo, big enough to hula with.

And in the hole in the middle of the halo is another place. Not the cybernism ship – another place entirely.

This miracle is not a dream, or a message or map.

It's a doorway.

20

GLITCH ENCOUNTER

Slowly, Pia and Ishan circle the halo. They peer down into the hole at its centre. Light warps into a ring shape around it, but the hole is absolute black, absolute silence. Like a well dug down to the bottom of the ocean.

For a long time there is only the drone of the nanite stacks around them, and under that the ship's deep thrum: two low notes of dread beneath Pia's drumming heart.

'What is it?' Ishan says.

'Hum's miracle.' She steps closer. It is big enough to climb through. 'I've never seen a halo like it.'

'What did it do to him?'

Pia looks at the tiny fragment of angel. Hum has fallen down into her palm, so small she can't make out his shape. Just a glint. A smithereen thrown from a steel welder. 'He wove it from his own light. His own essence.'

'But what is it he wove?' Ishan breathes in sharply as she puts a hand over the hole. 'Don't!'

'There's air, Ish. Rising up. It's *warm.*'

A sudden, horrible thought: the hole is a mouth, breathing on them. She shudders and wipes her hand on her dungarees.

'Don't, Pia.'

'Don't what?'

'Stand that close.' He motions her back. 'Use the lamp.'

Good idea. Taking up the numinous, she swings its beam downwards. The hole lights up. It's a riveted metal tube, rusty-brown and streaked with water stains. On one side is a bolted rung ladder that goes all the way down, beyond the reach of the lamp. Is that writing on the side? Some long serial number, in stamped black lettering.

Ishan blinks. 'That isn't . . . there aren't any vents beneath this cargo space.' He goes to his monitor and pulls up the ship's blueprints to double-check.

The back of Pia's neck tingles. 'It isn't beneath the deck, Ish. It isn't even on this ark.'

Ishan is too engrossed in his own theories to hear her. 'The angel must have zephyred around the layout of two ships or something? Or maybe . . .'

Pia shines the numinous lamp closer. 'Look at that bit of the serial number.' She reads it out loud. '1-17-US-WRDB.'

Ishan blinks. 'That's . . . that's . . .'

'It's a portal,' Pia says in wonder. 'To the Weapons Research Development Bunker.'

'But that's—'

'Inside the mountain,' Pia finishes for him.

'It's practically inside the *Seam*!' Ishan backs away. 'That's the delivery tube! They dropped the reality bomb down that nulling tunnel!'

'The wardrobe that leads to Narnia,' Pia murmurs.

'We need to report this. This is . . . this is . . . I don't know what this is.'

'What are you freaking out about? It's basically just a door.'

'Are you serious? *Basically just a door?*'

'How is this any weirder than zephyring?'

'Because a genie can't zephyr you to the hypocentre of an r-bomb blast!'

'It could if its beard was long enough.'

Ishan starts shaking his head, very much not able to deal with what is in front of him. Does Not Compute. Does Not Compute. Like his brain is overheating.

'Stop thinking *how* it is,' she tells him. 'Start thinking what we do with it.'

'OK . . . OK, what then?'

'Isn't it obvious? What else do you do with a doorway?'

And as if to demonstrate, Hum slips straight through her hand and down through the halo. Pia points the numinous lamp to light him up again. He twinkles inside the vent the size of a firefly. Waiting for her to follow.

Ishan sees the look she gives him.

'Uh-uh. No way, Pia. As in, absolutely not. As in, don't even think about it.'

His voice is like iron and his stare is unblinking. It isn't a bad impression of Siskin, but it's still just an impression.

Pia steps closer to the hole.

'Pia, stop!'

'Maybe the other angel needs rescuing,' she says. 'Maybe whatever hurt Hum is hurting the other angel too.'

'OK.' Ishan is holding up his hands pleadingly. 'OK,

yeah, maybe that's true. But you're not the one that goes down that hole. You haven't been authorised. They have to psych test you, you know that. It isn't just *dreams* that come real in the Seam, it's nightmares, phobias, buried traumas . . . What if you get mind-fray? What if you don't come out at all?'

Pia has already reached down and gripped the first rung.

'I've got an angel to guide me,' she says, swinging down one foot.

Ishan's hands scrabble at her dungarees, trying to haul her back but almost making her slip. She glares at him, hand balled into a fist. 'Do I really have to punch you again?'

He cringes away from her. His eyes are trembling with tears. 'You're so weird sometimes,' he says. 'I wish . . . I wish I didn't like you.' Then he turns and runs to his desk to ping for help.

Pia clips the numinous lamp to her belt and grips the floor and swings her second foot down through the hole and into the vent.

Warm, damp air rises up in gusts. It feels like climbing down some enormous throat. Again those same thoughts – mouths, throats, teeth.

'Bagrin, if that's you trying to scare me, stop it.'

The devil doesn't reply. It occurs to her that she is now a long, long way from the celestial ark. She doubts his powers reach this far or this deep.

Hum is flashing in red urgent colours for her to be

careful. She glances down at him as she steps on to the rungs. Bad idea. The vent has no bottom that she can see. The dark beneath her feet might be miles deep. She feels a weird nauseating wobble. A sick dizzy feeling.

Vertigo, she decides. *Or food poisoning.* How typically ludicrous it will be, if she has to climb back up to Ishan. *And the angels were abandoned, and the Earth was doomed, all because of one disastrous hot dog. The End.*

But it's only the motion sickness, or lack of it. Because she isn't on the ocean. The floor isn't gently rocking beneath her feet. She is on the island. Inside its mountain. Climbing down towards her angel, and the Seam.

Hum hovers up by Pia's face, changing from red to green. *Go*, the colour says to her, so she climbs down, counting the rungs as she goes. Ten, twenty-five, fifty.

She tries not to think about the glitch. When the r-bomb exploded, it didn't just create the Seam. Like any bomb, it threw out shrapnel. Debris. The official term for it is *glitch*. Little pockets of the universe where time stops working, or where matter no longer exists; where there is only one dimension, or seven.

This close to the Seam, the glitch will be orbiting inside the mountain, moving very fast. Tiny patches of it are whizzing through her even now. A larger one might swallow Pia up in one gulp. A lot of the original research team were gobbled up like that, never to be seen again. Others had been lost, only for the glitch to spit them out days or months later, mind-frayed or changed in other awful ways.

To reach the Seam, Seamers are taught paths and schedules through the glitch. Pia only has Hum to guide her.

Suddenly he flashes from green to red. Pia stops.

A second later, just below her feet, a patch of glitch rushes past. It thunders through the mountain and the vent like a Rhinosaurus rex. The same crushing roar of blurred fury. Except the glitch is not an animal, it is an emptiness. And in its vast cavern of nothing, Pia's own thoughts echo back to her.

Suddenly she can smell the apples as they rot in the angel's garden; can taste hot-dog mustard and salad and green tea and cobmist spray; can feel Ishan's lips on her lips, and her knuckles on his cheek, and night frost sprinkling on her shoulders; can see the blinding sunlight, Weevis's blackhead, Bagrin's chimeras, a squashed pea; can hear her father's ghost and the gargantulas clicking and Threedeep pinging.

All overwhelmingly at once.

A thunderous rush of memory.

She is nine again, and crying on the Rek. She is ten, and failing the psych test. She is with Wilma, teasing an old genie called Sesame by wishing for his wishes not to come true. She is listening to Gowpen talk about his unicorn.

Then the glitch is gone, leaving Pia alone in the vent again.

Her head reels. At some point in the last few moments (seconds? Minutes? Hours?) her legs buckled and she had nearly fallen. Hum is blinking green again, which means she has to go on before the glitch orbits back round again.

Step by step, rung by rung, guided by Hum: stop, go, wait, go, wait, stop, go. Each time she glances up, the halo is a little further above her. A faint circle, the cool-blue colour of Ishan's monitor light. She can't tell whether it is only a hundred metres overhead, or a mile. Her sense of distance is all skewed. There is no other way to gauge how far she has moved. The darkness and silence around her are an oblivion.

It's the mountain. All this rock, this stone. The crushing weight of it, pressing downwards and inwards for a billion years. Squashing the dark blacker than black, squeezing the silence deeper than deep.

Passing through the vent feels like it happens in one endless second that has been set in stone. Time here is like the silence and the dark. The weight of the mountain has fossilised it.

Then the vent comes to an abrupt end, and the ladder with it. Pia's foot gropes for a rung that isn't there, and she slips and falls in the darkness, falls into it like a dream.

And when she lands, it is softly as a feather, inside the Seam.

It's nothing like what she expected.

21
ANGEL SONG

Pia looks around the curved glasshouse. It is made of tall thin windows that arch from floor to ceiling, set in iron frames painted green. Sunlight angles through them. The long slanted beams fall warmly on Pia's skin.

She glances up. There is no sign of the mountain, or the vent she travelled down.

The glasshouse smells of waxed wood and washed linen and dry crumbly earth. Dark green, viciously spiked plants sit on the shelves in terracotta pots full of pebbles, soaking up the sun and sprouting extraordinary magenta flowers. Against the red-brick wall that the glasshouse curves against, vines dangle little bunches of purple-black fruit amongst their hanging leaves.

A wicker armchair sits in the centre of the worn and wobbly paving stones. And cushions. So many cushions. All piled up. Round, square, long, tasselled, buttoned, woolly, big, small. Like the chair is there just for the cushions to sit on.

Pia notices each of these things one after another instead of all at once, as if they aren't there and then they are; like someone is sketching the glasshouse in front of her eyes and slowly filling in its details.

She is tingly and tired. The warm feeling sinks into her skin as she stands there, motionless as a prickly plant, until she starts to think that some of the cushions might have to budge up and make room, because she feels like sitting on the armchair to rest or even nap.

And then it is like the cushions on the armchair have been rubbed out, because they are gone and in their place sits a woman, who is turning round in her seat and looking around the room with the same expression of pleasant wonder as Pia.

The woman has long grey hair, tightly plaited. It reaches the small of her back, where the brown wispy end has worked free of its hairband and is starting to unravel. Her fingers are long and knuckled, with nails clipped short, and large blue veins that wriggle across the back of her hands as she gestures. A plain gold ring sits on her littlest finger like a tiny halo. Her spectacles too are round and gold-rimmed.

The woman is Doctor Celeste Lalande, the inventor of the reality bomb, the leader of the first research team, who walked into the Seam thirty years ago and vanished.

'I like what you've done with the place,' Doctor Lalande says. She looks around and nods. '*Very* cosy. Much dustier than I normally have it. And one of us has a cushion obsession. But that's to be expected. With three of us here, of course, things can get a little crowded.'

Lalande bends her neck and inspects herself in the reflection of the mug of water she holds. Her outfit is the exact same one as the photo on Siskin's wall: a blue paisley skirt with a frayed grey T-shirt. And long white-green earrings, like little cuttings of watercress. The ones Urette must have lent her on the day she vanished.

'And I like what you've done with *me*.' Lalande beams. 'It's always a little nerve-wracking, meeting someone new. You *are* new, aren't you?'

'I think so,' Pia said.

'Well, sometimes newcomers make me just monstrous. The stuff of nightmares. But you've clothed me very nicely. I always like being dear old Doctor Lalande.'

The back of Pia's neck tingles. Wait. This woman *isn't* Lalande?

'No,' answers the woman, and Pia has the eerie realisation that her thoughts have just been read. 'Although Celeste is a part of me – everyone who enters the Seam is.'

Pia takes a step back. She is afraid. 'Who are you?' Even as she speaks, she knows it's the wrong question. '*What* are you?'

'Too many questions, Cornucopia. Questions in here can tie you up in knots.' The woman sips her mug. 'Just call me what you always call me. OK?'

It takes a moment before the name comes to her. Before it falls into Pia's head like a dream.

'You've gone all pale,' says the Seamstress with a kind smile. 'And look what a state you're in. Let me tidy you up a little . . . *there*.'

Something like an electric current runs through Pia. The rusted grime on her hands from the vent's ladder has gone, and her dungarees are free of sweat and muck.

'Now drink this.' The Seamstress's mug is suddenly in Pia's hand, and there isn't water inside any more, but something hot and rich and sweet and creamy.

'None of you kids know what *real* hot chocolate tastes like, you know that?' The Seamstress smiles. 'You just have that genie-thrinted stuff. But the research base? The WRDB? It still had supplies of the genuine article before the detonation.' She sighs. 'Oh, the taste of hot chocolate. One of Doctor Lalande's most precious memories. I make sure I hold on to it. You can see why, can't you?'

Pia finds herself drinking from the mug, though she hadn't been aware of raising it to her lips. The hot chocolate is tooth-hurtingly sweet and tongue-scaldingly hot and the most wonderful thing she has ever tasted in her entire life.

Now the Seamstress holds the mug in her hand again. 'Thank you.' She smiles. 'You've drunk a little of me, and I've been decorated by a little bit of you.'

She gestures around her.

'It's good to mix imaginations in here, and do it as often as you can. Otherwise, the realities drift apart. Yours and mine. Like cloth unravelling. Very dangerous. We wouldn't be able to see each other. Or anything, eventually. And you don't want to be in the Seam without some reality around you. That's like being on the ocean without a boat.'

She takes Pia by the shoulders and together they sit down on the armchair, which is now a scuffed, wine-coloured velvet couch with patched arms leaking cream-coloured fluff.

'Before we start,' the Seamstress says, 'would you please pass the cherry bowl? Thank you, Pia.'

Pia looks around. What bowl of cherries? Yet suddenly she is passing one over: a clear glass bowl filled with dark red fruit. Where has it come from?

'You wove it,' answers the Seamstress, reading her thoughts again. 'I helped too, of course, by asking. The question is the needle, the thought is the thread, and the cherry . . .' The Seamstress plucks up a cherry by its stalk and takes a bite. 'The cherry is the cloth.'

She chews, and her face sours.

'I always ask with newcomers.' She spits out the stone. 'But it seems nobody *truly* remembers how cherries taste. Or maybe nobody really loved them as much as Celeste did. Or perhaps it was another member of the research team . . . I forget whose memories are whose. It's hard to remember, in the Seam. You'll see.'

Pia just sips her hot chocolate, half sunk in the couch. Yes. She does feel forgetful. Why is she even here?

'So,' the Seamstress says in a business-like manner. 'Another unicorn imageration, yes? How's Moonbeam doing? Was it Moonbeam? Something like that, right? Any tweaks to the pattern?'

Pia sits up with a start. Now she remembers. 'I'm here for my angel. Not a unicorn.'

'Your angel?' The Seamstress raises her eyebrows. 'It's beside you. Do you not see? It's very small.'

And Pia spots Hum beside her. Has he always been there?

He shifts through his colours kaleidoscopically. 'Not that angel. The second one. The elder.'

'Oh,' said the Seamstress. She looks troubled. 'I thought you were here for the unicorn.'

'That's Gowpen.'

'Of course it is. Of course. I forgot about Gowpen. It's so easy to forget here. Have I said that already? That's why I need you children. To hold the pattern.' The Seamstress frowns. 'But you don't have the unicorn pattern.'

'No,' Pia says. 'At least, I don't think I do.'

The Seamstress peers forwards. Her frown deepens. 'No. Then why are you here?'

'Angels.'

'Oh yes, you said that, didn't you. Didn't you?'

'They both went missing. I'm looking for them. I found Hum, and he led me here.' Pia looks around. 'I was hoping to find the second angel. Have you seen it?'

The Seamstress looks around the glasshouse. Then she snaps her fingers, and Hum appears above her head, lit up like a light bulb.

'Angels! *Now* I remember. They showed up not so long ago. To help me with something . . .' Her smile fades. 'Help me to do what, though? Let me see, let me see . . .'

The Seamstress trails off, one hand twiddling absent-mindedly at the frayed edge of her sleeve.

'It's no good,' she says. 'Whatever it was has unravelled. Unless I kept it for safekeeping. Let me check my memory box.'

In the Seamstress's hands is an old hinged box. She puts

it on her lap, rattle and clunk. The lid comes up with a creak, and she rummages within. Pia leans forward to see what the box holds.

Reels and reels of pearlescent thread. A tray of them, each in its own neatly labelled compartment.

Gowpen, says one label. *Wilma*, *Zugzwang*, *Lian*, *Chen* . . . Each Seamer has their own reel of iridescent string.

'I unravel their memories of this place,' the Seamstress explains. 'Each time they leave. It makes them forget what they saw in here, which is unfortunate, but necessary. And I put all the unravelled memory to good use. My own thoughts are always wearing away. I'm always needing to patch myself up.' She picks at the grey arm of her T-shirt. 'Look.' She picks up a reel. With a silver flash, she frees the needle from the thread, and her long knuckled hands begin to darn the frayed hem. The hand that holds the needle moves back and forth across her arm like a concert violinist drawing their bow across the strings. The thread loops, draws taut then slack, as the Seamstress sews.

There is a beauty in her stitching. The beauty of a dance. As the needle pirouettes. As it spins its spiralled pattern.

And the threads themselves are shining, filling Pia's head with their light, and in that dazzling space in between the weaving fibres, she sees the Seamstress spinning, sees her true shape dancing, sees her ten legs clack, sees her body glitter-black. She is the maker, she is the loom.

'Pia?' says a voice. 'Come back.'

And Pia is in the glasshouse again, next to Hum, with

169

the cup of hot chocolate in her hands, blinking at the woman who is and is not Doctor Lalande.

'I'm sorry you had to see that,' says the Seamstress gently. 'I try to keep things here in the Seam as real as possible when I have guests. But it's a fragile thing.' She gestures to the glasshouse around them.

'You don't have to say sorry,' Pia says. 'Was that your true shape?'

'There's no truth in the Seam, Cornucopia. Just some things that are more real than other things.'

'It was . . .' Pia tries to find the words to describe that brief glimpse of the Seamstress. 'It was the most beautiful thing I've ever seen.'

'Then I am even more sorry to have to take it away from you. But it's best to forget. And speaking of forgetting, why is my memory box on my lap?'

'You're trying to remember why the angels were here.'

'Of course!' The Seamstress jumps up in her chair and claps her hands together. She pinches the edge of the tray with both hands and lifts it away. There is another layer beneath, more reels with less thread on. *Vivi*, *Tej*, *Britta*, *Minnie*. Zookeepers who had once been Seamers, years past.

And then Pia's throat goes tight, and she squeezes her eyes shut to keep in the tears. Side by side in the Seamstress's long, loopy writing, are her parents' names. *Yisel*. *Estival*.

'Hmmm . . .' Before Pia can say anything, the Seamstress lifts away the second tray. The third layer has memory threads from the original research team. There was *Arlo*, and *Urette*, and *Celeste*. Many of these reels are empty.

'I remember making a thread . . .' The Seamstress slowly taps her temple with one finger. 'A memory thread about the angels. About why I needed their help. But . . . I don't remember where I put it.' She rechecks all the layers. 'Hmm.'

'Maybe Hum knows.' Pia looks at the angel. He stays stubbornly pinned in place above them though, glowing red.

'*Et voilà,*' says the Seamstress, lifting away the last layer. Beneath all the trays is a single shining loop of string.

'Who put it there?' The Seamstress reaches forward and plucks it up. 'I must have, of course. But why hide it from myself? How curious.'

She uses the memory string to tie the loose end of her plait. As she tightens the knot, her smile falters. The sunlight streaming through the glasshouse goes dim.

'Oh. Of course. I remember now.'

'Why?' Pia feels suddenly cold. 'Seamstress? Why did the angels come?'

Her face is ashen. 'The same reason as always. Mortal peril.'

Pia edges to the end of the couch. '*Whose* mortal peril?'

'Everyone's.' The Seamstress cries out in sudden agony. 'And – my own.'

'Seamstress?' Pia leaps to help her as the memory box clatters to the floor. The Seamstress is doubled over on the armchair, hands clutching at a dark ragged hole in her side, the same as Hum's wound.

She just remembered that she's injured, Pia thinks. *That's why she hid the memory. To make herself forget that she was dying.*

'A terrible pattern,' whispers the Seamstress. 'Most terrible of patterns. And I wove it. I, the maker and I, the loom. But *he* gave me the threads.'

It is getting dark. Not just shadowy dark, but a nothingness, a void. The sky outside the glasshouse has vanished. Soon Hum is the only light.

'Seamstress!' Pia calls to her, trying to keep her anchored the same way she had with Hum. 'What pattern? Whose pattern? A voilà? What voilà? The unicorn?'

'A bad move.' The Seamstress's plait is loosening, her sleeve unravelling, the hole in her side widening.

'What bad move?' *That was the name of the reel of thread in Hum's dream.* 'Urette? Is this something to do with Urette?'

'The worm,' says the Seamstress, her voice faint. 'The worm.'

Pia holds her tight, but she is slipping, and their two imaginations are coming apart. Around them, the glasshouse begins to fray. The couch unknits, the cushions unwind. The mug jumps up from her hand, uncoiling like a tightly packed spring. It is all coming undone, gently and neatly, the way the sturdiest of a sailor's knots will collapse back into rope when given the right tug.

Emptiness rushes in on them, like a wave.

• • •

Pia finds herself in absolute emptiness. Nothing exists. Total null. No air to breathe; there is no gravity, no light: only her.

The Seamstress's words echo back from the void. *You don't want to be in the Seam without some reality around you. That's like being in the sea without a boat.*

Imagine; she has to imagine. But it's too much for her mind to hold. She is barely able to keep herself together.

She is going to die here. Just unravel and drift away into oblivion.

And that thought brings Hum.

She feels him.

There in the emptiness, singing.

Ishan has asked Pia to describe angel song many times, and the closest she'd come was this: *It's like what a cathedral must feel when a choir sings hymns inside it.* Angels sing songs that bypass your ears, that echo through the hollows of your bones. Songs you feel instead of hear. And in this awful darkness, Hum sings goodbye.

Pia feels it in the back of her throat and the pit of her stomach. Her heart aches with it. *Goodbye*, Hum sings.

Then he dies, the way stars die each morning when the sun comes up. He just fades away until he is gone. Behind him in his afterglow, one last miracle remains. It takes Pia in its palm and carries her home.

[Directive 3:3:2192]

FROM THE DESK OF DIRECTOR SISKIN

TO: ALL ZOO STAFF
DIRECTIVE: 3:3:2192

DEAR COLLEAGUES.

BY WAY OF UPDATE, PLEASE BE ADVISED OF THE
FOLLOWING DIRECTIVES:
*ALL ZEPHYR TRAVEL REMAINS SUSPENDED.
*EXTENDED CURFEW REMAINS IN PLACE BETWEEN
THE HOURS OF 1800 and 0600.
*AS OF THIS MORNING, A SECURITY DETAIL HAS
BEEN ASSIGNED TO EACH ARK AS AN EXTRA
PRECAUTION.
*IN LIGHT OF RECENT EVENTS WITHIN THE SEAM,
ALL SEAMERS AND NON-ESSENTIAL PERSONNEL WILL
SOON BE TRANSFERRED TEMPORARILY TO MAINLAND
FACILITIES.

THESE DIRECTIVES ARE TO ENSURE SAFETY,
SECURITY AND COMPLIANCE THROUGHOUT THE ZOO.

ADDENDUM

WITH REGARDS TO THE VARIOUS RUMOURS
CIRCULATING THE SHIP.
THESE ARE TO CEASE.

AS IN, IMMEDIATELY.

INVESTIGATIONS INTO THE DISAPPEARANCE OF CORNUCOPIA KRAVITZ ARE STILL ONGOING.

THE ONLY – REPEAT: ONLY – FACTS ESTABLISHED BY THIS INVESTIGATION ARE HEREBY SHARED WITH COLLEAGUES BELOW, FOR THE PURPOSES OF STOPPING ALL FURTHER RUMOURS, GOSSIP AND DOOMSAY.

FACT #1 – CORNUCOPIA KRAVITZ ENTERED THE SEAM LAST NIGHT FOR A PERIOD OF APPROX. SEVEN HOURS.

FACT #2 – CORNUCOPIA KRAVITZ IS NOW ON ARK ONE FOR THE PURPOSES OF OBSERVATION AND QUESTIONING.

FACT #3 – THE METHOD BY WHICH SHE REAPPEARED REMAINS UNDER INVESTIGATION.

FACT #4 – THE ALLEGED 'PORTAL' BY WHICH SHE GAINED ACCESS TO THE SEAM NO LONGER EXISTS.

FACT #5 – THE CELESTIAL VOILÀ *CAELESTIBUS AURORA*, KNOWN AS 'ANGELS', HAVE BEEN MISSING FOR APPROX. THIRTY-SIX HOURS AND REMAIN SO.

FACT #6 – THREE SEPARATE OBSERVATIONS OF THE SEAM HAVE FAILED TO RECORD ANY SIGHTING OF THE ENTITY/MIRAGE KNOWN AS 'THE SEAMSTRESS'.

IT IS HOPED THESE FACTS WILL HELP DISPEL SOME OF THE WILDER RUMOURS NOW CIRCULATING AROUND THE ZOO. ANY INDIVIDUALS FEELING EXCESSIVE ANXIETY, NEGATIVITY, DESPAIR OR PARANOIA SHOULD ARRANGE FOR TRANSPORT TO THE ARRIVALS ARK AND REPORT FOR MONITORING.

22

You are the Danger

At some point during all of the questioning, the monitoring and the endless observations, the grief hits.

At first, Pia feels numb. But the shock wears off, like anaesthetic. Grief holds back until it does. Then it sucker-punches her, right in her heart.

Hum.

He is gone.

She still has no idea how his miracle saved her. Probably won't ever know. Isn't that sort of what makes a miracle a miracle? She keeps waiting for her memories to become clearer, but a white haze hangs over them like fog.

All she knows, and all she has been able to tell Siskin, over and over and over again, is that she was inside the Seam. Trapped. No way out.

Then, the light. White and warm, beyond dazzling. Pia remembers shutting her eyes, but that hadn't shut it out. It shone everywhere. Light behind her eyelids. Light inside her head.

When it went away again, she wasn't in the Seam any more. She was in Siskin's office.

Holding his mended lamp.

Voilà.

And then the questioning started. Although maybe that is the wrong word. It feels more like an interrogation.

What happened inside the Seam?
How did you get there?
Where are the angels?
Are you sure?
Are you lying?
Do you have proof?
Can you repeat that?
Can you repeat that?
Can you?

Siskin sits at his desk as Pia repeats her story – a dozen times, a hundred – and each time it gets a little harder to tell, until she can't do it any more.

Oh Seamstress, oh Hum, oh please don't make me say it again, Siskin. They're gone, they're gone, they're gone, they're gone, they're gone . . .

'OK,' says Siskin finally. 'That's enough.'

Two bluebottles come to fetch her from Siskin's office. They hover there silently, or as silently as bluebottles can. Rotors buzzing, screens blank. Probably under orders.

'OK.' Siskin stands. 'Let's go, Cornucopia.'

Ark One's corridors have all been cleared as Siskin and the bluebottles march her down them in silence. Pia isn't wearing handcuffs, or being forced in any way, but she can't help but feel like a prisoner.

They come out on to the deck. It is early morning. The wind is up. It tastes of salt and burning plastic. The sun burns like a reactor fire over the irradiated sea and the mountain rises starkly in front of it. It isn't shimmering, it has no aurora. It is dark. Pia has never seen it look so . . . lifeless.

'How long has it been like that?'

Siskin regards her. 'Ever since you appeared in my office. Almost six hours.'

A small shuttle boat swings above the waves on a lowering crane, the same sort of boat Mum and Dad took her on when they gave her a peek inside the Seam.

'You're not taking me back there, are you?' Pia shudders. 'I won't go.'

'We're not going to the Seam, Cornucopia.'

'Where are we going, then?'

No reply.

They clamber in the boat. The pulleys whirr. Pia lurches as they descend down. It is choppy this morning. Cold spray spatters over the side and white foam caps the waves. A man and woman from security are on the boat. The woman hands Pia a life jacket and a breather. She puts them on.

'Turn over your wish-scripts,' says the security man.

'Why?' Pia looks from him to Siskin, who just raises his eyebrows. As in: *You heard the man, do it.*

She reaches into her dungarees front pocket and hands them over. Half a dozen creased-up rolls of paper. Now she can't zephyr, or even thrint herself a sandwich.

She puts the breather and life jacket on the chilly bench in the passenger area and looks out at the sun burning in the ash-coloured sky, and the waves like snow-capped mountains that peak and fall. It is an ugly and empty sea to look out on, but it is better than looking inwards at herself. At what she has done.

Hum dead, the other angel still missing.

The Seamstress wounded and dying in the Seam. Maybe even dead.

It's not your fault, Pia tells herself for the hundredth time. She tried to tell Siskin too, but he refused to listen. It is true, though. Something else is going on here: some vast and shadowy conspiracy. Pia has caught glimpses of it: the injuries to Hum and the Seamstress. Her references to a terrible pattern, to mortal peril for all. And the words muttered without explanation:

The worm.

Pia shivers. Someone wants to destroy the zoo and the voilà. She knows it.

And they're succeeding.

On the other bench, Siskin watches her and fiddles with his cufflinks. For someone who hasn't slept all night, he looks remarkably fresh. Pia is exhausted. The only thing keeping her awake is knowing she'll have nightmares about what happened in the Seam. Siskin, in contrast, doesn't even have stubble around his goatee.

'When did you even find the time in the last five hours to shave?' she asks, hoping to lighten the mood.

Behind his breather, Siskin doesn't smile. Pia decides to go for broke.

'You *moustache* your secretary to trim it for you, I suppose.'

Not even a flicker of amusement.

'*Moustache,*' Pia explains weakly. 'You know, like *must ask* . . . You *moustache* your secretary to . . .'

Maybe jokes are reflections of their owner, just like voilà. Maybe that explains why Pia's always crash and burn.

Siskin waits for Pia to turn a shade of red dark enough to atone for her terrible attempt at comedy. Then he clears his throat and says: 'You are not, just so we're clear, being accused of anything yet.'

Pia sits in her seat, staring straight ahead.

Accused?

Yet?

Siskin speaks up above the trugging of the boat's engine. 'And I've changed my mind. I *would* like to hear it.'

Pia pulls her knees up to her chest and hugs them.

'As in, your theory,' he adds.

'I know what you meant.'

'Then please oblige me.'

'I tried to tell you back in your office. You said it was irrelevant.'

'I hope I'm mistaken. I hope I'm mistaken about a great deal of things about you, Pia.'

He has never called her Pia before. Somehow, this frightens her.

She breathes deep. 'I haven't got it all figured out, OK? I just blundered into all this by accident.'

'That, at least, seems believable,' says Siskin.

'I think there's a bad *voilà*. It's a worm. But not like an earthworm. More like a serpent or a snake, probably.

A predator animal. I know this because it attacked the Seamstress after she wove its pattern, and then it attacked the angels when they appeared to help her. It left . . . *holes* in them. And now I think it's loose.'

'And if your theory is true, Pia, why haven't we seen this worm?'

'We can't see lots of voilà unless conditions are right, can we? Maybe you need numinous lamps to see it. Or something else.'

'How convenient.'

Pia bristles. She doesn't like Siskin's tone. 'Maybe that's what makes it a successful predator.'

'Hmm.' Siskin looks at the security guards. 'And who is responsible for this worm? A Seamer? Perhaps you would like to suggest a suspect? Since most of the Seamers are your friends?'

Pia shakes her head in frustration. Obviously it isn't one of the Rekkers. Whoever is behind this is lurking somewhere out of sight, like a gargantula in its silk mist.

'I don't know whose voilà it is,' she says quietly. 'But I know they hate the zoo.'

Siskin nods. For a long time he sits there, sliding across the bench as the boat see-saws over the waves.

'It's quite a theory,' he says at last. 'I still can't figure out how it is too that *you* know about the Seamstress, when all the other dozens of Seamers, across decades, cannot say for sure whether she exists.'

'Because she didn't take my memories.' Pia is trying her

best not to get frustrated. 'She unpicks them from everyone's head like thread. Said she uses them to stop herself fraying. And it's not good to carry around too much unreality in your head, either – she said that too.'

'You mean like *you* are, presumably?' Siskin asks.

Oh Seamstress, Pia hadn't thought of that. What are all these unreal memories doing to her mind? She remembers the story Urette told about the first research team. She thinks of Marie Curie, with her desk drawers full of radioactive test tubes.

Siskin chews his tongue and makes a sour face, as if the words he is about to speak taste bad in his mouth. 'Will you hear a second theory, Pia? Think of it as an alternative to yours. I haven't decided which has more evidence to support it.'

Pia swallows. 'OK.'

'Maybe you didn't *lose* our angels – maybe you *did something* to them.'

'What? Ow!' Pia has stood up from her seat and hit her head on the passenger-area roof. The two guards leap up with her. Siskin waves them back down.

'That's ridiculous!' she shouts.

'Is it? An accident-prone young zookeeper makes a mistake and tries to cover it up? Sounds plausible to me.'

'But I wouldn't do that! I didn't!' She hits her knees with her fists. 'I'm telling the *truth*!'

Siskin's voice is chilly. 'Apart from all yesterday, when you were lying?'

Pia has no answer to that – again. She looks past him at the churning sea, tears blurring her sight. The idea that she would harm any of her celestials – even Bagrin, that impish little twerp – makes her sick to her stomach.

'Do you really think I'd hurt my angels? My *mum's* angels?' She is unable to stop her voice trembling.

'You mean the *zoo's* angels?' corrects Siskin coldly. 'No. Not on purpose. But I believe you're very ill, Cornucopia. I believe you're very sick.'

'Sick?' It comes out a frightened squeak.

'This is why you were never made a Seamer. This talk about worms and glasshouses and memory boxes?' He shakes his head.

'I'm *not* mind-frayed,' Pia insists. Which is exactly what someone who has mind-fray would say. Oh facepalm, this is really bad.

'I've no doubt *you* believe what you saw, Pia. But I'd ask you to consider the possibility that the Seam did something to your head. Something that makes it hard for you to differentiate between reality and illusion. Maybe what you saw was your way of dealing with the guilt of something terrible. Something very similar happened after the prism breach, didn't it?'

Pia clenches her fists. So he's been reviewing her past nanabug reports, has he? So what if she insisted that her parents had been away on a trip to the mainland? It was easier than thinking about where they'd really gone.

'I was eight years old, Siskin. As if *you* could understand.

You zephyred me a card with *condolences* written on it. I couldn't even read a word that long.'

Siskin looks away, towards the great grey ship they are approaching. They must have been heading towards it for the past few minutes, but Pia has been too preoccupied with talking to Siskin to notice.

He doesn't care about her theory at all, she realises. He's just been distracting her. Now they are almost at the ark; the only ark that doesn't hold voilà.

'You'll be safer in here, Pia. Just for now. We all will. Even if you aren't mind-frayed. You break things. And I have too much to fix right now as it is.'

Pia sits there numbly. OK, so she'd lost her angels, but the quarantine ark? Siskin has reacted so so so much harsher than she thought he would.

She should refuse to leave her seat. Kick and bite and spit if security tries to move her.

Yeah, sure. Great way to convince Siskin she isn't crazy.

'This is a mistake.' She tries to keep her voice level and calm. 'The zoo's in danger, real danger.'

'I agree.' Siskin regards her thoughtfully. 'But I'd ask you to consider, Pia, that the danger might be you.'

And once again, Pia has no answer to that.

23
That Kiss

Wilma calls it the Quark. Whenever she says it, she juts out her elbows and flaps and squawks like some demented chicken: *Quaaaark! Quaaaark!*

The joke being that Gowpen's mum Fay came out of the Seam once years back and had to go into the quarantine ark for a while because she got a mild case of mind-fray and came out thinking she was a Fabergé chicken.

Pia used to find it funny when Wilma did that. She doesn't think she will again if she gets out.

When, she tells herself fiercely. Not *if*, when.

The Quark has one entrance: a grey auto-door on its deck. Two bluebottles buzz either side of it, waiting for her as she clambers off the ferry.

Will you comply? they both ask, and the left one flicks up its jabber and crackles out a little blue jolt.

Pia is too frightened and too tired to do anything else. She ought to turn back to Siskin and the guards, over by the ferry, and say something before she leaves them, but she can't even manage any sarcasm.

So she goes in, and the grey door closes behind her.

That's it.

She's in the Quark now.

She's a Quarker.

Quaaaark! Wilma goes in her head, strutting and pecking and rolling her eyes all crazily. *Quaaaark!*

Pia stands at one end of a long corridor. It branches off in many directions. The bluebottles buzz forward, one node swivelled around to make sure she follows. Every so often, the leader crackles its taser, just to remind her who is boss.

Pia ignores it. She tries to focus on how ridiculous this is. How funny a story it is going to make when she tells it to Ishan. After all the calamities she has caused with her lies, Siskin has put her in a cell for telling the truth. The thought makes her giggle.

Then she remembers Hum, and she stops laughing. This will never be a funny story. Never. The fact she has even just smiled makes her furious at herself, and a little scared too. Maybe she *is* mind-frayed.

'Has Siskin assigned someone to my genies' beards?' she asks suddenly. 'Solomon and Bertoldo are both due a trim today.'

The bluebottle doesn't answer.

The quarantine ark is decorated almost identically to Ark One. Same blank beige walls, same humming air con, same air of boredom. Pia almost expects to pass a secretary with an enormous blackhead on his nose sat goggling at a desk, but the beige-walled corridors are deserted. Every now and then, another bluebottle buzzes past.

Pia has never really given much thought to all the mind-frayed people who have passed through here: all the surviving original research team, all the 'genieers whose wishes went wrong, all the Seamers whose minds were warped and torn by glitch. Now she is one of them. The thought makes her shudder.

'Where is everyone?' she asks.

This time, the bluebottle does answer: **You are the only patient currently in quarantine. All other patients have been transferred to mainland facilities.**

The corridor ends, and Pia steps through into a prisoner bay that hums noisily. Looking up, she sees four more bluebottles hovering by the ceiling lights.

There are four cells either side of her, each with fuzzed glass fronts.

Last on the left, chats the bluebottle.

Pia ignores all the scary security around her and focuses on making this into not-such-a-big-and-terrifying deal in her head. This colossal mess is, in actual fact, just a minor spot of bother. She'll be out of here in a day. Whatever hurt the angels and the Seamstress won't stop. It will prey on more voilà, and Pia will be in here with bluebottles for her alibi.

Once that happens, she tells herself as she steps inside her cell, *Siskin will let me out.*

'Ugh.' Her good mood evaporates at once. 'Not *you*.'

Hello! ⌐(●ᴗ●)⌐ **It's me: Threedeep.**

'You don't have to introduce yourself to me every time we meet, you know.'

Would you like a tour of your room?

'Call it what it is, Threedeep. It's not a room, it's a cell.'

Saying that, Pia's cell actually looks pretty similar to her cabin. There's a cot, a desk, a chair. It even has a genie with the tiniest little beard, probably with just enough power to zephyr a couple of slips of paper or thrint a sandwich.

Do you know Jazzamin? Threedeep displays a big arrow, pointing to the tiny, timid genie peeking a blue flame from her lamp. **She is a very good friend of mine. Shall I get her to thrint you some water?**

'No.' Pia goes over to her cell's cot and flops on to it and kicks off her boots with her feet. 'Just go on standby. Please.'

Threedeep processes this request. **Sorry, Pia. As a minor, you are prohibited from being confined without full monitoring. I guess you're stuck with me!**

¯_(ツ)_/¯

Pia groans.

I'm sure you'll feel better after a nice snooze, Threedeep chats.

Ugh. The most annoying thing about nanabugs is how often they are right. Pia really is very, very tired.

'Fine, I actually am going to sleep right now, but not because you told me to, because I want to.'

Sleep tight!

(˘ ³˘)♥(ᵕ｡ᵕ)

Pia yawns. 'I need thread, though. And scissors.' She won't sleep until she does her remembrances for her parents.

Umm, says Threedeep. **Scissors are sort of a forbidden item in here.**

Perhaps I can do your remembrances for you.

188

Here.

(͡° ͜ʖ ͡°)=ε✂ | |

snip snip

How is that?

Pia stares at the screen. What does it matter anyway? The thought shocks her, and yet it won't go away. It *doesn't* matter. Nothing does. The Seamstress is dead and Hum is dead and her parents are dead. Cutting two little lengths of thread won't change that.

• • •

Pia falls asleep. She dreams about the kiss and its aftermath. Ishan and her on the Rek, in the starry dark. Her knuckles hurting. Him, holding his cheek. She's never dreamed a memory before.

She feels the kiss on her lips, hot and cool at the same time. It is not romantic or anything. Maybe if she liked him that way, it would've been a tiny bit romantic. But it is mostly awkward and not really even a kiss at all – more of a lip collision.

His mouth tastes really strongly of Pepsi and crisps.

She jerks away and *WHACK* – her fist flails up and bounces off his cheek.

'Why did you do that?' she yells.

Ishan blinks at her for a long while. Then at last he gives a sigh. 'I read a book on my goggles about bees.'

'*What?*'

The relief is just massive. A book about bees?! His answer is so weird, so Ishan, that her anger evaporates and she laughs. At once, the kiss is no longer something that might ruin their friendship. It is just another calamity in a long list of calamities: just another thing for two klutzes to laugh about.

But Ishan doesn't smile. Doesn't go all goofy. He just looks really, really sad.

'I thought I might learn something about the nanites: their hive structure and stuff. But the book was just about *solitary* bees. They were bees that didn't live in hives. I never knew there were so many different types. I don't know anything about nature at all, really. None of us do. Not even most of the grown-ups. Funny for a zoo, right?'

Pia isn't laughing any more. Ishan looks too serious.

'And then I asked Sixtip some more questions, and you know what? There were twenty *thousand* known species of bee before the mass-extinctions. Twenty *thousand*.'

Will every one of Ishan's kisses have this sort of rationale behind it? Be followed by a speech? Well, pointless questions, because she isn't finding out. There will be no more kisses, ever. No way.

'Do you know how many different species we've managed to make with the Seamstress?' he asks quietly. 'Ninety-five, not counting all the imagerations. About sixty of which survive. In just over thirty years. At that rate, maybe in a couple of thousand years, we'll have enough to replace all the *bees* we wiped out.'

He lets that sink in.

'That's why I've never created any voilà. Because I know the truth. Siskin wants us to believe we can save the world. But the world's already dead, and we're just the worms on its corpse.'

Pia looks away from him. Above the sprawl to the east, chemtrails criss-cross the night sky like scars.

'And when I realised that,' Ishan says, 'I asked myself: *What do you want to do before the world ends?*'

He shrugs.

'And that's why I did it.'

• • •

When Pia wakes the next morning, a bluebottle has been in the cell and placed three beige cards on her desk. Printed on them in capital letters are various wish-scripts: one to zephyr away dirt and sweat, another to kill the bacteria on her teeth, and a third to zephyr away her pee and poop from the cell's plastic pot. So the Quark doesn't even have toilets installed? Ugh.

She uses the pot (she makes Threedeep swivel her node the other way), then recites the scripts. Jazzamin grants each wish with a tiny, terrified squeak.

'You don't have to be scared of me, you know,' Pia says to the little genie.

Jazzamin peeks out from her shroud at Pia. 'But we is a redshirt,' she says in babyish Tellish. 'And thee is a Hyde.'

Pia doesn't know those phrases, and Jazzamin looks too young to know English. 'Threedeep, translate.'

Redshirt: Tellish, *noun*: An expendable individual who is often killed to demonstrate the powers of a nemesis. *SEE ALSO*: Nemesis.

Hyde: Tellish, *noun*: the evil version of a character/ individual.

'What the—?! Jazzamin, I'm not evil! And I'm not going to kill you!'

'Clichéd Hyde dialogue,' narrates the genie, vanishing with a puff back inside her lamp.

'Hey!' Pia rubs the lamp. 'Hey, I hadn't thrinted breakfast yet!'

Jazzamin won't come back out though, so Threedeep goes off to fetch Pia something to eat and comes back a little later with a drone-made sandwich. Pia takes one bite and leaves it. Nanabug sandwiches are the worst. The ratio of butter-to-bread-to-filling is always way, way off.

Threedeep pretends to busy herself cleaning the already spotless cell, but her node stays focused on the uneaten sandwich by Pia's side. Pia grimaces and takes a few more bites. For creatures that don't have any nerve endings, nanabugs are way too sensitive.

Time passes. Pia lies restlessly on her cot and stares at the walls. If breakfast is any sort of indicator, today will be about the same level of awful as yesterday. There isn't much left for her to do but sit and wait for it all to happen.

More time passes.

A whole bunch of it.

Would you like to read a story? Threedeep asks.

'No.'

Or we could do an educational quiz?

'No.'

Or—

'Or you could put yourself on standby.'

ʕ·ᴥ·ʔ **Do you know what I find helps when I am grouchy?**

'You don't have emotions, Threedeep.'

If I'm ever grouchy, I sing a song. (͡° ͜ʖ ͡°) ♪ ♫.*·。°

'You don't have a voice, Threedeep.'

That's OK! I've always thought music is something you feel, not just hear.

Pia's spiteful reply catches in her throat. Hum. Poor, poor Hum. Her bones still ache with his song. They always will. Why didn't she listen to Ishan? If she hadn't followed Hum into the Seam, the angel might be alive now.

Siskin is right. Jazzamin is right. Pia is the danger.

[Hen Coop]

The Fabergé hens sit like duchesses on their plumped velvet cushions, clucking softly. Fay moves down their aisles from perch to perch with the midday menu. Each hen pecks at the treat item it wants.

There is a whole range this lunchtime, from mother-of-pearl to sapphire dust. The hens will ingest each treat, and use it to gild the eggs they lay at the end of each month.

Fay leaves the coop and goes into the store vault at the back of the ark to gather up their orders. She hums as she works.

A strip light flickers in the corridor. It makes Fay jump a little. Her heart gives a flutter. She has felt on edge since yesterday. That stupid girl, Pia. She has messed up the whole zoo. Curfew. No zephyrs. Lost angels. All because of her stupidity.

Or maybe, as Fay whispered to everyone at breakfast, maybe it wasn't stupidity at all. Fay has never quite been able to shake the suspicion that Pia turned her purple *on purpose*. There is something about that girl. When things get back to normal, Gowpy will *not* be hanging around her any more. That is for sure.

Packing the last of the treats into her hamper, she leaves the store vault and makes her way back through the ship. She has been gone ten minutes, maybe twelve if you add the couple of minutes spent walking down the corridor from the storeroom to the coop.

Ten or twelve, it doesn't matter – it isn't enough time, not nearly enough time, for whatever has happened to happen.

When she reaches out a trembling hand, thinking this is all some terrible dream, the plumped cushions are still warm. Then the hamper falls to the floor, in a scatter of pearls and filigree swirl and shining blue dust, and Fay screams.

24

LUNCHTIME

Threedeep pings for her attention. Looking up, Pia sees a message scrolled across the nanabug's screen.

Lunchtime!

Pia rolls over. The hours of doing nothing have made her feel all bleary and tired and miserable. 'I'm not hungry.'

You'll feel better after a good meal. Come on!

Oh Seamstress, she won't be able to take it if Threedeep makes her another sandwich. Maybe the drone senses her dread, because it adds:

Siskin has transferred a canteen genie, Ajjimajji, here to the Quark. He has become a very good friend of mine. He will thrint you whatever snacks you want.

'Ajjimajji?' Pia's stomach suddenly rumbles. She has barely eaten anything since yesterday's lunch. 'Will he make me his brownie ice cream?'

Of course. I would have taken you there this morning for breakfast, but you were asleep and still being assessed.

Pia doesn't really want to think about what that means. Right now, all she cares about is thrinting a whole plate of fries and nuggets. And dessert too. She needs dessert more than she has ever needed it in her life.

'All right, Threedeep.' Pia hops off the bunk and pulls on her boots and follows Threedeep out of the cell. Still nobody in the corridors but bluebottles. It creeps her out. Some people might use the phrase 'ghost ship', but Pia has lived on a ghost ship most of her life, and this place is way spookier.

It's so weird, in fact, that Pia has a momentary freak-out when they get to the Quark's tiny canteen and she sees, through the window, three people sitting at the only table.

Then she double takes.

'Is that Wilma, Gowpen and Zugzwang?' Pia just wants to make sure she isn't going crazy.

That's right, Threedeep chats.

Her three Rekker buddies sit around Ajjimajji's lamp (an old can of whipped cream). They all have nanabugs with them too – even Gowpen.

'What are they doing here?'

Threedeep's node whirrs quietly as it zooms. **Ordering lunch, I believe.**

The nanabug is right: as Pia watches, the Rekkers all wish food from a nervous-looking Ajjimajji, and his 'genieer – who for some reason is Wanda. Today, Wanda has a very serious-looking bob cut. It isn't even dyed neon-pink or anything.

I shall wait out here for you, Threedeep chats. **Don't want to embarrass you in front of your friends.**

Pia looks at the drone. That is actually quite sweet. Threedeep's programming might have been reset, but somehow she has remembered the general rule that nanabugs stay away from canteen tables – something the other drones seem to have forgotten.

'Thanks, Threedeep. It's not anything personal, you know. It's just that nanabugs aren't . . . you know.'

Cool? chats Threedeep.

(•_•)

(•_•)~–■-■

(–■_■)

I beg to differ.

Pia actually laughs out loud. Sandwiches aside, maybe it isn't *so* terrible that Threedeep is with her after all.

There is a sort of hiccup in the chatter as she walks through the door.

Then Wilma yells, 'Peeeeeeeea!'

Pia shakes her head. 'That joke is really old and really not funny. But I'm still glad to see you guys.'

They all grin back, but their smiles are thin somehow, like they've been pasted on. And they don't get up or anything. Pia feels a little stung.

'What,' she says, 'not even a hug?'

'A slap in the face, more like,' Wilma says. 'Do you have any idea how much you freaked everyone out? Us included?'

'A little.' Pia sits down and Gowpen resumes his order, although he talks just a little louder than before, like he's trying to talk over the low hum of tension Pia has just introduced into the room.

Siskin must have told them then. About the angels, about her possible mind-fray, all of it.

'What are you guys doing in here?'

Again, they all glance at each other.

'Well, I'm *trying* to order rice and peas,' Gowpen says, folding his arms, 'but *someone* keeps interrupting me.'

'All right, all right.' Pia points to an empty chair at the table. 'But seriously, though. Which one of you guys invited the giant pink bunny?'

Not even Wilma laughs at that. There are nervous eye flickers and rictus smiles.

'Just to be clear,' Pia says slowly. 'That was a joke. I am not crazy.'

Wanda steps forward with a pad of wish-scripts. 'Why don't you, I mean, what would, uh, we were just . . .'

'We are ordering food,' Wilma translates. 'Why don't you skip to the front, Pia. You must be starving.'

'That's, uh, yeah.' A red flush is creeping up Wanda's neck. 'Hey, gal. What is it, um, can I get ya?'

This is *really* weird. What is Wanda doing here too? She isn't Ajjimajji's 'genieer.

'I'll have fries,' Pia tells the genie. 'Salted, sauced, no mustard though. And nuggets, hot cajun breadcrumbs. And a stim juice. And save some wish-power in that beard of yours, Ajjimajji, because I'm ordering dessert.'

Wanda scribbles out a wish-script, or tries – her hand is shaking so badly she can barely write anything. The others sit there with their own trays. Not talking, not eating, not even goggling. Just glancing at Pia and then glancing away.

Eventually, Ajjimajji wishes up Pia's food. Wanda passes

it over on a tray, but Pia doesn't get a proper hand on it, and the ketchup-covered chips slide on to her lap.

'OK.' Wilma looks to the others and relaxes. 'It's her.'

'Yep.' Gowpen looks down at the mess on the floor. 'No mistaking our Catastro-P.'

'Huh,' says Zugzwang, pulling on his goggles again.

Pia looks down at the ketchup splattered over her dungarees. Amazingly, she's *relieved*. It is lunchtime – she has been a klutz, and the others are grinning. This is maybe the most ordinary sequence of things that has happened since yesterday.

Wanda hurries around the rest of the table, and soon Wilma has her cereal, Gowpen has his veggie meal, and Zugzwang has a stim drink.

Pia, meanwhile, tucks in. She scoops the chips from her lap, shovelling food. It is just OK, but when you're ravenous, OK food tastes like heaven. She scoffs it all like a pigasus, not even caring that Zugzwang is staring.

'Sooo,' Wilma says conversationally. 'Pia. Or maybe I should call you *DoppelPia*.'

The others snigger nervously.

We have talked about name-calling, Wilma, says Fourcandles, hovering over to her.

'It's OK, Fourcandles,' Pia says with a smile. 'I'm not offended. I don't even get the joke. One morning in the Quark, and I'm out of the loop already.'

Wilma tilts her head. 'Thought Siskin would've told you.'

'Told me what?'

'About the rumours.'

'What rumours?'

Wilma glances at Gowpen, who shrugs, as if to say: *Tell her.*

'Urette's going around saying that you're not *you*. That you're just some weird voilà that *looks* like Pia, and you're here to destroy the zoo.'

Urette? That nasty old witch! And after Pia had been nice to her too!

'That is *crazy*,' she says. 'Urette should be the one inside here, not me!'

'Exactly!' Wilma makes a *pfff* sound. 'So what if you just came out of the Seam and randomly zephyred into Siskin's office. Big *deal*. Although, technically, I guess that *does* make you a voilà, right?'

Pia snorts into her hand. It feels good to sit here making fun of herself. It feels normal.

'Yeah,' says Gowpen. 'Which makes you property of the zoo, P. Siskin's trying to build a clumsy-proof enclosure for you as we speak.'

Even Zugzwang sniggers at that one. Wilma obviously has another joke lined up. She is so eager to say it she forgets she has a mouth full of cereal, and milk dribbles all down her chin and over the table.

'Get her in her dome quick!' Gowpen yells. 'The clumsiness is contagious!'

After that, they are all laughing, even Zugzwang, although he has his goggles back on, so it might be at something else.

But it doesn't matter. Laughing is good. It beats feeling guilty. Or scared.

They chat a while, about this and that. Gowpen says Sparklehorn's poop looks like rainbows, but smells even worse than the Rhinosaurus rex dung.

'Argh, Gowpy!' Pia facepalms. 'Don't tell me you let your mum convince you to change Moonbim's name?'

'Oops, sorry, I meant to say Moonbim.' Gowpen sunk his head on the table. 'Ugh. My brain is fried. Siskin woke all the zookeepers up as soon as you went missing, so everyone missed a night's sleep. All the grown-ups look like zombies.'

'Some of them are acting like zombies too,' Wilma says, then starts telling the story of how she managed to lock Fourcandles in a cupboard.

'The zoo's so stressed about the Seam and the angels that nobody has noticed yet,' she chuckles.

'But Fourcandles is there.' Pia points at the drone, huffing its rotor disapprovingly behind them.

'Yeah, she got out eventually.'

'Oh. Where's Ishan? Is he OK?'

Gowpen turns pinker. Wilma looks at her tray.

'He's fine, P.' Gowpen jabs with his spoon at the far end of the canteen. 'He would've come, but, uh . . .'

Pia lets him flounder for a moment, before she finishes his sentence for him. 'But he doesn't want to see me.'

'Aw, come on, Pia,' Wilma says. 'He had to evacuate the nanites from the cybernism ark. You know. Busy stuff like that. The zoo's in chaos. Emergency procedures in place and everything.'

'It's crazy out there,' Gowpen confirms. 'Siskin sent most of the other Seamers back to the mainland. We're practically the only kids left in the zoo.'

Pia thuds her head on the table. 'Ishan hates me.'

Wilma pats her on the neck. 'I'm sure he'll come to see you when stuff calms down.'

'Yeah.' Zugzwang's goggles spew out kaleidoscopic light. 'We almost got sent back to the mainland too, but then Dad ordered us to see if you—'

It was like Zugzwang had been speaking without paying attention to his mouth, because he suddenly shuts up, and Pia is pretty certain it is because Wilma just kicked him under the table.

Oh, she thinks.

Oh, right.

Pia puts her cutlery down slowly, and pushes away her tray. Now this all makes sense.

'"It's her." That's what you said, Wilma, when I did something clumsy. "OK, it's her." Siskin sent you here to check on me, didn't he? To see if Urette's theory is true.'

Zugzwang, Wilma and Gowpen all look at each other with the guilty looks of the busted.

'Is that why Wanda came along with you too? Because she saw me on the day I went missing.'

'Pia,' says Wilma. 'Listen . . .'

'And that's why you haven't asked me a single thing about

203

the Seam, isn't it? You were testing me with stuff that the *real* Pia would know. About Moonbim's name, and whether I knew Fourcandles. Who shouldn't even *be* here because a Rekker lunch is a no-drone zone. But of course, Fourcandles often comes along to punish Wilma, who has probably done something to deserve it. Is that enough knowledge for you? Do you want me to go on?'

The anger builds up in her until she can't stay sitting. Wilma's joke echoes in her head, taunting her. It *is* like she is the zoo's new voilà. And this is the enclosure they are keeping her in. These are the tests they are conducting.

Well, she doesn't have to play along. She stands up from the table and stomps towards Threedeep.

'I want to go back in my cell,' she says loudly. 'Me and my "friends" are done.'

Please don't be upset, Pia. Your friends are just trying to help you.

'What the drone said,' Wilma says. 'Siskin sent us in here so we could tell the others that you're really you. P! Hey, *P!* Don't be like that!'

Pia leaves the canteen and swipes the door shut behind her. She leans against the corridor wall and breathes in and out. She feels dizzy, not just with anger. More than that, she is afraid. She thinks back to being in her cell, to when Jazzamin called her a Hyde. At the time, that seemed crazy. But what about now?

You are the danger.

You're just some weird voilà that looks like Pia, and you're here to destroy the zoo.

Oh Seamstress, what if it's true? What if the real Pia never made it out of the Seam and I am just a copy?

'Pia!' The door opens and Gowpen runs after her. 'Wilma's right. You don't know how weird the atmosphere is. Security everywhere, arguments, and *Urette* . . . We had a meeting just now: Siskin got booed, and *Urette* got a cheer. It's like everything's turned upside down. A whole *load* of doomsay is going round. Mum's got obsessed over these mad conspiracy ideas.'

Something Gowpen just said makes Pia pause. She remembers all the times she sat with Ishan at the Rek, listening to him come up with all sorts of crazy theories.

'Is Ishan the one who came up with the theory about me?' she asks. 'Is he? Gowpen?'

Gowpen freezes. Then he slumps. '. . . Yeah. I think so. I haven't seen him.'

Pia turns from Gowpen so he won't see how upset she is. She feels the way she did when Hum died. That same ache. That same goodbye. Because friendship is as delicate and as miraculous as an angel. Something you feel in your bones, right down to the hollows. And like an angel, friendship can up and leave you, and never tell you why it went, or how to bring it back.

'I bet Urette's just twisted his words,' Gowpen says. 'You know how Ishan is.'

Pia puts her head in her hands. She can only think of the last time she saw Ishan, by the vent.

'I wish I didn't like you,' he said. And though there hadn't been a genie around to grant it, maybe the wish had somehow come true anyway.

[Megabunny Warren]

Flopsy munches at the new tunnel, grinding her teeth-chisels against the rockface. In the deep-black of the warren, Donna listens to the splinter and crack of stone. Megabunnies are virtually blind, but Donna keeps her headlamp off. Any light will only confuse Flopsy, making her think she has reached the surface, though that is impossible. They are almost sixty metres below the ground.

Donna doesn't mind the dark, though. The dark is always full of digging noises, enormous bustling furry bodies, snuffling and warmth.

Even better, you can't fill out Siskin's procedure reports if you can't actually *see* them.

Not everyone sees the positives, though. Most zookeepers outright refuse assignments to the megabunny warrens. They fake claustrophobia, fear of the dark, deficiencies in vitamin D. The real reason, of course, is that the warrens are located near the island: megabunnies are the only voilà in the zoo that cannot, for obvious reasons, be on an ark. Not an ark that has any hopes of floating, anyway. Megabunnies can grind a hole through anything. Even a ship's hull.

Donna doesn't even mind being on land, either. The warrens are on the little archipelago of islands that hold the Rek. In terms of distance, they aren't much closer to the Seam than some of the arks. And if anything does happen,

Donna has Houdini, her own personal genie that she carries in an ancient iPod on a chain around her neck, to zephyr her to safety.

Flopsy chisels off another rock chunk, then uses the sledger-teeth at the back of her mouth to gravel it up until it is small enough to gulp down. Behind her, her littler megabunnies scurry. Donna feels their noses poke her. They are more like trunks, really: very long and bendy, with three nostrils megabunnies use as crude fingers to grip and pinch.

Donna shoos them. 'Go help your mama.' The furry bodies bound away, though one of the littlers – probably Bugs, the naughtiest – continues to poke Donna. She gives his nostril a flick and he sneezes and goes to join the others.

As an almost full-grown megamama (Donna came up with that term and now it is part of the zoo's official classification system), Flopsy's shaggy bulk fills almost the whole tunnel, which means she can't turn around and clear the rubble herself. Megabunnies work as a family unit to clear tunnels, which is why they are constantly having littlers. Baby megabunnies are born with flat paws as big as shovels, to scoop and carry the rocks back up to the surface. No littlers means no one to carry away the rubble that Flopsy chisels, grinds up, swallows, and then finally poops out behind her.

As Donna is fond of telling everyone, especially Seamers, human children don't know how good they have it. Megabunny kids have to clean up their *parents'* poop.

Flopsy stops chiselling. Perhaps she's reached a granite

stratum, or maybe broken through into another part of the warren. It happens sometimes. There are four families now – Flopsy's, Peter's, Thumper's and Briar's – and there is always some criss-crossing.

The littlers have gone very quiet.

And it is suddenly cold. Donna shivers as a breeze comes down the tunnel. She reaches up and switches her headlamp on, knowing something is wrong, horribly wrong. The beam lights up the empty tunnel. Flopsy, Bugs, the whole family: all of them are gone.

Donna rubs the lamp at her neck with a shaking hand, but Houdini has vanished along with the megabunnies, and she is alone.

It's just her, underground, in the darkness.

25

JONAH

Pia hasn't been back at her cell for five minutes before Threedeep pings to say Siskin is coming to see her. She listens out, and soon enough she hears the rap of his shoes on the floor as he makes his way down the corridor. Tap, tap, tap, tap. You could practise cello to those footsteps.

The door opens. Siskin stands at the entrance, arms folded. A bluebottle is behind him.

'You are well, I hope?'

Pia scowls. 'As well as an evil mirror-image can be.'

(Ѳ∆Ѳ') **EVIL MIRROR-WHAT?** Threedeep chats.

'That hypothesis is false,' Siskin explains to Threedeep.

Pia is too angry to feel relieved. 'Don't make my own friends do tests on me, Siskin. I'm not a lab rat.'

♂_♂ I wish I was kept informed, Threedeep grumbles. **Nobody updates me on anything.**

'Or me, Threedeep. What are all these rumours about me, Siskin? I thought *I* was meant to be the crazy one.'

Siskin's jaw clenches. 'The disappearances have people frightened. Frightened people spread doomsay. Some of it involves you.'

'Okaaay,' Pia says slowly. 'So Urette starts up some cult saying I'm some sort of evil clone, and you put *me* in the Quark?'

Siskin looks down at the shine of his shoes.

'Wait.' Did she just hear Siskin right? 'Did you say *disappearances*? As in, more than one?'

Siskin takes a deep sigh and loosens his tie and rubs a spot on his temple just above his left eye, like he has a migraine. 'The *gallus aureate*,' he sighs. 'The Fabergé chickens.'

'Woah,' Pia says. She can't remember ever seeing him undo his top button before. Suddenly she notices that his pocket square is missing, and there are sweat patches under his arms.

'What's *happening* outside?' she murmurs. It had to be bad, for Siskin to look like this.

Siskin does his answer-a-question-with-a-question thing. 'Do you know what a *Jonah* is, Pia?'

'An old name?'

'And a sailor's term, taken from a Bible story. Threedeep?'

Siskin looks over and the nanabug displays the verse on her screen.

So the Lord sent out a great wind into the sea, and there was a mighty tempest, so that the ship was like to be broken. Then the sailors were afraid, and they said each one to his fellow, Come and let us cast lots, that we may know for whose cause this evil is upon us. So they cast lots, and the lot fell upon Jonah.

Siskin points at Threedeep's screen. 'This zoo is made up of ships like that, Pia. Ships full of very scared people. They are searching for someone to blame for their fear. Searching, in other words, for a Jonah. And they are looking at you.'

'Me?' Pia swallows. Maybe a couple of days ago, she

would've burst out laughing, but not any more. This is way, way past hilarious.

'For example,' Siskin continues, 'some people have pointed out the *real* Pia that went through the hole had *mustard stains* on her uniform. You don't.'

Pia looks down at her dungarees. He is right, the uniform is clean. No mustard stains anywhere.

'Jazzamin must have cleaned it,' she says.

'Did she also mend the tear on your sleeve that has vanished?' Siskin asks. 'And fix your hair?'

'My hair?' Pia says in a small voice.

'It has been cut.'

Pia knows that. She hacks it short herself, every few months, with a pair of scissors. Ishan helps do the back.

She puts him out of her mind. It hurts too much to think about him.

'Cut *properly*,' Siskin clarifies. 'I checked the security tapes from our psych-eval meeting yesterday morning. Why don't you check it yourself?'

Pia's fingertips trace her hairline across her forehead. It is straight. No kinks at all.

'I don't know why that is,' she says, voice rising up in a panic. 'But you can't seriously believe that I'm—'

'Of course I don't,' Siskin interrupts. 'It isn't *my* theory. I'm telling you because *others* believe it. Cornucopia, you are not an evil clone. Nor a Jonah. OK? Look at me and nod. *Look at me and nod.*'

She nods.

'There's no doubt that your angel's miracle changed you, though. Which, I think, gives us some clue as to the type of miracle it was. I think it was a *mending*, not a zephyring.' Siskin steps up to her. 'You were in the wrong place at the wrong time, and you were *corrected* to where you ought to be. Your hair, your sleeve, the mustard, and my lamp all got caught up in the miracle's aurora. They were fixed too.'

Pia swallows. Her heart slows a little. That makes sense. Thank the Seamstress for Siskin's ice-cool logic.

'Does that convince you?' Siskin says, and it takes Pia a moment to realise that he isn't talking to her.

He's talking to the boy in the doorway who used to be her friend.

• • •

Ishan steps into Pia's cell. His fringe is droopy and his eyes have a bloodshot stim-drink look to them. He looks shame-faced. Miserable.

Siskin clears his throat. 'I will wait outside. As in, you have two minutes.'

He walks out and waves the door shut behind him.

And . . . I am going on standby, Threedeep chats, rotoring down on the desk and blanking her screen.

Pia looks at Ishan, wondering what to say. She decides to wait for him to break the silence. Thirty seconds of their allocated two minutes ticks past.

'Are you going to punch me again?' Ishan says eventually.

She sniffs. 'Wasn't going to.'

Ishan looks surprised.

'I was thinking a headbutt, this time.'

Ishan looks her in the eye for the first time since she went through the vent. He can only hold it for a moment before he facepalms. 'You don't need to. I've been beating myself up.'

Pia nods. 'Me too.'

'I've given my stupid conspiracy-theory-spouting mouth a slap.'

'And I've given my stubbornness a karate chop to the face.'

'And I've given the bad friend part of me a massive pummelling,' says Ishan.

Pia starts grinning so hard it hurts her cheeks. Maybe the powerful whatever-it-is between them is not broken after all. Their weird, precious ability to joke and laugh over anything is still in one piece.

'I won't keep secrets from you again, Ish.'

'And I won't ever not trust that you're you.'

'Well, I promise not to whack you again.'

'I promise not to give you a reason to whack me.'

'OK, OK, it's not like this is a competition.'

He laughs. 'If it was, I would so win.'

'Really, Ish? I've basically wrecked the zoo.'

His smile vanishes. 'It's not you, Pia. Seriously. Things out there are *crazy*.'

Pia is a little freaked out by how freaked out Ishan looks.

'What do you mean *crazy*? I just saw the others, and they all said the same thing.'

Ishan shakes his head. 'I can't explain it. I only mentioned my stupid theory to the Rekkers this morning. Then Gowpen told it to his mum, and within an hour it was *everywhere*. And now people just *believe* it. We had a meeting half an hour ago, and Siskin was arguing with them – with Urette and Fay and a few others . . .'

Ishan stops for a while, and then his voice goes quiet.

'I saw a lot of doomcults, back in the sprawl. The look in their eyes . . . Fay had that same look. A kind of madness. And now her Fabergé chickens are missing, it can only have gotten worse. Siskin asked me if I'll go and speak to them myself, and tell them I made it all up. I said I wanted to come see you first. To apologise. And—'

Siskin marches back in, cutting Ishan off mid-sentence.

'Follow the security drone outside,' he tells Ishan. 'It will take you to Ajjimajji. Zephyr yourself to Urette and the other doomers. As in, right now.'

Ishan glances at Pia, then back at Siskin, and nods. 'Yes, sir.' He turns on his heels and leaves.

Pia flops down on her cell bed. 'I'm glad you've got everything under control, Siskin.'

He frowns. 'I wouldn't go that far. One disappearance is an anomaly, two begins to look like a pattern. And the *peculiar* behaviour of some of our zookeepers seems to be spreading faster than rat flu. And then, of course, there's the halo.'

The back of Pia's neck goosebumps at that word. 'Halo?'

Siskin nods. 'It was Threedeep who found it.'

Pia looks at the drone, who powers out of standby at the mention of her name.

/ ⦁ˎ_⦁ \ **He said not to tell you**, Threedeep chats.

'None of the observations back on Ark One picked it up,' Siskin continues. 'But your nanabug has a numinous lamp. Show her, Threedeep.'

(`-`)⧄, Threedeep salutes. The numinous light on her node flashes on, illuminating the cell in its silvery-violet light. The nanabug blanks her screen, making it into a mirror, and angles it towards Pia so she can see.

Her breath catches in her throat. The halo is pinned in place above her head. A sparkling, unbroken ring of light. What is it woven from? Not from sunbeams, or lamplight, or candle flame, or monitor glow. If it only shows up under numinous, that can mean just one thing: the light is *celestial*.

'You said that your angel died in the Seam,' Siskin says. 'But I think different. I think angels are made of light, and light is energy, and energy cannot be destroyed, only transferred. Threedeep says the halo is three per cent brighter than last night. It's weaving itself. Drawing ambient celestial light into itself, becoming brighter.

'Your angel didn't just *mend* you, Cornucopia. He gave you something to carry. Something made from himself.'

Pia reaches up to touch the halo with her fingertips. It sends a tingle through her. What is it? A message, like the one above Threedeep? Or something else?

216

She tilts her head to the left, to the right. The halo glitters. Silent. Inscrutable. For now.

With a quiet puff, a note from Ark One zephyrs in front of Siskin's face. He plucks it from the air, reads it once, folds the paper carefully in two, and slips it inside his shirt pocket.

'Evidence seems to be building for your theory that the Seamstress has stitched a new species of predatory voilà,' he says. 'Now the megabunnies have vanished too.'

Dread mixes with Pia's shock. Another disappearance? All her thoughts about her halo are put on hold. 'Did Donna see anything? She's their zookeeper, right?'

Siskin starts pacing in the cell, like he is the prisoner instead of Pia. 'She didn't see a thing. Her genie vanished too. And her monitor drone.'

Threedeep's circuits make a *blat* noise. **!!!** it chats. **Oneslip has disappeared? But Oneslip was my very good friend!**

Threedeep hovers in place, but messages keep scrolling across its screen.

Where did Oneslip go? I did not receive a notification. We are very good friends! Have you told Fourcandles? Fourcandles and Oneslip are very close. Oneslip is a good monitor drone. Please find Oneslip.

Pia feels a lump in her throat. Poor Threedeep. Poor Oneslip. Maybe drones *do* have feelings, or at least programming so advanced that they can mimic feelings perfectly.

'Why didn't it take Donna?' she says suddenly. 'Whatever's doing this, I mean?'

Yes, and why take Oneslip also? I am worried about Oneslip.

For the first time ever, Pia sees Siskin look afraid. He turns to stare at the door, to hide his fear from her, but she sees it.

The zoo is changing, she thinks. Stuff isn't staying put any more. Things run amok. Rumours. Angels. Monsters. Doomsay. Everything Siskin once found so easy to contain is now working its way loose.

'What do we do?'

Siskin looks back around at her, his expression normal again. Calm. Controlled.

'We?' he says. '*We* do nothing. *You* stay here. *I* review procedures.'

'But what about the zookeepers? Aren't you going to tell them what's happened?'

Siskin gives Pia a look so cold she actually got goosebumps. 'Did you not listen to anything I just said? Do you know what the most dangerous animals in the zoo are? Not the Rhinosaurus rexes, not the gargantulas, not your devil – the *people*. And they have only one zookeeper to try and stop them from destroying everything: me.'

Pia hears a *wompf!* sound as a genie zephyrs into the corridor: from the small grey fuzz she can see of it through the blurred window she guesses it is Blom.

'One moment, Cornucopia.' Siskin leaves the cell.

'I'm sorry about your friend,' Pia says to Threedeep.

The drone does not reply for a long time.

Thank you, Pia, Threedeep chats at last. **I am also very sorry.**

Then: **That is a kind thing to say.**

And: **I too do not believe you are an evil clone.**

Pia smiles and blows the drone a kiss. Threedeep blows one back:

(˘ ³˘)♥

Is Donna a very good friend of yours?

Pia shakes her head. 'She's older. And she spends a lot of time in the warrens. Sometimes we saw her when we hung out on the Rek. Wilma always says she's quite funny.'

Oneslip was also highly amusing. Oneslip invented very funny faces. Many of us got our emoticons from Oneslip.

My favourite ever is this one:

(∩｀-´)⊃━☆ﾟ.*･｡ﾟ

I have never had an opportunity to use it, though.

Then the drone receives a ping. And another, and another, and then a whole pinball rattle of them: ping-ping-ping-ping-ping!

'What's that?' Pia asks.

ᕦ^ᴥ^ᕤ Don't worry, Pia. Nothing to worry about. Not in the slightest.

'Uh . . .' Pia gets up from the bed. 'Why did you tell me not to worry?'

Because you shouldn't. Everything is fine.

'I *know* everything's fine.'

(b^_^)b

Just don't worry.

Pia facepalms. 'You realise when you tell someone *not to worry*, it's really worrying, right?'

Oh.

⊙﹏⊙

Well . . . You just have some visitors, that's all.

Outside the cell, Siskin zephyrs Blom back to wherever the genie came from. He comes into the cell again, jaw clenched.

'We have a problem. Urette and her followers have just zephyred here. As in, they're on the deck of the Quark. And they have Ishan.'

Pia's heart starts to thump. 'What do you mean, they *have* him? You mean, like a hostage? What do they want? Siskin? Siskin?'

Siskin stands there, jaw clenched.

'They're demanding to see you,' he says.

[Smellephants]

Three boulder-shaped creatures sit huddled in the corner of their enclosure. Their enormous nostrils quiver and drip as they taste the air around them.

'What are they scared of?' asks the security guard.

Vashti edges up to them very slowly, holding out her hands and going *shhh*. She gets why Siskin has posted a guard on each ship, what with the disappearances and the weird doomsay that seems to be filling the heads of the zoo staff, but she doesn't feel safer with this guy on board.

The security guard has a beetroot face and white-blond hair and a thick neck pinched tight by his black collar. It looks like his uniform is trying to strangle him. Or make him explode.

'They smell something coming?' The security guard looks around the enclosure, his hand dropping down to the gun that hangs from his shoulder strap. 'Is that it? Huh?'

'Like I already said,' says Vashti carefully, 'they're smelling *you*. You know that old cliché about being able to smell fear? That's not a cliché if you're a smellephant. Stop getting spooked by them getting spooked by you being spooked.'

The security guard frowns as he tries to make sense of that.

'Just – be less scared,' Vashti tells him. 'OK?'

She can see that annoys him – a fat zookeeper in sandals

telling his big-strong-soldier-of-a-self to be brave. The smellies catch a whiff of his anger, and that sends their wafters unfurling up like palm fronds.

'Uh-oh,' Vashti mutters.

'*Scared?*' says the security guard. His face turns a dark purply colour. A vein on his neck stands out like a cord.

Vashti backtracks. 'OK, you're not scared.' She tries to say it as gently as she can. 'But you might want to try not being angry either, because . . .'

'How about you don't *make* me angry—' There's a rustle as the wafters all shudder. The security guard whirls around. 'What was that?'

'Ah.' Vashti winces. 'Please don't threaten me either, because the smellies are really protective of . . .'

She trails off. This isn't working at *all*. It's like saying to someone, 'Don't think of a smellephant'. That's exactly what they just go on and do.

She starts to think that maybe there is something wrong. This guard looks ready to snap. He wasn't like this when he first zephyred on board.

'You are winding me tight, woman,' he growls.

And for whatever reason, this tips the smellephants over into full-on skunk mode.

Vashti sees it coming and buries her nose in her shirtsleeve. She yells at the guard to do the same, but her voice is muffled in the crook of her elbow. Her zookeeper suit has a special wad of odour-neutralising cotton sewn there.

'What did you just say to me?' the guard snarls.

222

'They're about to skunk, hold your breath!' She turns and runs for the red button by the door to trigger the emergency extraction. But running triggers something in the security guard too. A paranoia that has come from nowhere.

'Hold it right there!' he bellows, and raises his gun.

Very bad idea.

An orchestra of farts. That's how Vashti always hears it. Deep parps and high piping squeaks and everything in between. Three waves of the vilest stinks sweep outwards from each smellephant. Bad eggs, rancid meat, chemical fumes. Three gusts of brain-rotting, gut-churning stench. They hit the guard right in the nose.

'Ugh!' He reels away, clutching his face as if struck. 'Oh man. Oh *man* that smells bad. That—'

Then he pukes.

Then he faints.

In his puke.

Vashti peeks over her arm at him. He's been skunkfunked good and proper. The stink is so powerful it has knocked him out. Still holding her breath, Vashti feels light-headed too. She slams on the industrial extractors above the enclosure that are designed to suck the smellies' skunking out of the ark. Then she hauls the security guard up.

He is groaning, still half out of it. She looks at him, frowning. Then she reaches over carefully and ejects the bullet clip from his gun and puts it in her dungarees pocket. Maybe he escorted some Seamers to the island a few days ago, and got himself mind-frayed or something.

The extractors above them whir to a stop. The smellephants cower in the corner. Gradually their frantic skunking starts to slow as they realise they are safe. Then their boulder-shaped bodies rise up on their stubby legs, suddenly curious. The smallest and wrinkliest smelly steps forward, wafters unfurling shyly, and sends out a new aroma. The other two wait a moment, then do the same.

Vashti looks back at them, keeping her face jammed in the crook of her elbow. 'What are you guys introducing yourselves for? You know me, sillies.'

The three smellies ignore her and patiently repeat their names. Vashti can smell their scents even through her elbow, she knows them so well. The first smellephant's name is a smoky, charred smell: Old Campfires, the older grandma of the other two.

'It's OK.' Vashti reaches out a hand to stroke the smellephant's leathery sides. 'I know. You did right. I don't know what came over him, pointing his gun like that. Crazy. Like the whole zoo right now.'

The second smellie, fresh and zingy, is called Peppermint. The third, just a babe, has so far called himself Turned Earth. Smellephant names age as they do. Old Campfires had once called herself the scent of Dry Kindling, and one day she might be Embers-and-Ash. Who knows what Turned Earth's scent will become? A flower? A herb? Something else?

Vashti shakes her head. 'You three are acting funny too. *He* won't remember your names – you've put him in a skunkfunk.'

Old Campfires takes another step forward, trundling past Vashti. Her eyes are very small and black and solemn. And they are not looking at Vashti. But at someone else. Something else. There in the enclosure, behind them all.

In a flash of light, they vanish. All three smellephants, gone in an eye blink. Vashti cries out and falls backwards. She is alone in the enclosure, with the unconscious guard and three fast-fading scents. Old Campfires. Peppermint. Turned Earth.

26

BEAST WITH SIXTY EYES

Beside the Quark's main door, Siskin makes Pia pause.

'You don't have to go out there,' he says. 'You understand that, don't you? Look at me and nod.'

Pia has her ear turned to the door, listening to the crowd outside.

'Look at me and nod,' he repeats, his voice hard as iron.

Pia nods. She forces herself to breathe deep. To be cool. Anger won't help anyone – Ishan, least of all.

'Is he on deck?' She glances at Siskin. 'Is he OK?'

The boss nods. 'Security drones are monitoring him. You know I can get security to handle this.'

'No way.' Pia shakes her head. 'The last thing anyone needs – Ishan included – is a bunch of bluebottles charging in.'

Siskin concedes the point. 'We could try and mount an emergency zephyr.'

Pia shook her head. Zephyring *yourself* might be an easy wish, but zephyring *others* was much trickier – and more dangerous.

'That's a last resort and you know it,' she states. 'I'm going out there.'

Siskin still looks unhappy. 'Threedeep? Link your display with security, so Pia can see for herself what she's getting into.'

The drone pings a link-up request to one of the bluebottles outside. Siskin authorises it, and suddenly Pia sees the quarantine ark, floating on the nanabug's screen. On the deck are a crowd of about thirty zoo staff: keepers, admins, 'genieers, and even a few security officers. Pia goosebumps. Does that mean there are guns out there?

'Zoom,' Siskin says. 'Let her see the faces. Let her see the look.'

'What look?' But the question dies on Pia's lips, because it's there on the screen, in all of their eyes, in everyone.

The exact same look. Like Pia isn't standing in front of Fay and Britta and Tej and Vivi any more, but just one thing, one big animal with thirty pairs of eyes, and thirty times the anger and thirty times the fear. An animal called a *crowd*.

And this crowd is like a beast, powerful but stupid, and in its stupidity it could be directed to do terrible things.

And Pia is afraid. Now she knows the reason for Siskin's skewed tie and missing pocket square. Something has gone terribly, terribly wrong with the zoo. Not just with the voilà, but with the zookeepers themselves.

'Are they ... *doomsick*?' she breathes. She almost can't believe it. No one at the zoo has *ever* fallen doomsick. How has this happened? How is it so widespread, and so *quickly* too?

A sudden possibility sends chills through Pia. Maybe when the Seamstress died, hope died with her.

'Show me Ishan,' she says, and he comes up on screen. She breathes out with relief. He doesn't look hurt in any way. His expression is more confused than anything else.

'He's totally surrounded.' Pia gazes at the screen. 'There's no way he's getting away from them by himself.'

Beyond the doors, she hears a muffled shout, and then a roar of approval. An actual roar, like a Rhinosaurus rex would make. So the crowd is an *angry* beast too. Pia's knees are juddering and her heart is thumping and Siskin is watching her.

'This is not a good idea,' he says. 'I can't let you go out there.'

'It's just adrenalin!' She takes a few deep breaths. 'I can do this. I can convince them. I *need* to do this. Whatever the zoo is facing, we won't survive it if we're not together. You have to let me try and talk sense to them.'

Siskin stares at her for a long time. 'I can't let you go out there on your own,' he says at last.

Which is not *quite* what he said before, and Pia knows she has him.

'So send me in with backup,' she says.

Siskin raises his eyebrows. 'As in, security?'

'As in,' Pia corrects, 'my friends.'

• • •

It takes maybe ten minutes to bring the Rekkers up from the canteen and brief them on what is about to happen. Zugzwang, Wilma and Gowpen share looks with Pia as Siskin speaks. The sort of looks that say: *What the actual is going on? And why did you have to drag us into it?*

The whole situation feels so weird and tense. Somehow, Pia can't put her finger on why. She puts it down to the fact that the zoo's adults have gone crazy and are holding her best friend hostage, whilst believing her to be an evil doppelganger from another dimension. That is *probably* it . . . But still. Weirdness.

'Bottom line: no risks,' Siskin tells them. He looks at Gowpen. 'As in, ignore your mother.' He looks at Wilma. 'As in, no jokes.'

Wilma rolls her eyes. 'What if they're really, really funny, though? Like, legitimate screamers?' She holds up her hands quickly. 'I'm kidding, I'm kidding. I'll shut up. This situation is hilarious enough already, right?'

She looks at Gowpen, but he hasn't taken his eyes off Threedeep's screen. A grainy image of Fay's face stares back at him.

'Mum was *fine* this morning,' he says, then reconsiders. 'Well, maybe not *fine*. But she wasn't like *this* . . .' He trails off, staring. Fay stands in the crowd, cheeks marked with make-up and tears, her eyes vacant.

'Fay loved those Fabergé chickens almost as much as you, Gowpy,' Wilma says. 'Now they're gone, her chickens have literally left the roost – sorry, Gow. That wasn't funny. I am actually shutting up now.'

Siskin looks at Pia. 'Are you *positive* you want them with you?'

'Positive. I want them with me. They're my best friends, Siskin.'

Siskin hands out the breathers, and slips his own over his face. 'Are you ready?'

Pia breathes deep. 'I think so.'

'Remember what I said.'

'I remember.'

'They're acting strangely. They're not themselves.'

'I know.'

'If you—'

'*I know.*'

Siskin frowns, like he's giving this idea one final assessment in his mind.

'I'm proud of your bravery, Pia. And you, Wilma. And you, Gowpen.'

Then he authorises the door open and steps through. The noise and anger of the crowd floods in and it washes over them like a wave.

And Pia finally realises what the weirdness was. All through that whole discussion, Siskin didn't so much as look at his son. Zugzwang has his goggles pulled up on his forehead, but as Pia glances over at him, he pulls them down, like he doesn't want Pia to see what's in his eyes.

She takes a deep breath, and leaves quarantine, out into a world of hysterical mobs and unseen monsters.

Yay, freedom.

It is sunny outside. Strong and warm and beaming. The kind of day angels love weaving halos out of. Around the quarantine ship, the sea is blue and calm. So unlike the seething crowd on the deck of the Quark.

Siskin stands beside her, with Threedeep and the Rekkers. Bluebottles hover above with their jabbers out, ready to swoop, but Pia is still scared. She looks for Ishan, but she can't see him. Not at the front of the crowd, anyway.

The crowd simmers down to silence as Urette steps forward. Every beast has a head, and here is the crowd's. Urette looks unrecognisable from the sweet, lonely lady Pia accidentally had tea with only two nights ago, like her personality has disappeared the same way the Fabergé chickens and the megabunnies have, and someone else has moved in. Someone crueller and colder.

'We only want to know the truth. That's all. The truth.' Urette pauses, and the crowd mutter *yeah* behind her in a way that makes everything she just said into some kind of threat. 'We think we deserve that much. After what we've lost. After the directives we've been given. After the lies we've been told.'

Urette turns her gaze to Siskin. He flinches. Actually flinches. Everybody sees it, and it puts a smirk on the lips of the crowd. Weevis, that horrible twerp of a secretary, has the widest and nastiest smile of all. Pia might have known *he* would join this bunch of crazies.

'There's a darkness come into our zoo,' Urette says, almost chanting the words. 'We all feel it. Even out here, in the sunshine. It's a darkness that only the *truth* can light up.' She looks at Pia. Everything else about her is crumbling and cobwebby, but her eyes are quick and dazzling. And there is something else in them too. Something Pia recognises. What is it?

'And so I'll ask you. Just this one time. What have you done? What did you do to *them*?'

Pia doesn't reply. Not immediately. If the crowd is a beast, then words are the only way to tame it. She weighs up each one before she speaks it. Takes a deep breath.

'I'm hearing a kind of truth in this silence,' Urette interrupts, before Pia has a chance to speak. 'Because truth is simple, isn't it? Truth just needs to be said. You only have to wait and think about what to say if you're about to *lie*.'

The crowd nods and scowls. Pia inwardly facepalms. She walked straight into Urette's trap, there.

'No, listen,' she blurts. 'You have to listen. You're right – there *is* some sort of darkness in the zoo, but—'

'She admits it!' Urette's bony finger points at Pia, and her voice begins to rise up, like a kettle boiling on a hob, like a preacher at the end of a sermon. 'There is a darkness! There is! You heard her say it! And how does she know? Because she loves the darkness, because she serves the darkness, because she *is* the darkness!'

'What the *actual*?' Wilma mutters.

ヾ(ツ) **Excuse me?** Threedeep buzzes in between Pia and the crowd. **I am compelled to remind you that doomsay, especially directed towards an individual, is discouraged under directive SIS: 0004. You should know better. Pia is a child.**

'*That*,' Urette said, looking at Pia, 'is not a child. It is a demon, come from the Seam to cause our doom.'

'Okaaaay,' Wilma says sideways at Siskin. 'I know I promised to shut up, but: can you put us back in the crazy ship now?'

'We stand against the darkness!' Urette cries at the doomers, never once taking her eyes off Pia. 'We are the light!'

'Mum?' Gowpen steps forward, tears in his eyes. 'Mum, where are you? Stop this, it's crazy.'

'You are full-on mind-frayed!' Wilma says in disgust. 'Doomers, all of you! Nothing but doomers!'

'Wilma, shut up!' Pia elbows her. Things are spiralling out of control. She can feel the hysteria on the deck rising. Gowpen's crying for his mum, and Wilma is hurling insults into the crowd like they're stones, and Zugzwang unbelievably is on his goggles, watching a vid.

We seem like the crazy ones, Pia thinks, looking around.

'That's *enough*!' Siskin strides forward, face full of fury. 'Urette, the rest of you, back to your arks.'

Urette just babbles nonsense. About dark and doom and death and decay, and Siskin starts bellowing back at her, spit flecking from his mouth.

'As in, LEAVE!' he yells. 'As in, GO! As in, NOW!'

But Urette steps closer to him, and the crowd moves with her, shuffling on its sixty legs, clenching its sixty fists. And Siskin looks almost deranged with anger, because no one has ever disobeyed him before, not ever, and yet here is

Urette, frail and old and unpopular, defying him. Not just that – *goading* him.

Cold, clear-thinking, keen-edged, implacable: Siskin is ice, through and through.

But rigid too. Stubborn to his core. Ice is brittle; it breaks before it bends.

When it happens, it happens fast. Siskin takes Urette by the arm and twists her round towards quarantine. Maybe he is trying to break up the crowd: knock out its head in the hope its body will scatter.

Or maybe he has just had enough. Maybe he has snapped.

The crowd rushes forward. Fay gets there first. Fay, the most timid woman in the zoo, whom Wilma reduced to tears during a chicken-naming contest. Now she runs at Siskin, fists flying. She isn't that big or strong. Doesn't have to be, when running at that speed.

She tackles Siskin to the ground, and Urette falls too. The three of them collapse on the deck in a furious tangle of arms and kicking legs.

The roaring crowd surges over them. Pia catches a last glimpse of Siskin, struggling up, arms reaching out like a man drowning.

'Ishan!' Pia screams. 'Ishan!'

Wailing their sirens, the bluebottles swoop down and fire into the crowd. There are screams. People start to slide unconscious on to the deck. Stun darts. They hit with hollow slapping sounds.

Something metal spins through the air to them. A

wrench. It clips the rotor of one drone. There's a crack and a metallic whine and the bluebottle spins down into the waves.

Wait – the crowd has brought *weapons*?

Pia grabs hold of Wilma and throws her towards the entrance to the Quark. She takes Gowpen too and drags him back. Zugzwang is watching the deck like it's a level on a video game, all bug-eyed and gawping. Pia yells at him, then joins Wilma and Gowpen in hammering on the metal door. They have to get away before the doomers remember her. Without Urette, focus is scattered. Half of the crowd are trying to bring down the bluebottles by hurling bottles, kitchen knives, tools. The other half seethe around where Siskin fell.

Pia catches a glimpse of Urette as the crowd haul her up. Her mouth is bloody from the fall. An expression is fixed on her face: she *wears it*, like a horror mask.

It is delight.

She *wanted* this to happen.

A hand takes Pia by the wrist. She kicks out, feels her boot connect with a shin, and twists free of the grip. It was Tej, who just yesterday had been smiling and joking with her. Now his face is glazed with madness. He bear hugs her and hurls her on the floor.

'Dad!' Gowpen is yelling. 'Dad, stop!'

Pia's knee jangs on the deck. She bites her lip, tastes blood. Tej reaches down to grab her again.

Something butts him off his feet. Tej flies sideways and hits the ship's rail with a clunk. Threedeep, with (ง•_•)ง flashing in neon colours on her screen, has rammed into him at full speed. The impact sends the nanabug's rotor snapping off and whizzing up into the air. The rest of her falls on to the deck with a crack and skid of plastic, and the emoticon on Threedeep's screen vanishes, and the little plastic box of a drone is still.

'Threedeep!' Pia scrabbles on hands and knees towards the drone, but rough hands grab her, pulling her to her feet, yanking her in all directions. Wilma tries to pull her towards the Quark. Pia is wrenched away.

Panic and pain, wailing in her head like sirens. Jutting elbows and barging shoulders. People she knows all around her. Wanda, the 'genieer. Vivi, the doctor at arrivals. The canteen guy whose name they didn't know. The one Wilma nicknamed Pasta La Vista because he only ever ate ravioli. Now he has Pia in an armlock and is wrestling her towards Urette.

She passes Weevis, lips moving as he chants to himself. Oh Seamstress, they are all completely doomsick. How has it happened so suddenly, spread so fast?

Then Pia notices Blom floating unshrouded beside him, and she realises Weevis is speaking a wish-script under his breath.

Blom bows. His mouse-tail beard tumbles down his cigar puff of a chest. The genie lights up briefly, the way thunder flashes inside a cloud.

'And so it is granted,' he says.

Pia has no time to close her eyes or take a breath. There is a heaving whirligig of light and sound around her as she zephyrs away.

27
PLAN C

Pia is below deck somewhere, in a large dark hold. On an ark, she guesses. Which one, she doesn't know.

Weevis is there, with Blom.

And Threedeep's broken box of a body too.

Pia can't say or do anything, though. She just lies there, trembling from the adrenalin. With the savagery of what happened to Siskin, and *almost* happened to her. If it hadn't been for Weevis and Blom . . .

She checks herself over. Her dungarees are torn, her knee aches, her lip feels fat and tender, but she is OK. She is OK.

But Threedeep . . .

The drone's blank screen flickers on.

I fƎEℓ Ⓦ℉ᵼirD. ÐïÐ þïå jµ§† §ï† ðñ mê?

'Threedeep!' Pia throws her arms around the broken drone, not even caring that a nanabug can't feel hugs. The hug is as much for her as it is for Threedeep. 'I thought you were busted!'

i SuR ⓋïⓋ℃D Yⓞur ʙutt, dᵢdₙ't ᵢ? Cⓞmₚ⋒Rℂd tⓞ that, thᵢₛ W⋒S ⋒ⓞtℍᵢ⋒g.

'Are you OK? Your text looks a bit garbled.'

I åm a††℃mpting tⓞ яêpair mySe1f.

Pia looks up at Weevis. So he hadn't been a doomer. Siskin must have put him in the crowd to spy on them, the way he'd put Wilma and Gow and Zugz in the Quark to spy on Pia. Thank the Seamstress. He saved her. She guesses she should sort of hug him too—

'That's not necessary,' he says as she puts Threedeep down and her arms come up to embrace him.

'Oh. Good.'

Pia looks around. The gloomy ship's hold is warm despite its size. The walls and floor are all painted with black fire retardant, a bit like the Sunset Pagoda. The only thing Pia can see in the entire enclosure is a big pile of rocks over in the corner. It looks like a miniature mountain, twice her height.

'Where did you zephyr us to?'

'Talk later,' Weevis says. 'I have to wish-script the others out of danger. Who else is back there?'

'Wilma and Gowpen,' says Pia breathlessly. 'And Zugzwang!' She almost forgot about him. Then she swears. 'And *Ishan*! Do Ishan first!'

'They'll come in the order they come,' Weevis snaps, and goes back to muttering with Blom.

Pia has never seen someone wish-script from memory before. She always recites from paper. But as she listens, Weevis builds up a custom multiple third-party zephyr wish-script *from scratch*, without even writing it down.

'Threedeep?' Pia whispers. 'Do you know where we zephyred to?'

(눈_눈) ï doη'† εvεη kΠow whåt håppênêD. Threedeep's chat seems a little clearer now. **Somê of my mêmoяy filêS åяê mISSIng, pяêSumêd cяuShêd**.

238

'I'll fill in the gaps for you,' she tells the drone. 'Basically, you just became a very good friend of mine.'

i̱ di̱d? HΘΘray! DΘuble thumȻs up!

'You don't have thumbs.'

Do tΘΘ.

d(͡⁔ ͡⁔)b

See?

Pia laughs. 'I actually *like* these settings on you, Threedeep. You were always way too stern before.'

The monitor drone looks at her with her node. **ʕ˚ℤ˚ʔ Now I'm just wåy tΘΘ cute!**

'Don't push it.'

There is a sudden commotion as Wilma, Gowpen and Zugzwang appear. The three of them had been running somewhere in the moment they zephyred, which means they all yell in confusion and trip over in a heap.

'WHAT THE ACTUAL IS GOING ON?' Wilma yells, face down on the floor.

'It's OK, Wilma.' Pia helps her up.

'Who zephyred us? Where even are we?'

'Weevis did. You're safe.'

'They're mind-frayed.' Gowpen sits up, wiping his tears. 'Mum and Dad didn't even recognise me.'

Zugzwang shakes his head in amazement. 'Every damn grown-up,' he mutters. 'Gone crazy-crazy-*crazy*. This is something *else*.'

'They chased us down into the Quark,' Wilma says. 'This

bluebottle appeared to guard us, and I'm like, *ah, we're safe*, then WHAM! It gets fried.'

'It was like some VR game.' Zugzwang looks at his goggles. Both the lenses are smashed from where he fell.

Gowpen sniffs back tears. 'A VR game that *sucks*.'

Wilma swallows. Her eyes are wet and shiny. 'I am finding it very hard to be funny right now.'

Then Ishan appears in the midst of them, curled up on the floor with his hands over his head, and sneezes.

Pia runs up and throws her arms around him. She brings Wilma in too, because otherwise it is weird. Gropes for Gowpen and pulls him in as well. Even Zugzwang.

For a long time, no one says or does anything. They just hug. Still breathing. Still there. Still friends. Still Rekkers.

Wilma sniffs. 'My snot's all over your dungarees, Ishan.' Her voice is muffled in Pia's shoulder.

'That's OK,' he says.

'I think there's some dribble there too.'

Gowpen starts to giggle. When they break away, Pia knows that they are all OK. Not for ever, but just for now. They are OK.

'Is there anyone else coming?' Pia looks around at the six of them: Wilma, Gowpen, Zugzwang, Weevis, Ishan and her. Plus Threedeep and Blom.

'Is that it? We're the only non-crazies in all the zoo?' Wilma moans, and mimes blowing her own brains out.

'They're more than crazy, they're *doomsick*,' Ishan explains. 'I went to—'

Pia cuts in. 'We know. It's Urette. *She's* doing it.'

'Old spider lady? How?'

'CAN YOU ALL PLEASE SHUT UP,' Weevis bellows. 'Just because *you're* safe, doesn't mean that others are.'

He turns back to Blom. Wilma makes a face like *oooooOOOoooh*.

Gowpen grins. '*Some*one's moody.'

Perhaps it is puberty, Threedeep chats. **I do not know much about that, though. It is a little above my current settings.**

'Threedeep,' Pia says. 'Stick to being cute and saving my life, OK?'

(•ᴗ•)ᕤ Yes, ma'am.

'What's the secretary doing?' Zugzwang mutters, giving Weevis dark looks.

'Wow,' Ishan breathes. 'Is he wish-scripting from memory?'

Gowpen makes a *wow* whistling sound. 'Didn't know he was a 'genieer.'

'He's a freaking *nin*'genieer.'

Zugzwang scowls. 'Thought he was top of our list of enemies? Whatever.' He stomps off.

Wilma looks at them and rolls her eyes. 'I better go after him. Hey, Zugz! Need some hugz?'

Gowpen, Ishan and Pia stand and watch Weevis and Blom. It's not like they know what else to do. After maybe a minute, Weevis trails off. He turns to face them, ashen and hopeless.

'The wish can't find the Director,' he says.

'What do you mean, it can't find him?' asks Pia.

Weevis wipes sweat from his eyes. He looks exhausted. 'I keep trying to zephyr him here.'

'Relax the script parameters?' Ishan suggests.

Pia doesn't know much about 'genieering. She is about fifty per cent sure that parameters are the rules you give to a wish to bind it, and make sure it works in the way you want it to work.

'The parameters are fine,' Weevis snaps. 'You're missing the point. It's *Siskin*. That's the only explanation for the wish not finding him.'

'What do you mean it's Siskin?' Pia asks.

Weevis doesn't reply. But Pia can see what it means, just from his expression. They all can. Siskin isn't in the parameters.

He's gone.

Siskin – the Director – the boss – Mr Ice-cold – Zugzwang's *dad*.

'Oh Seamstress,' Pia whispers.

'Do *not* tell Zugzwang,' Weevis hisses. 'Not until we know for sure.'

The three of them barely have time to nod before Wilma and Zugzwang come back. Both of them are scowling.

'Why the actual have you zephyred us here?' Wilma says.

Pia hears the buzzing of wings. Something tiny perches

upon Wilma's fingertips. Now it is hovering by Ishan's ear. Pia glimpses a flash of jade, a thrum of wings.

A creature with little onyx-coloured claws.

'What was that?' Ishan jerks around. 'Something just—'

'Ow!' says Wilma as it tries to steal her nose ring. She bats it away. The creature hovers above her head, a trail of smoke snaking out of its snout, like a wisp from the end of a cigarette. The long neck corkscrews. Twin candle-flame eyes regard the kids and Blom. Then it is gone, leaving behind the smell of burnt matches.

'He zephyred us to the *hummingdragon* aviary,' Wilma says, indicating Weevis. 'Great. Just *great*.'

'Maybe you would've preferred me to have taken my time and made the perfect wish-script,' says Weevis acidly. 'I'm sure you could have dodged all those weapons for a few minutes longer, no problem.'

Wilma folds her arms and tilts her head at Weevis. 'Nice comeback. I don't know whether I want to punch him, or high-five him.'

The first hummingdragon had obviously gone to alert its friends, because there are now about a dozen of the things zipping around in the air above their heads. They look like colourful precious minerals; turquoise and amethyst and azurite, with throbbing molten cores and little glittering wings that vibrate too fast to see.

'Null! *Off!*' Wilma swots another hummingdragon as it dive-bombs for her nose ring.

'Chill, Wilma,' says Gowpen. 'They're not dangerous.'

'Tell that to my nostril.' Wilma covers her nose ring so it can't get snatched. 'They're scavengers, right? Don't they hoard rubbish?'

'Precious metals and minerals,' says Weevis.

There are now about twenty hummingdragons, swooping and flitting like bats. One of them notices the shiny fragments of Zugzwang's smashed goggle lenses, strewn across the floor.

An almighty squabble starts up: high-pitched roars that are more like squeaks, and little jets of blue and yellow fire. It is utterly vicious. Everyone steps back.

'No one has any shiny tooth fillings, do they?' Ishan says, throwing his own goggles to the scrabbling hordes of hummingdragons. 'Or necklaces? Or belt buckles?'

'Nope,' says Gowpen.

'Not any more,' says Zugzwang, regarding his goggle remains miserably.

Wilma hurriedly stuffs her nose ring in her pocket, out of sight.

'Threedeep, turn your screen off,' Pia whispers, and the drone goes dark. Now she is just a dull plastic box.

'They're scavengers,' Weevis explains. 'We were hoping they might be used in recycling plants – hey!'

Three hummingdragons have called a truce and teamed up to sneak into Weevis's pocket to steal Blom's genie lamp. They go soaring clumsily over the heads of the zookeepers, barely keeping the cigarette lighter aloft. Pia jumps and makes a wild grab that misses completely and accidentally hits Gowpen in the face. Blom and his lamp disappear off towards the big pile of rocks at the end of the room, whilst the other hummingdragons squabble after them, spitting out little fireballs the size of orange pips.

'Get Blom back!' Weevis orders. 'As in, right now!'

Wilma rolls her eyes. 'We get it, you're the boss. You can stop the Siskin impression now.'

Weevis glares at her.

'Where'd they go?' Pia looks around. The air surrounding them is empty. Just the smell of ozone and a dry heat.

'Their hive.' Ishan points. 'At the other end of the enclosure.'

So that's what the rock heap is. Looking a little closer, Pia sees that each stone is riddled with little finger-sized holes. 'Genieers must have zephyred away the centres of the rocks too, hollowing them out, because the hummingdragons have all crawled inside them, making the rocks glow like lanterns.

'Don't panic,' Ishan says. 'We're in their enclosure. That lamp isn't going anywhere.'

'Neither are we, without Blom,' Weevis says.

'Let's just bang and yell until someone comes,' Gowpen says, pointing over at the loading-bay door on the far wall.

'I'm not leaving without Blom,' says Weevis.

'You can stay, then.'

'Did you forget about all the grown-ups going crazy?' says Wilma. 'We start hollering that we're here, we don't know who is listening, and whether they're all, you know—' She does her best impression of a chanting, doomsick maniac.

'If we don't have a genie, we're pretty helpless if we get into trouble,' Pia agrees.

'OK,' says Zugzwang. 'So we go over to that hummingdragon hive and get Blom back. Fine. *Then* what, huh?'

Nobody speaks. Pia realises after a moment that they are all looking at her for the answer.

'Me? Why do I have to decide?'

'Because all the grown-ups are nullin nuts,' says Ishan. 'And you seem to be the only one with the vaguest idea of what is going on.'

Pia doesn't feel like she knows anything at all, but she launches into a quick explanation about her journey into the Seam, and her meeting with the Seamstress, and everything else that's happened since.

The others listen quietly, except for Weevis, who keeps making impatient huffing noises and eventually goes off to the hummingdragon hive to look for Blom himself.

'So you think there's a voilà on the loose?' says Wilma when Pia finishes.

She nods. 'A predator. And it's preying on other voilà. The Fabergé chickens, the megabunnies . . . Maybe others too, that we don't know about.'

'What sort of person would make a voilà like that, though?'

'Has to be a Seamer,' says Ishan grimly.

'Why a Seamer?' Wilma folds her arms defensively.

'Because of security. No one else would be able to get on the island.'

'I did,' Pia points out.

'Predator or no predator, I still don't get how this explains what's happening to Mum and Dad and the other grown-ups,' says Gowpen.

'And I still have no idea what we *do*,' Wilma says. 'Anyone?'

They all fall silent.

Pia facepalms. 'You're all looking at me again, aren't you?'

'Yup,' says Wilma.

'Sort of,' says Gowpen.

'Uh-huh,' says Zugzwang.

'Always,' says Ishan.

Pia screws up her face in concentration. A plan. Any plan whatsoever. She feels the others getting impatient with her. Ahead of them, by the hummingdragon mountain, Weevis lets out a little shriek and furiously pats some part of him that has just caught alight.

Wilma giggles. 'I like him,' she whispers conspiratorially.

Gowpen wrinkles his nose. 'Ew!'

Wilma gives him a *don't even care* look.

'But he's gross,' Gowpen says. 'And really rude.'

'Well, duh. That's what I like about him—'

'OK!' Pia interrupts. 'A plan. Here it is. Nice and simple: find Blom, zephyr to San Silicio – no, it's not too far, I've seen him send letters there – and raise the alarm.'

'Bad plan,' says Wilma.

'Uh-huh,' agrees Zugzwang.

'I'm not leaving without Mum and Dad,' says Gowpen. 'Or Moonbim.'

'Or my nanites,' says Ishan.

'OK, OK.' Pia doesn't want to leave her genies either. Or Bagrin, even though he's been ignoring her since she left Urette's. 'How about Plan B: find Blom, zephyr to the island, get the Seamstress to sort this out.'

'Umm,' says Zugzwang.

'Didn't you say the Seamstress was sort of dead?' says Gowpen.

'Worse than Plan A,' says Wilma.

'Agreed,' says Ishan.

'Plan C, please,' says Gowpen.

Pia throws her hands up. 'Look, I don't have any answers, OK? I know this has something to do with Urette, but I don't know what. If I could be a fly on the wall and—'

The others look at each other.

'Ding ding ding!' says Wilma. 'We haaave a winner.'

'Plan C it is,' says Ishan.

Pia squints. 'Sorry, what? I thought I just said I don't have any answers?'

She looks at Ishan, who grins. 'You said it yourself. We need a fly on the wall. Threedeep, you still got that vid-link with that bluebottle?'

Please, Ishan. They prefer to be called security drones. But yes, I do.

'OK, get ready to ping it.'

(b^_^)b

'How high up is your authorisation, Weevis?' asks Wilma, calling over to the secretary.

Weevis looks insulted by the question. 'Very, very high.'

Gowpen grins crookedly. 'Is that a surveillance-authorising level of high, or . . . ?'

And suddenly Pia understands.

'Oh,' she says suddenly. 'You're right. Plan C *is* pretty clever.'

ds on the deck of the Quark in the aftermath of the ba Around her, the splattered shells of bluebottles squelch under the feet of her followers. As she watches, another of the security guards aims his rifle at another security drone. The air shimmers and wobbles as the heat beam builds and boils. The bluebottle tries to fly out of range, but it melts mid-air into a black gloop and hits the deck like tipped paint. Even with a breather on, the air smells thick with the stink of burnt plastic.

Urette's followers cheer. Now the security forces have joined her, the bluebottles have retreated. There is no one left who can stand against her now. She hasn't just built a movement: she has built an *army*.

An army that has conquered the zoo.

Victory is bitter, though. In her mouth, she can still taste it: the iron tang of her blood, spilled during her battle with Siskin. The Whisper has taken away all the pain from the bruising, though. It can do things like that. Take bad feelings away. Sorrow. Fear. Loneliness. Doubt.

Whenever it happens, Urette's followers call it a miracle. But it isn't. She knows. A miracle is given freely. What the Whisper does has a cost.

What else happened, up there on that deck? It was less than an hour ago, but already the memory is hazy, as if her thoughts are covered with cobmist. All she can remember is the feeling of everyone listening. Of people around her. Of not being alone.

All the things the Whisper promised.

It was wonderful, at first. The way they listened. The way they looked at her. Not in a fearful way, like they had before. But with attention. Respect. Even worship.

It hadn't even mattered that the words tumbling from her mouth weren't even hers, they were the Whisper's. She barely even remembered them after speaking them. Something about darkness, about light, about a child. A load of doomsay, really. Who cared? What did a few lies matter, if they brought the zookeepers comfort?

It became easier not to listen. To just stand there and bask in the adulation. One by one, the zookeepers came to her hourly meetings. She was amazed how quickly it happened. Within a day, almost all the zoo was with her. *Going viral*, they called it in the old times. She remembers. It is just like that. Viral.

She even has *followers* now.

But not friends.

No, that isn't true. There was a girl. When? It seems for ever ago.

But she drank Urette's tea and politely pretended to like it and asked Urette about the photos on her wall, and that memory isn't fuzzy at all.

None of her followers have ever done that. Not Vivi, not Wanda, not even the Whisper. Only that girl.

What was her name?

Pia.

And Urette can't remember what she has done to Pia, but she knows it is something terrible.

But no, that wasn't her. *He* did that. *He* said those words.

Urette gets shakily to her feet. Enough. No more. She will go to the others, and tell them that this is all just foolishness.

No sooner has she decided than He comes back.

But we had a deal, Urette.

He isn't a Whisper any more. He is louder now. Stronger. A *Voice*.

'I've done everything you wanted,' she whimpers. 'Just leave me alone.'

You wanted to be listened to, says the Voice. *You wanted to be heard. Didn't you? Didn't you?*

Urette's skin goosebumps. Fear lays a thousand tiny eggs under her skin. 'Not any more,' she says.

Ah, buyer's remorse. We know it well. But a deal is a deal. A deal is a deal is a deal is a deal is a deal . . .

And Urette feels herself slipping, feels the Voice taking control again, and she can't stop it.

'Leave the bluebottle,' she hears herself say to her followers, who are trying to shoot one of the few remaining drones hovering nearby. 'Get below deck. Get control of this ship's autopilot. Direct it towards the celestial ark. To defeat the darkness, we must free the light.'

28

Alpha Queen

Urette's words are picked up by the bluebottle in fly-on-the-wall mode, transmitted back to Threedeep and converted to text on the nanabug's screen.

Leave the bluebottle. [inaudible] Get below deck. Get control of this ship's [inaudible] towards the celestial ark. To [inaudible] the darkness, we must free the light.

'Free the light?' Ishan turns to Pia. 'What light is on the celestial ark? Does she mean those old genies you've got?'

But Pia shakes her head. She feels a sick plunging feeling as she falls towards a realisation. It hits her with a smack.

'Oh Seamstress,' she whispers. 'Oh no, oh no, he – he *couldn't* have . . .'

Wilma raises her eyebrows. 'Who couldn't have what?'

'That's why I couldn't hear him,' Pia breathes.

'Couldn't hear *who*?' says Gowpen.

'I led him right into the spider parlour, and he went and made a deal with her . . .'

'Pia?' Ishan takes her by the shoulders. 'Let's have some proper nouns please.'

'Bagrin.' Her heart thuds. 'The zoo's devil. It's him. Urette's just the puppet, and Bagrin has hold of her strings. She must have signed herself over. Now she has to obey everything he says. Like an employee obeys their boss. All this chaos: the doomsay, the disappearing voilà too, I'd bet . . . It's Bagrin trying to get free from the infernal prism.'

It seems almost obvious now. Back on the deck of the Quark, she noticed how Urette seemed to stand on a stage in front of them and read lines from a script. There had just been too many other weird things going on back then for Pia to zero in on it.

'We have to stop the doomers,' she says. 'Bagrin's been recruiting them like a personal army to bust him out of jail.'

'Hold on, hold on!' Weevis comes back over and butts in, bogging them down with questions, but Wilma pulls him aside and does the explaining: how the prism only keeps Bagrin's body in one place, but that devils have the ability to project their voice, and send chimeras, and even make deals with people far away.

'I thought the lead door blocks out his temptations, mostly?' Ishan says.

Pia screws her eyes shut with the shame. 'It's, uh, a little bit open at the moment . . .'

Gowpen facepalms. 'Oh, Catastro-P. Seriously?'

'If he gets free . . .' Wilma trails off. Everyone knows what happened the last time a devil escaped its prism, but no one wants to say it.

'How is he kidnapping all the voilà, though?' Ishan says.

Gowpen shrugs. 'Dunno, but he's probably doing it to send everyone nuts.'

'Not everyone. *We're* OK.' Wilma looks upwards, as if inspecting her own brain. 'I think?'

Ishan nods. 'Yeah, how come he's only sending the grown-ups doomcrazy? Why not us too?'

Zugzwang coughs. 'Devils, man. Tricky, tricky.'

'We can solve *how* and *why* later,' Weevis snaps. 'Bagrin *cannot* be freed. We have to get Blom and zephyr to the celestial ark to stop the doomers. Urette told them—'

'Bagrin,' corrects Wilma. '*Bagrin* told them.'

Weevis glares at her. She smiles sweetly back.

'*Bagrin* told the doomers to turn the Quark towards the celestial ark. That means they don't have enough genies with them to zephyr there all at once.'

'Yeah, it's just Boppity-Boo on the Quark, I think,' says Pia. 'Other than that, there're only genies with no beard length at all.'

Weevis thinks. 'If they zephyr there one at a time, the bluebottles will stun them. They need to swarm the place in numbers. That gives us time. But we have to hurry.'

They all nod solemnly. An image flashes in Pia's mind: a single blazing eye, sat burning in its crystal pyramid of a prison, waiting to be freed.

They turn in the direction of the hummingdragon hive. To rescue Blom. To stop Bagrin. To finally put an end to this colossal mess.

• • •

The hive is quiet as they come close. A few hummingdragons flit from their rocks and zoom around them, but their curiosity wanes when they realise no one carries anything shiny. Soon the tiny creatures crawl back into their holes and are gone again.

'They're all sleeping inside those rocks,' Weevis says sourly. 'On little piles of trinkets.'

Ishan regards the pile of rocks. It is twice as tall as any of them. 'It'll take hours to look inside all those holes.'

'We don't have the time.' Weevis points at one singed eyebrow. 'Plus I already tried that.'

Why not summon their Alpha?

'Threedeep!' Pia hisses. She carries the drone in her arms like a child. 'Turn your screen off! It's too shiny!'

'Hold it,' Weevis put up a hand. 'What does your nanabug mean, an "Alpha"?'

'As in, the leader of the pack, right?' says Wilma. 'Like what you're trying to be.'

Weevis glares at her. 'As opposed to what *you* are? Which is a total and utter—'

'OK, OK, OK,' Gowpen says. 'We get it.'

Weevis scowls, and Wilma blows him a kiss, which he doesn't quite know what to do with.

Hummingdragons operate on feudal principles, Threedeep chats, regardless of Pia's attempts to quieten her. **The specimens you saw are of the peasant caste. They pay a tithe of all riches gathered to their Alpha, who typically resides at the top of the hive with the warrior caste.**

'Could've told you that, if I'd had my goggles,' says Zugzwang mournfully.

'My mirrorangutangs have an Alpha too,' says Wilma. 'He's a total pain in the neck. Thinks he's the boss. I have to be super polite if I want them to do *anything*.'

Yes, politeness will be key. Hummingdragons are very sensitive voilà. Nevertheless, I am sure we can bargain for Blom's return. Hummingdragons speak in fire and smoke, not sound, but it is possible to replicate the flame patterns via my screen. I have Zookeeper Arlo's translation files.

Weevis narrows his eyes suspiciously. 'Why have you got those if you were assigned to the celestial ark?'

Pia knows the answer before it even rolls over the screen. 'Threedeep is *always* well prepared when it comes to making new very good friends.'

'OK,' Wilma says. 'Chat to these little fiery bird-things, get Blom back. This will be easy. Three cheers for the drone.'

☀ヽ(^‿ᵔ^)ノ☀ Hip hip hooray!

Pia grins at the nanabug. 'Is there a risk they'll go for you though, Threedeep? You saw what they did to Zugzwang's goggles.'

'Don't talk about that,' Zugzwang moans. 'It's still too raw.'

It depends on the nature of the hummingdragon Alpha, Threedeep chats.

'We don't exactly have many other options,' Ishan points out.

Very true. Pia nods. 'Fine. But everyone get ready.' She looks up at the miniature mountain. 'If this Alpha turns

257

nasty, they might send their whole kingdom to war with us. It's going to take everything we have just to beat a devil. We can't be battling dragons too. Even tiny ones.'

Pia holds up Threedeep to the very top of the pyramid, and the drone's screen lights up. A sequence of yellow pixellated fireballs appear, like a kind of Morse code.

Seconds later, an emerald-coloured hummingdragon flits from its hole. It hovers in front of them, an arm's reach away, and coughs out three fireballs that fizzle in the air. Pia wrinkles her nose from the chemical smell. Wilma puts her breather back on. The hummingdragon flies off towards one of the very top rocks in the hive.

'Did you do it?' Pia asks Threedeep. 'Is the Alpha coming?'

I hope so.

Nothing happens for a moment. Then a dozen ruby-red hummingdragons shoot out into the air and hover in a formation of two straight lines.

'What are they doing?' Ishan whispers.

Wilma grins through her mask. 'Rolling out the red carpet. You did it, Threedeep: we're getting a visit from royalty.'

'Non-cybernetic organisms . . .' Ishan shakes his head. 'So *weird*.'

Down the corridor of air between the red hummingdragons appears one of royal-blue. The honour guard spout rainbow-coloured flames as the Alpha passes, in what Pia imagines is a kind of fanfare. Unlike the rest of their species, the Alpha flies slowly. Almost lazily. All except for its wings, which are a rippling glow either side of its body.

The Alpha flies right up to Pia and Threedeep, so close and stationary that Pia's breath catches. The majesty of it. The perfect interlocking scales, the mouth filled with needle teeth, the eyes that burn with white-purple fury like peepholes to a furnace. Staring into them Pia felt that if in their squabbles for treasure one hummingdragon was to cut another, it would bleed molten fire from its wounds.

The Alpha coils its neck. Its tar-coloured tongue licks the air and breathes out a long arc of blue flame.

Threedeep's node whirrs and a clunky translation comes up on the nanabug's screen: **[I is Queen Yrekk'n, Third One. Tribute, where is? Offer shiny.]**

Pia raises her eyebrows. A queen? That's how the Alpha saw itself – *her*self? Not just as a leader, but as a *monarch*? So Wilma had been right in her interpretation of the ruby-coloured hummingdragons. A red carpet, huh? What other royal symbols might this dragon be interested in?

'Tell her to give Blom back,' Weevis tells Threedeep, whilst Pia is still thinking. 'I'll get Blom to thrint her a – I don't know – a diamond or something. Whatever she wants.'

Pia winces. That doesn't seem like the right way to speak to royalty . . . But Threedeep's screen has already translated Weevis's words into flames and fireballs.

Queen Yrekk'n reads everything with her head tilted sideways, one eye narrowed to a slit. Tiny threads of smoke and heat simmer from her nostrils as she replies.

[I is Queen Yrekk'n, Third One. Mightiest of Three. Summit of the Mountain. Holder of {translation: error} Humans be unworthy mush-sacks! OFFER SHINY!]

Weevis huffs irritably. 'Tell her I will *give* her shiny. But she has to give *me* my genie back. And tell her we're in a *hurry*.'

This time, when Threedeep translates, Queen Yrekk'n erupts in fury. Her twelve ruby servants fly forwards in a blur, circling the Rekkers and belching fat sizzling globs of napalm. Ishan gets one on his collar that Wilma has to tear off and throw on the floor. Gowpen shrieks and ducks down with his hands over his head. Zugzwang roars out, 'What the null, man?' and brandishes his fists.

'Wait! Wait! Everyone, stop freaking out!' Pia tries to calm them. If anyone knows what an impending disaster looks like, it is Pia. The hummingdragons might be small, but there are hundreds of them, and they can breathe fire, and apart from Threedeep everyone is highly flammable, so they do *not* want to annoy the queen any more than Weevis already has.

'Zugzwang, don't you dare! Gowpen, stop screaming! Weevis, shut up! Threedeep, tell the great and terrible Queen Yrekk'n that the unworthy mush-sacks beg for her mercy.' Pia bows low as the drone translates her words.

At once, the fireballs stop. Queen Yrekk'n turns her head and regards Pia with her other blazing eye.

[Queen Yrekk'n has big fury with mini mush-sacks. No shiny given. Much rude. Other {translation: error} see.]

'If you had just actually *listened* to my—' Weevis gets no further, because Wilma clamps a hand over his mouth and says into his ear: 'Shush now.'

Pia gives Wilma a grateful look. A plan is forming in her head. If there's one thing she has learned from Bagrin, it is this: in negotiations, you have to tailor your chimera. Find out what someone desires and offer it to them. Queen Yrekk'n already wants shiny – but she also wants something else too. The same thing every queen wants, no matter what their species: respect.

'Threedeep,' says Pia, 'tell Queen Yrekk'n that we mushsacks are very sorry. We are very stupid and unworthy, and wish to pay her a very great shiny indeed.'

Queen Yrekk'n tilts her head. At once, her rage seems to cool.

[Great shiny what is?] The colour of her flame is a coy pink.

Pia ignores the question. 'We would have given it sooner, but we did not recognise the great Queen of the Hummingdragons at first.'

At this, Queen Yrekk'n puffs up her chest, and the ruby warriors behind her hiss and snap their jaws.

[I is Queen Yrekk'n, Third One. Mightiest of Three. Summit of the Mountain.]

'Yes, I realise that *now*,' Pia says quickly, aware this is the riskiest part of her plan. 'But where is your crown to prove it?'

Queen Yrekk'n cocks her head.

[Crown what is?]

And Pia smiles.

'A great precious shiny. It can only be given to a queen, who wears it on their head.'

[I is Queen. Give crown now.]

'We would be honoured!' Pia is getting dizzy from all this bowing.

Queen Yrekk'n cranes her long neck from Ishan to Wilma to Pia. She's impatient. That's a good sign.

[Crown where is? Tribute now. Give great precious shiny. Only Queen can has.]

'I shall show it to you first . . .' On her next bow, Pia whispers to Threedeep: 'Turn on your numinous lamp and light me up.'

Threedeep's node swivels, and suddenly a beam of silver-violet white shines blindingly in Pia's face. The Rekkers gasp around her, and she knows that Hum's halo is sparkling above her head.

'Woah!' says someone. From all the shrieking sounds coming from the hummingdragons, she guesses they're just as impressed.

[Very great shiny!] breathes Queen Yrekk'n. **[I take!]**

Her ruby-coloured royal guard rush above Pia's head, then utter hisses of confusion. Their claws just snatch at empty air.

'Quick, turn off the numinous,' Pia tells Threedeep. 'That ought to be enough to tempt her.'

The numinous lamp winks off, and Queen Yrekk'n lets out a tiny squeak of a howl.

[Crown where is? There but not. See now gone.]

'A thousand pardons, great Queen.' Pia tries to keep the grin off her face and is mostly successful. 'But we need our genie Blom, inside the lamp one of your loyal subjects took. Only then can we make the crown real, and make it fit your head.'

Queen Yrekk'n reads the translation on Threedeep's screen. She turns round to her ruby guard and barks out a series of fireballs.

'So,' Ishan murmurs to Pia as the ruby guard go to find Blom's lamp. 'What, you're a saint now?'

It takes Pia a moment to realise he is talking about the halo. 'Hum gave it to me,' she mutters back. 'Before he died.'

'Like inheritance?'

'I guess. I only just found out about it.'

'Does it let you do miracles? Maybe it'll let you do miracles.'

'I dunno. Let me see if I can magically get you to drop the subject without asking you directly.'

'Celestials.' He shakes his head. 'So. *Weird.*'

29
DEVIL CHAT

Five minutes later, Weevis has Blom back in his hands. By that time, the whole group is prepped, and the crowning ceremony goes off without a hitch. Blom and Weevis make a load of impressive fireworks to dazzle the onlooking hummingdragons whilst Wilma digs her tiny nose ring out from her pocket and slips it to Pia, who pretends to find it on top of her head, 'magically shrunk'.

With much bowing and ceremony, she presents it to Queen Yrekk'n. The tiny golden ring fits perfectly atop her scaled head.

The little queen is delighted. She immediately announces a parade around her hive, to show off her new crown. Away she flies, with her ruby royal guard puffing fireball fanfares around her.

The Rekkers watch her go. Then they turn to Pia.

'That was . . . impressive,' Weevis admits grudgingly.

'P-*nomenal*,' says Wilma.

'Pia-fection,' says Gowpen.

'P's on earth, and goodwill to all hummingdragons,' says Zugzwang.

'We're all doing puns?' Ishan looks around. 'I'm no good at puns.'

Ishan: impossible, chats Threedeep.

'Stop droning on,' says Pia, grinning madly.

Yrekk'n I should stop?

'Yeah, you're nanabuggin me.'

Weevis huffs irritably. 'Can we get going, please? This is really starting to *drag on*.'

They all looked at him, dumbstruck. Then everyone except Zugzwang cheers.

'What's so – oh,' he says. 'I get it. *Dragon*.'

For the first time for a long time, Pia feels like she's done something right. Fixed something instead of broken it. For a moment, it is almost possible to believe that the zoo might finally have stopped falling apart.

'On to the celestial ark then, I guess,' Ishan says.

That kills their smiles. Because now everyone remembers what they have to do next. Getting Blom back is just the start of it. Stopping Bagrin, now *that's* the challenge.

Weevis goes off to form the wish-script with Blom. The rest of them sit around, listening to Ishan spout theories about what is happening and why the zoo is falling apart.

'Maybe it's like when you cut yourself and your immune system fights any infection that comes in,' he says. 'Because the Seam is a wound in reality, right? So maybe *reality* is getting rid of all the voilà that come in.'

'And making the grown-ups crazy too?' Wilma makes a *pfft* sound. 'Next!'

'Or it might be the timefrogs? They could be hopping from now to the future, and kidnapping the voilà as they go.'

'Have you ever *seen* a timefrog, Ish?' Pia holds up her

hand. 'How does a little slimy thing as big as my palm carry off a megabunny?'

'And make all the grown-ups crazy too,' Wilma repeats.

'Or it could just be a poacher? A really really good poacher?'

'I'm just gonna keep on saying *all grown-ups crazy* until I go mad too, OK?'

That gives Pia a thought. 'How exactly are we going to *stop* all these crazy grown-ups freeing Bagrin?' she asks.

'Go shut the lead door you were talking about,' Wilma says. 'It'll block Bagrin from controlling Urette. Without her leading them, the doomers will back off. We win. Boom.'

Pia shook her head. 'Too dangerous. I made a deal with Bagrin to keep the lead door open for a whole night – but then we don't know what sort of deal he made with Urette. It could be *linked* to my deal.'

Wilma shrugged. 'So?'

'So you have to keep your side of the bargain with a devil. I know that sounds stupid, but deals are the only way to get a devil to do *anything*. Bagrin's only staying in the infernal prism because of a deal. And he's clever. If he made sure there was some kind of link with my deal in his deal with Urette, and I break the agreement, he can break his. Shutting that lead door would be as good as freeing him.'

'Oh.' Wilma frowns. 'So we actually have to fight the doomers then?'

'Wait, what?' Gowpen goes pale.

Ishan scrunches up his face. 'How the null are we supposed to—'

Then Blom says, 'And so the wish is granted.'

And they zephyr to the celestial ark.

• • •

Everything is really dead, Threedeep chats. Then she underlines **really**.

Pia slips her breather on and grimaces, looking out on the deck of the celestial ark. There's almost nothing left of the garden, just some withered brown stuff that used to be grass and a faint glow from the remains of the angels' house.

'Let's hope that's not a sign of things to come,' Wilma says with a nervous laugh.

Ishan points. 'There!' The quarantine ship has appeared round the island's rocky western shore, a couple of miles away.

It won't be long.

What do they do?

Oh Seamstress, they are all looking at her again, like she is some sort of leader. After her stunt back at the hummingdragon hive, she guesses she kind of is.

'Can I remind you,' she tells them all, 'that my nickname is Catastro-P.'

'Yeah, but you *also* have an invisible glowing halo hanging over your head,' Ishan points out.

Pia has no answer to that. She has no answers at all, in fact. She just flounders, and all the time the Quark gets nearer, churning up the ocean to foam as it comes.

'We need to buy ourselves more time.' Weevis steps forward. 'Get Threedeep to see if she can ping the ark's autopilot and get us moving away from the quarantine ship.'

I can do that, Threedeep says, and gives a ping.

'Scrip,' says Weevis to Pia. She just stares at him dumbly. '*Scrip!* Give me some!'

'Uh,' she says. 'In my cabin?'

He rushes in and comes out again with a fistful of pink zookeeper scrip and a pencil. 'Below deck!' Weevis yells.

The Rekkers look at each other. It isn't like anyone else has a plan.

They follow him down into the ark's corridors, feet slapping and squeaking across the shiny floors. Pia, lugging Threedeep, can't keep up. The drone's sharp corners bash her as she runs. She loses sight of the others as they hurtle down the first flight of stairs. The sounds of their running fade away.

And in the silence, her cheek grows warm.

Ah, it's Pia.

How nice to see you before we leave.

She grits her teeth and ignores the whisper.

All this time, you've been saying there's a monster loose in the zoo, says Bagrin. *And now you think it's Bagrin.*

'I *know* it's you,' she pants as she runs. Her arms ache and her head feels dizzy. She stumbles down the first flight of steps. A peeling poster of Dibsy grins at her at the bottom of the stairwell.

We have never done anything that a human being has not put their name to and signed, Pia.

Think about that.

And now tell me who the real monsters are.

We think you know.

They're the ones on the quarantine ship.

The ones coming to get you.

Cold fury burns in her. 'You've *made* them into monsters.'

Who are you talking to? chats Threedeep, which Pia ignores. She swings another door shut behind her and locks it. Another and another.

You think we did this? Bagrin sounds quite flattered. *They're sick, Pia. Sick with the zoo's newest voilà. I think you know its name, don't you?*

'The worm,' she says between lungfuls of air. 'Its name is the worm.'

That's right, it is. You suspected it was here, but no one believed you because they couldn't see it. Of course they can't. No one can see the worm. You can only see its symptoms.

Pia knows she ought to shut Bagrin's voice out. But the devil's words are too seductive. Not because they are lies, but because they are a mix of lies and truth.

Thou art sick, Hum said.

The picture of the worm in Threedeep's dream.

The way it spread so fast through the crowd.

The worm is a virus.

A virus that transmits doomsickness.

That's right, says Bagrin. *You wondered what could wound an angel? Angels aren't just made of light. Part of them is hope. Pure hope. And doomsickness is a kind of despair. It killed*

269

*your little angel's hope. With a wound like that, it's a wonder
it lasted as long as it did.*

Killing hope.

Very clever.

We wish we'd thought of it first.

There has to be a reason he is telling her all this. Stalling
for time, perhaps? Distracting her? She ploughs on. Ahead
of her, the others have stopped, somewhere near the Sunset
Pagoda. Weevis is barking out orders like a general.

*We're honoured you thought Bagrin powerful enough to
create such a voilà,* the devil continues. *Of course, if we could
do such a thing, we would've escaped this prism years ago.
We're just taking advantage of fortuitous circumstances.
Unlike Gotrob, we have been patient.*

Pia stumbles down the last few corridors. The Sunset
Pagoda is just ahead. And beyond that, Bagrin himself.

Look.

*Believe us or don't believe us, but we didn't make the worm.
If we did, we wouldn't have made children immune. Strange
that, don't you think? That only children haven't caught this
contagious virus?*

*It's almost as if the worm's creator didn't want to be
infected . . .*

'We're done here,' Pia manages to gasp. 'Go away.'

We haven't made all the voilà vanish, either.

'I *don't* believe you.'

Very well.

Your loss.

Must dash. My little minions are almost aboard.

Oh, one last thing.

Did you know there are already viruses called worms? They're a type of cybernism. There was a very famous one called Megalolz. You might have heard of it.

Yes, they're very common in computing.

Isn't that interesting?

Why don't you ask a gogglehead about it?

You know one of those, don't you?

30
Ouroboros

By the time Pia reaches Weevis and the others, they have already built a small barricade out of old *dib$* crates. Blom zephyrs them up from the hold, one after another, each square block dropping into place with a wompf and a smack.

Zugzwang grins. 'Like minecraft, bro!'

No one gets the reference, except for Ishan.

Ishan.

Pia just stares at him. Trying to tell. Is it true? Has he made the worm? This virus that kills hope, that killed her angels? And not just the angels, but probably the Seamstress and maybe some voilà, and definitely some zookeepers?

She feels sick. Her skin crawls.

Her friend.

Her best friend.

She remembers that night again. The words he said. *The world's already dead, and we're just the worms on its corpse.*

'Get this side, P!' Wilma holds out her hand and nods at the corridor. 'It's long, well lit, straight . . . They'll have to charge us. We're building a barricade. Weevis says we can pick them off before they reach us.'

Dumbly, Pia takes Wilma's hand and clambers over the crates. She plonks Threedeep down to one side. 'What are we supposed to fight with?' she asks. She can't think straight.

Bagrin has gotten into her head and stirred up all her thoughts.

'Hothothothot!' Gowpen comes rushing out of the Sunset Pagoda to their left with his arms piled up with lamps. He drops them like they are hot coals. Two aluminium cans, an old tuna tin, a rusty bike bell, an aerosol and an i-era smartphone clatter over the corridor floor.

'We're fighting with *genies*?' Pia watches the others pull their sleeves over their hands and scoop up the lamps and rub them. 'Guys, this won't—'

Before she can rubbish the plan, Solomon and Bertoldo shoot out in spouts of lilac- and lime-coloured flame. They immediately start gabbling with Threedeep, their 'very good friend'.

'Good beard lengths,' Weevis looks up briefly from the wish-scripts he is scribbling. 'This might work.'

The other genies make less of an entrance. Zugzwang takes up the smartphone, of course, but it sends out nothing but a shower of sparks. He throws it down and rummages through a *dib$* crate for a weapon instead. Finds himself a novelty gun that fires rolled-up Christmas T-shirts.

Ishan takes up the old tuna tin that is Hokapoka's lamp. It burps out a puff of smoke, but nothing else.

'Um?' Ishan looks around. 'Did I do something wrong?'

'I don't know,' Pia says abruptly, staring at him hard. 'Did you?'

He gives her a confused look. She decides just to come out with it. To just ask him straight.

'Who made the worm, Ishan?'

The ark judders. A groan runs through the whole ship. The corridor shakes. Pia falls over, obviously.

Threedeep pings. **The autopilot informs me that the quarantine ship is alongside us.**

'They'll be boarding,' Weevis says. 'We don't have long.' He holds out the pink paper scrip. 'Choose your weapon—'

'Wait!' Pia yells, and everyone freezes. She fixes Ishan with a stare. Raises her eyebrows up, as if to say, *well?*

'Pia, what's going on?' Ishan scrunches up his face. 'The worm?'

'The worm, the virus, the voilà, whatever you call it!' Her anger is making her voice tremble. 'Did you send them all doomsick, Ishan?'

Ishan just blinks at her. Then he sneezes.

'Oh Seamstress.' Pia presses the balls of her palms to her eyes. 'You're not denying it.'

'P, what is going on?' says Wilma.

'Could we not do this *after* we stop the doomers?' Gowpen pleads.

'*No!*' Pia is so angry she slobbers a bit. No one laughs. 'He said the world's dead, and we're just the worms on it.'

Ishan is trying to speak, but she is shouting over him.

'I should have known from all your doomsay. Facepalmit, you even monologued at me! Like a pantomime villain! It's so *obvious* now.' She turns to the others. 'He said the name for a group of humans ought to be a *problem*. Well, he just created something to take that problem away! He made a doomvirus – a virus to bring about the end of the world – and look what it's doing to people—'

'Wait a second,' interrupts Wilma. 'A problem of humans? Ishan didn't say that.'

Before Pia can react, Gowpen frowns. 'Hey, where's Zugzwang going?'

Pia stops yelling and looks around. Zugzwang has leaped the barricade and is running away from them, full pelt down the corridor, carrying his T-shirt cannon with him.

Zugzwang.

The zoo's joint-number-one gogglehead with Ishan, who is also a Seamer, running away from a discussion about who made the worm virus.

Pia feels a terrible sinking feeling. Oh Seamstress, she's messed up. Why couldn't she keep her stupid mouth shut? Ishan didn't make the worm – it was *Zugzwang*. The kid with the anger issues, with the jealousy issues, with the dad issues. The kid who hacks security systems, the kid who watches who-knows-what all day long on his goggles, the kid they all feel sorry for and mostly ignore.

The kid who never really does anything.

Except now, he has.

He's made a monster.

'Why?' Pia yells after him. 'Why did you do it?'

Now she knows why Bagrin told her. To distract. To divide. Now they aren't ready. Now they are one less. And Ishan is looking at her, his confusion turning to hurt.

'Zugz?' Gowpen calls, but no one chases over the barrier after him.

Wilma shushes them. 'Hear that?' They all go very still, and crane their heads upwards.

Footsteps on the floor above them.

At once, they are done with discussions. Pia has just split the Rekkers and maybe ruined her friendship with Ishan *again*, but there is no time to talk about it. They are beyond that now. Her heart hammers with adrenalin as she throws herself behind the barricade of crates. Threedeep displays the message **BE CAREFUL** in big neon letters across her screen. Pia tries to steady her breathing. She shares a look with Gowpen. With Wilma. With Weevis. With Ishan.

'I'm sorry,' she starts to say. 'I was wrong. I know you didn't do it. Bagrin spoke and I—'

The lights go out. Only the glow of the genies and Threedeep's screen in the otherwise pitch-dark corridor.

They've cut power, Threedeep chats, somewhat obviously. Pia hauls the drone on to the top crate, and her numinous lamp cuts a beam of violet light, straight ahead. Above Pia's head, her halo casts a golden glow.

'Quick, take a wish-script, take a wish-script!' Weevis waves the scrip frantically in his fist. Pia snatches a random one and strains to read Weevis's writing in the dark. It seems to be a wish that increases an object's *slipperiness*. Suddenly she realises she doesn't have a genie.

She scrabbles for the rusty bike bell from the floor, and wakes Kadabra. Somewhere ahead she can hear the slamming of doors, the echo of feet on stairs. The doomers are coming.

'Come on, Kadabra, wake up, wake up.'

The ancient genie crawls out, a feeble candle-sized flame. He looks around in bewilderment. He is so old that his chin is completely bald, and he only has a couple of wisps of moustache hairs. Barely any wish-power there at all.

Blom is talking to the other genies: some stirring speech in Tellish. Whatever he is saying is getting through – Solomon's and Bertoldo's faces burn brighter, and even Kadabra lets out a few sparks.

'Here they come!' Wilma yells.

A silhouette comes running down the corridor towards them.

And yelling out: 'I'm sorry I'm sorry I'm sorry I'm sorry!'

It is Zugzwang, pale and sweating. He leaps back over the barricade, chest heaving, face twisted with misery in the numinous light.

'I didn't mean for any of this to happen,' he gasps.

Then the doomers rush down the corridor after him and the battle begins.

• • •

The doomers wear cloaks of genie-woven shadows. They come in a slow wave, shoulder to shoulder, one mass silhouetted shape of doom. It seems as if darkness itself charges towards the barricade.

Pia stares at Kadabra and starts to go through her wish-script. Slowly, clearly. Praying the genie can hear and understand. He'd been a mighty genie in his day. A powerful wish-granter. She hopes he still remembers that.

'How do I set the parameters of my wish?' Wilma is yelling. 'I can't see who anyone is!'

The doomers keep coming, shrouded beneath their pitch-dark cloaks.

'Facepalm facepalm facepalm,' Gowpen mutters.

Zugzwang peers over the top of the barricade and fires his T-shirt cannon. A red T-shirt flies out in a tightly-packed roll. It hits a doomer in the face. The doomer falls over, their shadow tangling about their shoulders. It's the ravioli guy from the canteen, holding a shovel as a weapon.

'Anyone know Pasta La Vista's *actual* name?' Wilma yells.

Weevis shouts back something that Pia doesn't catch. Wilma and Gowpen rattle through their wishes. Before the doomer can get up, the two wishes are granted: Pasta's shovel zephyrs from his hands, and he falls fast asleep.

The other doomers just stagger over him.

One down, fifty plus to go.

Zugzwang fires his T-shirt cannon again. It *doing*s off someone's shoulder harmlessly.

Pia, says a whisper.

It's hopeless.

Give up now, and we will make sure the doomers don't hurt you.

Deal?

Deal?

Do we have a deal?

Then Pia finishes her wish-script: '. . . all this, I wish.'

Kadabra peers up at her with eyes crusted with years-worth of ash.

And nods his head.

And grants the wish.

A whirl of upwards motion, as if the doomers have all turned to ravens, flapping their wings. Then the thumps and thuds as they fall back down in a tangle of legs and arms, their cloaks pooling around them like an oil slick.

'Yes!' Wilma fist-pumps, and falls flat on her face too. Ishan wobbles and goes down and starts spinning on the floor like he's a malfunctioning game character. The slipperiness of the entire corridor floor has increased a thousand times. They're all on their butts, Pia included. They flounder there like fish out of water. It probably looks hilarious.

In her hand, the rusty bike bell is cooling. Kadabra has gone out with a bow, and one final, crazy wish-granting.

Pia tries to clamber on to one of the crates. As soon as she pushes against it, it drifts away from the barricade. Pia hauls herself on as it floats across the floor like a giant hockey puck, towards the doomers.

It doesn't matter. Pia can see the fight is over. A few doomers are shouting and cursing and trying to get back to their feet, but most are just lying there. It took so little to defeat them. With their cloaks gone, Pia can see why.

It was all an illusion. The cloaks made it seem like they were an army, but really the doomers are a wretched bunch. They moan and thrash on the floor. Some still mumble incoherent chants, others cough or retch or sit drooling into their laps. A few are lying flat out, chests rising and falling rapidly in a really scary-looking way.

Pia gulps. It looks like humans can't live without hope any more than angels can. For the first time, she starts to see the doomers for what they are: not an enemy, but sick people who need help.

Eventually, Weevis and Blom manage to wish the lights back on. Pia looks out at the mass of bodies carpeting the corridor. There has to be a hundred of them there now. Zookeepers, 'genieers, security guards, admin staff. Practically every adult in the zoo. Pia can see Gowpen's parents, and Britta and Vivi and Donna and Wanda and Arlo and Vashti. Even Siskin is there. He must have caught doomsickness in the crowd, or maybe even before it. Perhaps that was why he struck out at Urette. Either way, he wasn't himself when Weevis tried to zephyr him. Was that why the wish couldn't find him?

For a few minutes, Wilma and Gowpen slide clumsily back and forth across the floor, Solomon's and Bertoldo's lamps in their laps. They zephyr away the doomer weapons and send them all to sleep one by one.

Pia just stares at Zugzwang. He won't meet her eye. Just like she won't meet Ishan's.

'We need to zephyr these people to the mainland,' Weevis says. 'They need a hospital.'

Pia looked at him. 'Can Blom handle everyone over that distance?'

'I don't know.'

'Won't they just turn all the doctors doomsick too?' Ishan says. 'You've seen how quick this thing spreads.'

Weevis narrows his eyes. 'So we just leave them here, to die?'

'No!' Gowpen is by his mum and dad, trying to get Solomon to thrint some water for them to drink.

'I didn't say that,' says Ishan. 'I just don't think introducing this thing to the sprawl, if it's a virus like Pia says, is a good idea.'

'What do *you* think, Zugzwang?' Pia snaps. 'How about a whole city of two hundred million people all falling sick to your worm?'

Zugzwang puts his hands over his eyes like they are goggles, and doesn't answer.

Pia looks away in disgust. Now she knows the answer to the mystery, some things are starting to fall into place – but what good is that? The angels are still gone. The Seamstress is still gone. The voilà are still gone. Pia hasn't saved any of them. How is she going to save the doomsick around her?

Her cheek grows warm again.

If it makes the boy feel better, you can tell Zugzwang that his solution certainly worked out for Bagrin.

'You're staying in your prism,' Pia mutters at him. 'We beat your doomers and it was easy, even with your distraction.'

Ah, but the doomers were *Bagrin's distraction. From the zephyring that happened just behind you.*

A great licking grin of fire flares up in Pia's head.

'Guys?' Pia looks around, panic rising up. 'Can anyone see Urette?'

She scans the sleeping doomers.

Uh-oh.

'Anyone?'

The others are looking from face to face, but no one shouts out.

'Maybe she waited behind,' Gowpen says. 'Like a general sending out troops.'

'Or maybe . . .' Pia feels a heat building up behind her. 'Maybe Bagrin sent her on ahead.'

She turns her face towards the lead door just as it flies open and Bagrin breaks free. The mirror above his prison swings down and shatters. A glare passes over them. A blue flaming eye, a mouth of roaring teeth. A smell of sulphur and hot metal and burnt nylon.

Goodbye, Pia. It's time for us to take our business elsewhere. There're ten billion potential deals out there in the world, just waiting to be struck. If you ever need us . . . just call. Or, even better . . . whisper.

Bagrin's voice fades to silence.

Above Pia is a small round circle of sky. The devil burned a hole through the corridor's ceiling on his way out. Strings of melted plastic ooze down the vaporised edges like slime.

They find Urette down in the devil's enclosure, standing

by the shattered infernal prism with a hammer in her hand. Not a hair singed on her head. Bagrin has been as good as his word.

'He let me go,' Urette says weakly to them. Then she faints amongst the crates of smiling Dibsys.

31

LOOSE THREADS

They stand in the waiting area outside Siskin's office, all of them: Wilma, Weevis, Gowpen, Ishan, Zugzwang, Urette and Pia. Threedeep hovers beside them. They wait for her ping.

None of them talk. There has been enough of talking, these past two weeks. First the debrief, then the inquest, then the psych tests, then the further questioning. It took a long time.

Time is something everyone has a lot of, though, now the voilà are gone.

Sixty-four species, mined from the Seam. Angels, devils, hummingdragons, megabunnies, Fabergé chickens, smellephants, salamadders, phoenixes, singing hippos, gargantulas, the doomsickness worm, the genies and more besides.

All vanished, one after the other.

Even the ghosts are gone. Estival and Yisel have left Pia for a second, final time.

It isn't like before, though. There's no grief, or anger. She'd been so mad back then: at Gotrob, at Siskin, but most of all at her parents. How *dare* they leave her.

This time, it feels like a release. Not just for Pia. For her parents too. They are finally free of their endless loop.

Threedeep pings at last, pulling Pia from her thoughts.

Director Siskin will see you now.

And then, in super small font, she adds: Good luck.

Pia looks down at the floor as they troop in, one after the other. They don't need luck, they need a miracle. But the miracles are all gone.

Siskin stands behind his desk. It looks even emptier than usual. Not even the standard scattering of slim pink files. His antique lamp is packed up in a cardboard box.

Siskin looks different too. He's not wearing his suit – just a T-shirt and jeans. Pia has never seen him dressed so casually. It is weirdly disconcerting – the equivalent of seeing someone else arrive for work in their pyjamas.

As they enter, Siskin is taking the picture frames off his wall. The black and white portraits of voilà and zoo-keepers and arks and the island. They leave dark beige squares on the office wall. Like ghosts of pictures. Again, Pia thinks of her parents, and where they are now. Lately, that question of Estival's has been keeping her awake again. *Where else do we go?*

Siskin turns his head towards them. 'Come in,' he says. 'As in, don't be shy.'

They all crowd around his desk. There's nowhere to sit. Everyone stands, looking nervous. Even Weevis. Especially Zugzwang. He stands apart from the rest of them, gaze focused on the floor.

Pia wonders what it's like to have Siskin for a father. It's hard. She pretty much said that to Zugzwang himself once. *I can't imagine what it's like to have the boss as your dad*. Zugzwang's answer has been in her mind a lot recently. The way he just shrugged and said: 'He's mainly dad to the zoo.'

She has tried to remember that over the last few weeks of questioning. It helps soften her feelings towards Zugzwang a little. Towards what he's done. Pia knows what it feels like to have parents who don't see you. She can imagine how that feeling might build up, years and years of it. How it might drive a kid to do something stupid and dangerous. Just to make them, just for once, just *notice*.

'You'll be pleased to know,' Siskin tells them, 'that the Free State of California holds none of you responsible for the incidents of two weeks ago.'

He waits for their collective sigh of relief before continuing. Ishan, ever the doomsayer, has been predicting trials, prison, public-shaming. Gowpen got so worried about it Wilma had to promise him she would get them all diplomatic immunity via her parents.

'In fact,' Siskin continues, 'you are to be commended on your creative thinking that enabled you to save the lives of your fellow zookeepers, admin staff, security officers, 'genieers . . . and director.'

That was all down to Urette. After they found her beside the infernal prism, released from Bagrin's control (he'd *terminated her contract*, apparently), Urette observed that she was the only non-doomsick adult in the entire zoo. Yet she'd been around the doomers more than anyone.

It hadn't taken them long to figure out why. Weevis and

Blom zephyred small amounts of cobmist into the corridor, and they let the gargantula's ultra-powerful antibodies get to work on the virus. Most of the doomers were awake again a few hours later, all paranoid madness wiped from their minds.

By that time, though, it was too late. All the voilà were gone. Even Blom and the genies.

'So,' Siskin says with a brief smile. 'Your futures look bright. The future of our zoo, however, is considerably less so. The arks will be leaving the island and sailing back to San Silicio today.' He holds up a hand to stop their protests. 'As in,' he says, 'the decision is final. A zoo without animals is not a zoo. Unless you can convince my superiors otherwise.'

'We'll get more voilà,' Ishan says. 'From the Seam.'

Siskin's eyes go shiny, and Pia is astonished to see him wipe away tears. His famous stare has gone the way of the ice caps, and melted.

'None of the twelve missions we have conducted to the Seam since Pia's visit there have yielded any voilà,' he says. 'It has been concluded that the unreality has become too unstable for any new extractions. All visits there will cease.'

Pia feels a lump in her throat. It can't end. The zoo is the only home she's ever known. Sometimes, it has even felt like an enclosure itself. How will she survive in the jungle of the sprawl, amongst the shantyscrapers and failing ohtwo factories?

'What happens to us?' she asks. 'Where else do we go?'

Siskin resumes taking the remaining pictures from the wall. 'Back to your families.'

Pia's eyes brim with tears. 'This *is* my family.'

'Yeah.' Gowpen is crying with her. 'My family is here.'

Zugzwang speaks, very quietly. 'So is mine.'

'I've not been informed of all the details,' Siskin snaps, some of his old frostiness coming back. 'The zoo project has been terminated. So has my directorship.'

'But what about the voilà?' Urette says. 'They're missing, we have to *search* for them—'

'No one in San Silicio cares about the voilà,' Siskin says, voice rising. 'The voilà *failed*. Every one of them. Every species. None of them were a solution. Most of them weren't even *useful*.'

'They shouldn't have to be *useful*,' Urette snaps back at him. 'They're living creatures—'

'*Were* living creatures,' Siskin corrects. 'As in, you have no evidence that any of the voilà are alive now.'

No one has an answer to that.

'This is your fault,' Urette mutters at Siskin. 'This whole experiment was yours. It was sick. It was cruel. It wasn't a zoo – it was a laboratory, a factory. All you were interested in was your precious *solution*.'

Siskin, facing the wall, slumps his shoulders. His head hangs down, staring at a photo of Zafira, the first genie to voilà, all those years ago. It is hard to imagine that time now. When the Seam was full of possibility, instead of empty and silent. A time when the world might be saved.

'Well,' Siskin says, 'you are right, Urette. I did only care about a solution. We shall see how the world gets along without one in the years to come.'

'Badly,' says Urette flatly. 'Some mistakes you can't fix.'

Siskin looks at her, and Zugzwang, and Pia. 'I think we've all learned that,' he says. 'Now, if you'll excuse me, I have an office to pack.'

'Hold on hold on hold on.' Wilma puts her hands up. 'You're saying that no one is paying for *any* of what happened?' She points at Zugzwang. 'Not even *him*?'

Unlike Pia, Wilma has not softened towards Zugzwang over the last two weeks. If anything, she has hardened. Perhaps other voilà might have survived somewhere, but not the mirrorangutans. During the doomsickness, whilst the Rekkers were in the hummingdragon aviary, someone destroyed their generator, plunging the mirrorangutans into darkness and snuffing out the creatures that lived in light in an eye-blink.

No one remembers who'd done it, or how. Wilma says it doesn't matter, that Zugzwang is to blame regardless. She hasn't spoken to him for a week now. Neither, in solidarity, has Gowpen.

'He just gets away with it?' Wilma's mouth purses tight with fury.

Siskin looks at her in surprise. 'You think Zugzwang was the only one who did any wrong? We all did, Wilma. Will you make Pia pay for trying to cover up the angels' disappearance? Will you make Urette pay for her deal with

289

the devil Bagrin? Will you make Ishan pay for his foolish theories? Or what about Gowpen, who created a unicorn not because it would save the world but just to make his own mother happy?'

Gowpen blushes. They all do. Wilma juts her jaw and stays silent.

'We all did wrong.' Siskin steeples his hands. 'All of us. But you're right. Someone has to pay.'

Behind Pia, the door to the office opens. The two security guards standing there don't speak. They just let the bluebottle hover into the room, raise up its jabber and crackle it once.

Will you comply? it chats.

'Yes,' says Siskin. He turns and put the picture frames down on his desk. 'I'd hoped to clear the office before you came, though.'

That is not necessary. You will follow now.

'Dad?' Zugzwang takes a step forward. 'Dad, what's . . . *Dad?*'

Siskin looks at his son. Something passes between them, something like an angel's presence, something that cannot be spoken, only felt. Then Siskin nods and steps past them, holding up his wrists for the guards.

Wilma gawps. 'What the *actual*? They're arresting *Siskin*?'

Siskin nods, his face expressionless. 'Of course. I was the one who ordered Zugzwang to voilà a doomvirus.'

The sentence seems to make time stand still. Pia is stunned.

Siskin? *Siskin* ordered Zugzwang to make the doomvirus? For a moment, she can't believe it, won't believe it.

But then she thinks: this is the man who once zephyred away two thirds of a city's population to save the rest. What if that wasn't by accident? What if Siskin has *always* known the suffering and sacrifice required to truly save the world? Pia imagines him talking to his son, telling Zugzwang, giving him the seed of the idea to take into the Seam.

And wouldn't Zugzwang do it? Zugzwang, the boy who would do anything to please his father?

Or maybe – maybe this is one last lie. Because Siskin is right – someone has to pay for this. There'll be trials, and prison, and shame. And perhaps Siskin can't bear to see his son go through that. Perhaps he is taking the blame.

Looking at Zugzwang's face, Pia can't tell. Siskin's face too is a mask.

'Goodbye, everyone,' he says. The two guards cuff him and take him by the elbows. 'Look after the lamp,' he tells Weevis, nodding over at his desk. 'It's antique.'

Then they lead him away and the door slides shut and the Rekkers and Urette are alone.

'Is that true?' Wilma says to Zugzwang. 'Did Siskin tell you to make the doomvirus?'

Zugzwang just stares behind the desk, at the emptiness his father occupied just moments before. 'Dad got my name from chess.' His voice is strangely quiet, as if talking to himself. 'It's a position players sometimes encounter during

291

a game where all moves are bad. Move this piece you lose, move that piece you lose.'

They all stare.

'What the null is that supposed to mean?' Wilma asks.

Zugzwang doesn't look away from the desk. 'This whole thing has been one zugzwang after another. Even now. Whatever I tell you, you'll still hate me. What difference does it make?' He shakes his head. 'Game's over. Game's over.'

The floor beneath the office begins to shudder and tilt. It is the autopilot, adjusting course, heading for the shores of San Silicio.

'Wait, wait,' Wilma says, turning to the Rekkers. 'That's it? It's over?' She shakes her head. 'Null this. *Null this*, you hear me? We didn't save the zoo, we didn't save the voilà, we didn't save anything. All we did was *survive*.'

It's hard not to feel like she's right. It's all ending. No more Seam, no more zoo, no more Rekkers, no more miracles. And what about hope? Is that gone too? What do they live for now, if not that?

32
THAT LAST SLICE

That night before they reach the city, with the ocean churning in their wake, Pia stands on the deck of Ark One and looks up at the tiniest sliver of a crescent moon in the sky and sees the shape that she saw in her dream. The one given to her so long ago now, by angels long dead. She understands it now. She gets it at last.

'It was a birthday cake.' She says it aloud to herself, over the engine and the wind and the waves.

They are still a few hours from San Silicio. The coast is not yet in sight, but all evening the city's yellow glow has spread slowly up from the horizon more and more, like a fungus, to blot out the stars. Once she sees the moon, once she feels what is about to happen, Pia goes quietly to her temporary cabin, an old 'genieer lab on the lower levels, and unclips Threedeep's numinous lamp.

(눈_눈) **Pia? Are we there yet?**

'No. Go back to standby.'

We intelligence prefer the term—

'Asleep. Sorry, yes. That's what I meant. Go to sleep.'

(-_-)ˢ

Pia takes the lamp and heads back up on deck. Some part of her knows that it must end as it began. In moonlight.

On her way through the corridors, she passes a few zookeepers and 'genieers. Most of them ignore her. A few shoot her dark looks. They probably still blame her for everything.

Out on deck, the city glows brighter than ever. Pia makes her way carefully to the stern, where the horizon is still black and starry and the moon casts its silver spell on the waves rippling out to infinity behind them. She stands there for a long time. It is very beautiful. The night. The sea. This Earth and her moon. She feels the beauty as a kind of pain in her heart. As a kind of grief.

And then that feeling swells and changes. It becomes triumph instead, and relief. And Pia knows then that it is here, and she switches the numinous lamp on, and looks up.

The halo has gone.

And in its place:

'Hello,' she says to the angel.

It is sitting in her hair like a newly hatched bird in a nest. Gently, she tips her head forward and lets it slide down into her cupped hands. It has no shape yet. Just fuzz and radiance and feeling. She cradles it in her palms, all fluffy and warm in the violet of the numinous lamp.

Maybe being made of light means angels are outside of time. Maybe they experience past and present and future all in one moment, and know how their end will come even as they go to meet it. Maybe they saw Pia holding this newborn angel beneath the crescent moon, even as they wove her the dream on the night they left. And perhaps they had decided to celebrate, and cut her a slice of the moon.

A birthday cake.

'Hum wove you in the Seam,' she tells it. 'And gave you to me to look after.'

The angel shapes itself ears to listen to her words.

'Hum,' it says, forming a voice that is just like hers. 'After.'

We didn't save anything, Wilma said, back in Siskin's office. *All we did was survive.* Like that was nothing, less than nothing. But look. A new life. A second chance. Sometimes, just surviving is miracle enough.

'You're the start of a brand-new zoo,' Pia tells it. 'I'll raise you and teach you and make you strong, and one day you'll miracle the whole world back to life.'

She feels giddy with the possibilities. Pia looks around, to see if anyone is watching. Who does she tell about this? Who is in charge, now Siskin is gone? She has to find out. She has to show them. They have to sail back to the Seam and—

Her thoughts stop dead.

The second angel is there. Hum's sister. Hovering above the ocean waves.

She is older now, and bigger. The angel is clearer than Hum, with none of his fuzz. But she has her brother's lustre. The same pearlescent glow. And on one side, like a scar, is a dim circle of light.

'You,' Pia breathes.

'You of the yew,' answers the angel. 'Me of the tree. And the little makes three.'

'Yoomeethree,' echoes the baby angel.

'I thought you were dead.' Pia steps up to the rail. 'By the doomvirus. Or in the Seam, with Hum. But you're alive.'

Not just alive – the angel has grown up. How? They both stayed as children for two *decades*. Ever since Mum brought them out of the Seam. What changed? Maybe, for angels, growing up is a choice.

The angel floats closer. 'We were watched pots, children seen but not heard through the grapevine.'

The words are just as cryptic as ever, but there is something different about the *way* this angel speaks. If Hum is a pane of frosted glass, this angel is clear. Somehow, it is easier to see through the riddles and allusions, and glimpse the meaning.

'*We* kept you kids!' Pia cries out. 'The numinous lamps, the constant monitoring . . .' She thinks back to one of the first lessons Dad ever taught her. 'Angels draw most of their power from being *unseen*.'

The angel glows with satisfaction at her understanding.

'But if that's true, why have you come back?' Pia looks down at the baby angel in her hands. 'Oh.' Suddenly she is ashamed of her previous thoughts. There will be no new zoo. No turning back towards the Seam. For a moment, she has an urge to hold on to the tiny baby. To at least show it to a few others first, to bring back some *hope*. Then she realises the ludicrousness of trying to hold on to a being of light, and she laughs aloud.

'Go on.' She opens up her hands. 'Look, there!' she says to the baby angel. 'She's just like you.'

The angel shapes itself a pair of eyes to see, and a pair of wings to fly. It floats up and away from Pia to the older angel waiting for it.

'Did you come to stop me?' Pia says to the older angel. 'I was going to show it to everyone. Did that put the little one in mortal peril? Is that why you came?'

'Savings plan,' says the older angel. 'Safety deposit down and listen, they'll last if all's lost.'

Pia processes what that means. 'A plan for saving? A plan for saving what, though?'

'Less whatnot, more hoodoo, a new Q!' says the older angel.

'Less what?' Pia snaps her fingers. 'Oh! You mean the right question is: a plan for saving *who*?'

'And there we are! The there it is.'

What? Who are the 'there it is'? The realisation blooms in her like one of Solomon's and Bertoldo's fireworks.

'Voilà!' she shouts into the night. '*There it is* . . . that's a literal translation of *voilà*! Are you saying you took them? Oh Seamstress, you *are*. They weren't being poached, they weren't being killed off by the doomvirus . . . they were being *rescued* by *you*. From *us*.'

Pia facepalms, utterly flabbergasted. Of course. As the zookeepers began to fall into madness and violence, the angel came to each voilà to miracle it to safety.

'We were the danger,' she says to herself. She thinks back to what Siskin said once. 'We've always been the danger.'

She thinks about the mass-extinctions. The seas drowning in plastic. The land eaten by sprawls. A problem of humans. Suddenly she knows why Zugzwang said that.

But unlike his gloominess, Pia is filled with hope. The zoo had been wrong. Siskin had been wrong. All this time spent looking elsewhere for a magical solution to save the world. But the answer doesn't lie in angels, or genies, or hummingdragons, or any voilà. It is in people. They have to change people. Not for the worse, like Zugzwang's doomvirus: for the better. Not with despair, but hope. Not with madness, but sense.

'The problem must solve itself,' agrees the angel gravely.

'Are they all safe?' Pia leans against the railing of the ship, her face wet with spray and tears. 'Even the mirrorangutangs? The genies? Where did you take them?'

The angel gives no answer, which is a reply in itself.

'You don't want us to find them, do you?' Pia nods. Then her throat goes tight, and she can hardly bear to ask the question in her head. 'Are Yisel and Estival ... are my parents OK?'

When the angel finally replies, it is not with words. Words fall short when it comes to such a question. The answer is in song, and it is on a loop, cycling through Pia on endless repeat. And it is the song of a spring afternoon, four years ago at eight minutes past three. And it is the song of two people and the love in their hearts.

That is the beat of the song. That is its soul. The very first note, the refrain at the end. There when it finally loops back again. It is love, it is love, it is love, it is love.

This is the song of the ghosts of her parents. This is what lingers. This, their remains. Love is what lasts. Love haunts hearts. That's what the angel sings.

Yisel and Estival are more than OK. Have been, always, and always will be. Pia thought of them as trapped. Now she finally understands. Wherever they are, it will forever be spring, they will for ever be laughing, and for ever in love.

• • •

Surely the angels are leaving now. With each eye-blink, Pia expects them gone. But they linger. There, between the churning water and the serene sky. They seem to be waiting on her to do one last thing for them, though she doesn't know what it might be.

'Hum,' says the older angel eventually. With its left hand it points at itself, with its right it gestures at the baby. 'Who waits in a queue? Queue waits for the who?'

'Who?' Pia feels her throat tighten. 'Yes. OK. I understand.'

The first glimmering lights of the city rise behind her, as Pia faces the moon and names the angels.

33
Yes

After they are finally gone, Pia switches off the numinous lamp, heads back to her room, climbs into the cot set up by Threedeep and sleeps. This time she has no dreams. Not of the angels, nor the ghosts she named them after. Not even of the voilà, wherever they are right now. Her world is blank and featureless until Ishan comes and wakes her with a hand on her shoulder.

Once upon a time, that would make her yell and fall out of bed and quite possibly punch him in the nose.

Now she just opens her eyes and stretches. 'What are you so nervous about?'

She can just tell. He has that look on his face, like he is about to sneeze.

'It's not big,' he whispers. 'And it's not in a great part of the city. There's pollution and noise from the transit and roaches the size of your thumb. But my big sister is moving out of her pod, and the government still want me to do nanite stuff even when I go back, so Mum and Dad don't need to rent it. What I'm trying to say is, I think you'll like it. I mean, they can be grouchy sometimes and there's arguments and stuff, and don't expect either of them to thrint you a meal like you used to get at the canteen, but it'll be OK. Maybe not amazing, but OK. At least until you figure out somewhere else you'd rather be and—' He sneezes and stops talking.

Pia gets up on to her elbows. 'Are you saying I can come and stay with you and your family, Ish?'

He blinks. 'Yes.'

'Even though I thought you'd created the doomvirus?'

He blinks. 'Yes.'

'And even though—'

'Null it, Pia, yes! Yes!'

Threedeep's screen flickers on. **Am I invited too?**

Ishan blinks. 'Of course. I'm looking after a city of seven trillion nanites and I need your parenting advice.'

ᕦ(ò_óˇ)ᕤ Let's do this.

Pia finds herself grinning. There are so many reasons to, despite everything. She lists them in her head.

I still have a best friend.

My parents are at peace, and I'm about to get a new family.

Angels exist.

They're out there, alive. And the devil is too, but hey – so are the voilà.

And the world might be dying, but there's hope. I can feel it. Not a foolish or deluded thing, but fierce and real. Echoing through me like an angel's song.

Hope.

'So what do you reckon?' Ishan pulls at his fringe with one hand.

Pia smiles. 'Did I ever tell you that, for me, angels feel like getting away with a fart in an elevator?'

'Umm.' Ishan frowns. 'No. You didn't. Did you . . . did you hear what I said about coming to stay with me?'

And Pia laughs and tells him yes, yes she will go with him, at least for now. Then she goes back to sleep, knowing that somewhere, beyond the ship and beyond the sprawl, a hidden pocket of the world hums with life. A place that still holds miracles, in many and wondrous a form. Where tiny jewelled dragons flit and giant rabbits dig and hippopoperas drift through the air.

Where two angels are building their house from the sunsets and dawn.

Where a single unicorn called Moonbim treads delicately across the ground, her silver horn sparkling.

Where the ghosts of her parents remember themselves, in a loop of laughter and love.

And where genies sit, pulling boons from their beards, talking in Tellish about new beginnings; about hope-not-lost; and about the last threads of life, running endless and stubborn, through the ever-weaving tapestry of the Tale.

Acknowledgements

Eloise Wilson and Becky Bagnell – who brought this story out of the Seam with me.

Sue Cook, whose copyedits are eagle-eyed and crystal clear; Kate Grove and Tomislav Tomić, who are cover-wizards of the highest order; Erin, who planned out times for me to skulk off to my writing cave; Mum and Dad and Mazda, who took over when it was my turn.

With love and thanks!

THE
SNOW
MERCHANT

SAM GAYTON

ILLUSTRATED BY CHRIS RIDDELL

Lettie Peppercorn lives in a house on stilts near the
wind-swept coast of Albion. Nothing incredible has
ever happened to her, until one winter's night.
The night the Snow Merchant comes.
He claims to be an alchemist – the greatest that ever
lived – and in a mahogany suitcase, he carries his
newest invention.
It is an invention that will change
Lettie's life – and the world –
forever. It is an invention
called snow.

'A delightful debut . . . full of action
and invention' *Sunday Times*

'A germ of JK and a pinch
of Pullman' *TES*

9781783441778

Lilliput

SAM GAYTON

'Have you heard of the tale that's short and tall?
There's an island in the world where everything is small!'

Lily is three inches tall, her clothes are cut from handkerchiefs and stitched with spider silk. She was kidnapped and is kept in a birdcage. But tonight she is escaping.

Join Lily as she travels over rooftops, down chimneys and into chocolate shops on a journey to find the one place in the world where she belongs … Home.

'An undertaking of which Swift himself would have approved'
Irish Times

9781849397483

Hercufleas

SAM GAYTON

Greta is a girl on a mission: to venture to Avalon
and bring back a hero who can save her home from
destruction by the monstrous giant Yuk. Many heroes
have tried before now. Many have failed. What Greta
needs is a hero whose courage and self-belief are
greater than himself. She needs Hercufleas.

The only problem: he is a flea, no bigger than
a raisin. But the smallest person might just have
the biggest effect . . .

'Gayton is an exciting
new talent'
Books for Keeps

9781849396363

His Royal Whiskers

SAM GAYTON

ILLUSTRATED BY PETER COTTRILL

Something bad has happened to Prince Alexander, the only heir to the mighty Petrossian Empire. Something worse than kidnapping. Something worse than murder. Somehow, the Prince has been miraculously transformed into a fluffy-wuffy kitten.

Why has this terrible catastrophe happened? Who are the boy and girl brewing secret potions down in the palace kitchens? And how are they possibly going to avoid getting their heads chopped off?

'An outstanding story packed with magic and mayhem'
Abi Elphinstone

9781783443826

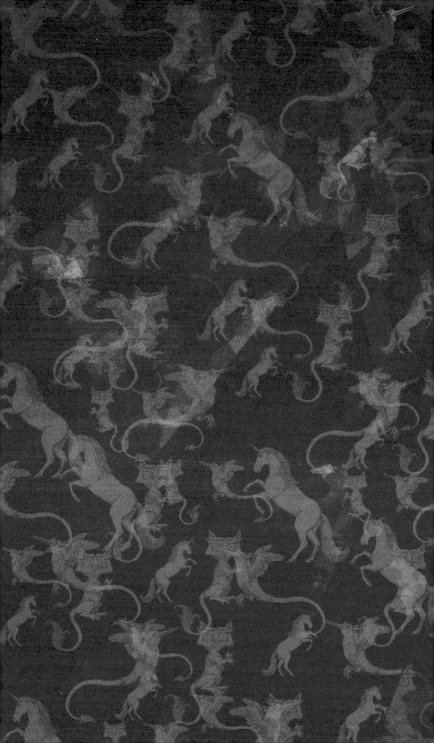